by Wanda Coleman

Mad Dog Black Lady (1979)
Imagoes (1983)
Heavy Daughter Blues (1987)
A War of Eyes and Other Stories (1988)

WANDA COLEMAN

A WAR OF EYES

AND
OTHER STORIES

BLACK SPARROW PRESS
SANTA ROSA / 1988

Grateful acknowledgement is made to the editors of the following: *Negro/Black Digest, Neworld, The Village Advocate, Enclitic, The Kansas City Star* and *The Available Press/PEN Short Story Collection.*

LIBRARY OF CONGRESS CATALOGING-IN-PUBLICATION DATA

Coleman, Wanda.
  A war of eyes / Wanda Coleman.
    p. 246 cm.
  ISBN 0-87685-736-5 :   ISBN 0-87685-737-3 (hard signed) :
  ISBN 0-87685-735-7 (pbk.) :
    I. Title.
  PS3553.047447W3   1988
  813'.54—dc19   88-14714
                           CIP

In memory of Spencer Coleman

CONTENTS

A WAR OF EYES
& OTHER STORIES

WATCHING THE SUNSET

FOR A black man he was runty.

He looked out on noisy New York from his drab apartment.

His students called him Mister Wilson. Behind his back he was known as Weasel Wilson. He accepted his nickname stoically (at least he'd successfully convinced himself that he did).

Gray sky struggled to become rose.

He moved to his desk. There were books. Lots of books. They were history — dark reflections of America's early development. The Civil War. It fascinated him.

That's where I was lost, he thought. That's where my history begins. I can't go back any further as a people.

War held special significance for him. He'd been turned down in forty-two. He was twenty-four then. It was a good way to make a living, the Service. The conflicts were fewer in those days. He could avoid uncle-tomming. In his mind Viet Nam was a nimbus.

Something stirred.

Gray-rose falling prey to blue-black.

A woman moved across the street. Her healthy behind bounced obscenely in tight slacks. Big women scared him. He was small, like his mother. Unobtrusive; high yellow — a part of that frustrating race that's neither black nor white.

Father was a word. His parents separated early. All he'd known was that his dad had been a civil service worker in Pennsylvania. And mama said he was a nice white man.

Mama died ten years ago.

Nervously he ran his hand through his straight black hair. Hmph! Straight. He hated it. Others had marveled at his caucasian handsomeness as a youth. It had long ceased being an asset.

11

Fifty-two years. What's happening?

A siren.

He remembered his brief career as an air raid warden in lieu of the Service. The atomic bomb made that occupation obsolete.

Women.

He didn't like to look at himself nude. His slight frame was wiry, thin. But not too bad looking for a man his age. And he was hung like a horse, but . . .

Women.

There'd been a few. Very casual affairs. In wry amusement he often recalled the young blonde girl who begged him to marry her. He was young, so light at the time. She hadn't been aware of his blackness. His gray eyes fooled her, for a while.

Light negroes darken with age.

Perhaps if he could've had sisters or brothers.

Very black women never seemed to like him. When they did it was usually for the wrong reasons; they'd have pretty children, he could always get a job faster than his black peers. They disgusted him.

He was tired, tired of teaching. A new cut of student faced him. They questioned everything he said, every move—even the private ones. It was difficult being always on the defensive.

He'd retire soon.

Then what?

Write a book, maybe. On black history, maybe. No one knew much about that past, passed. Who was his white great grandfather?

He liked church. Going there was like going home. He hadn't been in several weeks. Most of his angry black students denounced church.

He never argued with them. He didn't know how.

Suicide?

Long ago he tried from the top floor of the administration building at Penn State. Somebody in the crowd shouted, "Jump, nigger! The only good one is a dead one!" He graduated youngest in his class two years later, with honors. Mama had been proud.

Blue-black had won. Night.

Lights that were not stars began illuminating the night sky. Neon glistened.

He closed the window.

The world was passing him by.

12

THE BUYER

KURT'S stomach dug through his lower intestines as the intercom buzzed. Kathy's sassy drawl told him not to forget his one o'clock lunch appointment at Rollo's. It was past noon.

Reluctant, he tore his eyes from the vista. Day had gone fast. Arriving before dark, he had watched sunrise. At intervals he returned to the office window and looked out, longing. Watching the city's baptism in morning light thrilled Kurt. She was as exciting as any woman he had ever loved—angel and whore.

I want yah, flesh and blood. . . .

It gave him a high watching her populace flow into the streets. It infused him with power. In his own way he touched them all, no matter size or complexion. Few black men could make that claim.

His stomach crudely growled out the cost of privilege.

How'm I gonna get through this one!

He felt into his vest pocket for the packet. It was still there. He fingered in for it, easing it out. It was a tiny plastic storage sack barely two inches squared. Within its protection were five yellow capsules.

It'll be difficult to eat after this but not impossible. Least I'll be able to hear what the man has to say. God, it's great to be able, to wear a custom-made suit, sit across a desk and be addressed as "Sir." And I wanted this. Well, shit! I've got it.

He'd spent the night at the office. Not the entire night, but most of it, having let himself in with his private key at three in the morning. Hard work had won him most-trusted-employee status. C.J. et al made beaucoup profits off his sweat, cashing in on a poor-boy-from-Saint-Louis-made-good. The key had been both a thank-you and a crack of the whip.

13

He shaved in the men's washroom, then completed his review of the advertising layouts. He'd promised them to C.J. & Company that morning along with three campaign ideas. There was always one primary idea—what he really wanted—and two alternatives. That's what The Boys Upstairs demanded and what their Prize Buyer delivered. Usually he presented his preference as one of the alternatives. Usually they picked that very one; therefore, he was careful never to show enthusiasm. It kept him from having to scrape and bow. There was a good deal of ass to lick in this outfit and once one started, no end in sight.

So far, so good, Kurt, my man. It takes surgeon-like precision to extract fair pay from C.J.'s nut-crackin' gang of rogues. Once they get you by the balls, it takes quite a dance to avoid castration.

Kurt was doing his share of dancing lately. In his own gamble for success, he found himself aswill in an unsavory middle. The strain of keeping afloat was showing around his eyes. They were becoming pinched and tired. Such a shame. He had magnificent eyes.

Kurt took more after his paternal grandfather (Scotland via Beale Street) than either of his fair-skinned parents. He kept himself in peak form and in expensive clothes. His features were thick and darkly caucasian. Wavy sable hair with flecks of amber had been his mother's joy and the envy of his classmates. On first glance the uninitiated thought him white. The tan of his skin was not quite a full blush of gold. His natural smoothness and superb cool seemed more suited to the jazz lounge than the executive suite. And then, there were his killer green eyes.

His lime-colored lights laid waste the resistance of any woman he chose. Mated with charm and sophistication, his was the perfect combination for manipulating women, and men as well. His feverish history was laced with difficult romances and attempted suicides; assaults on body and psyche spanning puberty to manhood. It was a remarkable power. Time had taught him the dangers of using it too often too well. He had learned to be kind, to enjoy the object of his desire without destroying her.

But in business charm had its limits.

Squeezing against the soft plastic, he coaxed one of the capsules out of the sack. He laid it on his tongue and held it there while he resealed the packet and slipped it back into hiding. He

14

poured a glass of water from the cooler he kept behind him on the credenza. He took the "upper" on a swig, leaned back in his deluxe swivel chair and closed his eyes. As the high took hold, he envisioned his route along Hollywood's streets. It would take ten minutes to arrive at Rollo's, park and squat. He tried, but couldn't remember what Bo Wells looked like. They'd met at a cocktail party earlier that week. Kurt recalled a black-like-me man of medium build in a white stetson and white fur coat. They'd spoken briefly and had shaken hands. Wells had said, "Why don't we discuss this over lunch?" Something about the man had prompted Kurt to accept. But what? And now, no face came to mind. Odd.

Odd because black clients were so few. Most of Kurt's dealings were with white male Big Shots and up-and-coming Big Shots. He knew well enough how to handle them; was surprised, at times, by how easily they handled once he got past the bluster. Then there were the ones like C.J., his boss. The ones he could not fathom. The ones Kurt could barely keep company with for longer than five minutes. A conference with such a man was agony. C.J. was one of those milk white gentiles, the kind of soft man whose whiney manner and oozy mushiness were his strength. He set off chaos in Kurt. He had shaken C.J.'s hand once. It had felt like squeezing a bag of pus. Whenever C.J. came near, Kurt took pains to avoid contact.

Kurt's strongest impression of the faceless Bo Wells was a liking for the man. If he could use his influence to help one of his own, he would certainly do so. In the back of his mind, Kurt hoped there was something for him in this encounter. Perhaps a friend. Someone he could dog the streets with. He hadn't had that kind of buddy since college days. If not, he'd settle for having paid his pittance toward furthering the race.

As he left his office, he noticed Kathy at her desk diddling with her makeup. Kurt stood watching her. She had a body that stopped clocks and hearts alike. She dressed to show off her dark sexy flesh in hot pinks, hot limes, hot blues—everything she wore generated heat. But all her action stopped at her neck. Her head seemed completely foreign, as though from another, dissociated body. There was an undefinably mawkish and masklike quality about her; not African—more some kind of totem creature—a cross between bear and toad. In contrast, her civilized, pressed, dark brown hair was nicely paged at her shoulders. She wasn't

15

what one would call ugly, but she certainly drew one's attention. What was more, she flaunted her appearance, aware of the effect it had on those drawn to the extraordinary. Fascination for her face had been his primary reason for hiring her. Someday, when he had time to play, he'd unravel her mystery.

As Kurt waited for the elevator, C.J. zipped past carrying a thick manila folder, looking overly constipated. He had a heart condition, and it was on Kurt's secret agenda to see to it that one day C.J. suffered a final massive stroke. At times, Kurt fantasized C.J.'s dropping dead mid-conference.

That would be too tasty.

C.J. glared at him then promptly disappeared into a corridor ahead, his brown pin-striped trousers bagging against ancient thinning legs. That such a gray scraggle of humanity had ascendency over him doused Kurt in cold loathing. Sure, he "hated" racism. Sure, he "hated" what he had to do to survive. Sure, he hated it all. But he had never *hated* an individual as deeply as he did C.J. A black man might dislike white people in general. But that was something so distant, so removed, a cultural program with little reality until some incident occurred, targeting certain offensive individuals. In general, one was wary of them.

Kurt's stomach quivered. On seeing the old man he relived their clash the night before.

Early that week, Kurt had received slides submitted from advertising. Kurt sent C.J. a memo stating that when he had finished looking over the slides, he'd forward them for C.J.'s consideration. The week was unexpectedly busy and he hadn't been able to get to them. Around seven that evening, Kurt let himself into the art production office and laid the slides out for viewing. He was leaning along the vertical light table going over them with his loupe, studying each magnified shot carefully, jotting notes. The door opened and someone quietly entered. He assumed it was security inspecting the building before lockup. Intent on his task, Kurt didn't look up, eager to finish and get going. There was a lady waiting whom he did not want to disappoint.

To his annoyance, whoever had entered began easing, snake-like, into the less than one foot of space between himself and the light table. It was C.J.

Kurt saw red.

16

It took a minute to regain his vision and for his blood pressure to subside. Unable to move, he watched C.J. squeeze in front of him without their touching. Fingering his own loupe, C.J. proceeded to examine each transparency as though Kurt were not there. Kurt engaged himself in battle, throwing off the urge to grip C.J.'s cantaloupe of a head and smash it through the light table. When done, C.J. weaseled out of Kurt's space and left the room without glance or comment.

C.J. had been fifteen minutes gone before Kurt recovered sanity. It descended so hard he shook. Was C.J. inviting murder? Was it purely ignorance or purely arrogance? Both? It would not happen again. Could not.

Kurt managed to finish up and leave the office in time to keep his rendezvous, his stomach in acute dyspepsia. The scene stayed with him. It replayed itself again and again. Anger caused him such turmoil even his favorite lady failed to incite his lust. He cursed himself for having missed the opportunity of a lifetime — to go to prison a happy man. He left the lady wanting and returned to the office, hoping to channel his outrage constructively.

Thus his day had begun. And it had continued relatively well, despite his state of siege. It was now past noon and sleep kept coming down on him. He was betting on the "yellow jacket" he'd taken to dispel it.

The elevator doors wrapped him in steel gray and swept him down to the first floor. He exited toward the garage. It thrilled him each time he made that walk. He looked toward his parking slot and what sat there waiting to jump to life. It was long and sleek with a subdued gloss and it hugged and crouched. It was his. He jangled his keys and smiled.

The price paid. Amen.

It was his first new automobile, one that hadn't been broken in by someone else. It smelled of him, brand new and successful. It smelled like the sky opening up and raining coin. It smelled like thighs opening up and pouring out pleasure. The door did not close, it snugged. Inside was a symphony of wood, cashmere and leather — all the things that made one feel rewarded.

Kurt eased in, ignited it, and took off.

He arrived at Rollo's five minutes before Bo Wells. It put him at whatever advantage arriving early put one at. It allowed Kurt to appreciate the gold, red and white interior, the elegantly set tables, and the musings of a singer at the piano bar. It allowed the drug to finally take hold. Kurt was alert if tense.

"My man—my man!" Bo Wells stormed up to the table with exaggerated flourish, implying an intimacy that did not yet exist. Kurt was cool but receptive. "Good to see you again."

Bo was a contrast of white fur against black shirt and black denims. The white stetson was cocked over his narrow mocha face which boasted a waxed handlebar mustache over a blaze of teeth. His eyes were fresh, widely childlike despite their thirty years, with long curled lashes. His nails were manicured and glossed.

Bo offered his hand and Kurt took it. He liked the firm grasp of it, mate to his own.

They ordered drinks. Bo was into Scotch. Kurt was also, but thought he'd best play it safe and do chablis. Bo pulled out all stops on a medium-well steak and baked spud. Kurt went for the same, admonishing his stomach to hush.

Quickly, they dispatched their tastes in women, taking a minute to eyeball what was feminine within immediate range. Bo liked his women arrogant and bitchy. Kurt preferred his cunning but soft. Sports came next, but still no common ground. Bo was into fisticuffs, football, track and field, and basketball. Kurt liked horses, sports cars—anything that smelled of risk. Eventually they got to business.

"So look, man—look at this here furniture." Wells unearthed a fat briefcase and extracted photos, brochures, fabric and wood samples. "I want ya'll to move it for me. I make the best stuff of this kind in the nation and I know it will go cuz I knows what people want—especially black folk. You guys've got that special distribution network set-up. I want in." He waved a prospectus and Kurt took it.

"I've seen your work around." The man designed primitive living-room sets in a lovely pseudo-African motif. It had its appeal, would and did sell. But would Kurt's outfit go for the deal? Maybe. He was certain he could swing C.J., but some of his lieutenants were tough on cultural kitsch. Kurt decided to play it square on this one. His power lay in C.J.'s distaste for coming into direct contact with any of their clients, especially a black one.

"I like it, but I can't promise anything beyond my best presentation. Give me two weeks and I'll see what I can do."

18

"Two weeks? What presentation? What's that s'pose to mean? I've got product. I've got sales records. What more do you have to present?"

"They've got to want your business. And that's my job. To make them want you. As simple as that."

"I've got the figures, man! Convincing figures. My shit's uptight. I mean, damn, this ain't no rat hair coat I'm wearin'."

Kurt looked at the coat. It was ermine. He was a long way from that kind of flash, not that he was so disposed. Some things were sheer matters of taste. "I'll talk to my people and get back to you pronto."

"Hey, man — don't jerk me around. I can't use no jerkin' around."

The man was practically in Kurt's face.

Was he expectin' me to jam him for a kickback? Is he confused because I haven't asked for one? No — he doesn't like me. What is it? My eyes? That's it! I'm not black enough for him. I swear. Bro-ther, you ignoramus — I tried.

"Is yesterday soon enough?" Kurt said acidly. To think he could afford friends in his business was a mistake, a sign of weakness, of tiredness. He had to watch those kinds of slips. They were dangerous.

Wells slapped the table, drawing startled stares from other patrons. "I'm tired of these jive changes. What is this bullshit anyhow? I'm offerin' a good deal here. What's a man got to do, beg?"

Kurt refused to allow Bo to incense him. He appreciated Bo's outrage. It was justified. Wells had a hot item which sold handsomely on the local market. He wanted to go national with his product. There were only two networks available to him. One was run by organized criminals, the other was Kurt's turf.

"No. You don't have to beg. Manners might help."

Narrowing his girlish eyes meanly at Kurt, Bo hissed through his teeth, "I'm warnin' you, *niggah*. I'll kill you if you cross me. I'll *kill* your ass."

The noise of clattering plates and afternoon restaurant chit-chat diminished the threat. Nevertheless Kurt turned to ice. He knew the man could not and would not touch him. The threat was a bluff. It had nothing yet everything to do with Kurt. It was one of those peculiar residuals of slavery.

"Bo, do you know who you're talking to?"

19

"*Who* am I talkin' to?" Bo snapped.

"The buyer. I make all the buys. And if I say make a buy, they make a buy. I run this city."

"You? A niggah? Don't con me. You ain't got the power! Naw. You set it up for me to talk directly to the white boys runnin' it. Who are runnin' you. That's what I want."

"You've got me wrong, Wells. There's no one else. I'm it."

"Oh? We'll see about that. Be sure and get back to me tomorrow mornin'. I'll be expectin' your call." Wells leapt to his feet, tossed several bills on the table, and flew from the restaurant, briefcase in tow, ermine flapping.

Kurt sat in silence, staring at the dead presidents, the tossed soiled napkins, the half-eaten food. The lingering sweetness of Bo's heady aftershave mingled with the stink of cold grease. The wine, the amphetamine, and the meal were having a raucous party in his gut. He felt woozy, glutted and depressed. Kurt yawned. He was going to drop if he didn't get some rest. What he needed to do was catch up on his sleep.

And that's exactly what I'm gonna.

Late afternoon the next day Kurt returned to the office. Kathy was in the midst of primping her hair. She gave him a smile and the morning's messages. Kurt flipped through the numerous little slips, picking out those requiring immediate attention. There were four calls from Bo Wells. He made a face.

"That Wells guy keeps calling. He's off his rocker. He keeps demanding to talk to The Boss Man. I told him you were out. He said 'The real boss, not the negro imitation.' "

"What'd you say?"

"I took the message." She was a good soldier, eager to prove her loyalty.

"Good."

"Didn't ya'll have lunch yesterday?"

"We did. I was cool enough. Too cool. He's a sad man, sick with hate. He actually threatened to kill me."

"Serious? We ought to call the police."

"No, he's harmless, just confused. He'll stop calling when he gets the idea."

"I'm glad it's nothing bad."

"Thanks, Kathy. I appreciate your concern. 'Deed I do." His eyes mirrored his gratitude. Kathy purred with a coyness that made her rather lovely. She couldn't have been more

20

willing if he'd stroked her with his hands.

Amazing. His self-confidence went up another notch. He promised her with a wink. The phone rang, interrupting them, and Kathy answered. She listened, cupped her hand over the receiver, and silently mouthed out the caller's name, "Bo Wells," waving Kurt away as she again took the message.

In the privacy of his office, he ignored the work awaiting him on his desk and went to the window. He drew back the drapes, took a deep breath, stretched, and expelled a little gas. There she was, his city—his lust. Her garish beauty was a fallen white rudely violated by mauves, rusts, golds and a living scar of traffic.

Both angel and whore. But all mine, Baby. For this moment. My moment. Darlin', I know you won't be true—can't be true. Ain't I the fool? No matter. I loves yah anyway, Baby.

I'm hangin' for yah.

REBA

SHE sat in the dark. Day long she sat. Night long she sat. Sometimes she made a little blues song. Sometimes she made a moan, the low fierce movement of earth shifting. Sometimes she'd rock and rock and tear at herself and make her skin bleed a little. Sometimes her eyes rolled back into her head and she gibbered. Sometimes she beat her head against the wall. Most times she was on one long drunk.

Reba walked the streets but was not a streetwalker. She stood in front of store windows and stared at pretty things for hours. Her hair was gone wooly and she didn't bother to clean herself unless it got so she couldn't stand her own stink.

Her family had lost track of Reba. She wouldn't look for help so Reba got none. Yet she survived. One day she lucked across a man so lonely he put up with all of Reba's strange sorry ways.

Old Sam found Reba sleeping on the concrete floor of his gas station after closing. At sixty, he was widowed and childless so he took her in. Reba accepted his kindness. And when the urge took him, Sam had his way with Reba. She never refused him, but she also never responded with like passion.

The men under Sam's hire laughed at him. Behind his back they called him Monkey Sam. It was said that only two women in life had ever loved him, his mother and his wife, both long passed. The unkind joke was that Sam had uglied them to death. And his sin was not only in ugliness, but in his blackness. He was as black as the bottom of an old pone pan. The cowards never dared say such to Sam's face because he was every bit as powerful as he was ugly. He was quick with his fists and quicker with a tire iron. He had led one of the local gangs in

23

his youth and his reputation for violence still lingered.

Sam was quick and shrewd. He had salted away a good deal of money and was well-off though he lived sparely. Above all things, he was lonely. Till Reba.

He burned the rags he found her in. He bought her new dresses and shoes and lacy underthings. He loved her with an intensity that silenced his men with awe. He yearned with all he had in himself for Reba to someday return the love he poured into her. But Reba had no love in her. And he wondered and he worried, but could not decipher her. And Reba would not say. She was a dead woman. Yet there she was, walking around, breathing. But dead to all worlds except her inner one of unspoken pain.

Sam had his own house and he delighted that someone again shared it. In spite of her silence, Reba filled its emptiness with warmth. Sam couldn't get enough of her. Sometimes, when she sat in the dim light of their bedroom window, looking out at the western horizon, he watched her. He loved the play of twilight on her moody face. Reba never smiled. She wasn't more than twenty, he figured, twenty-two at most. She was a beauty. A sumptuous mahogany. But her loveliness was concealed in a death mask. Sometimes, he saw the pain as a soft angelic pensiveness. Sometimes hers was a hellish countenance, eyes red moons, skin aflame. More often than not she smelled of death, befouled and rotted.

Reba didn't do — either for Sam or herself. Old Sam took to bathing her. He'd undress her, quelling his lust until the task was done. He'd run the tub hot with water. He'd prepare it with perfumed soaps and foamy oils. He tried to make her brush her teeth and sometimes she complied just to avoid his fuss. He enjoyed lotioning down her body to keep it from gathering ash, gently rubbing her skin until it glowed. He took her to the beauty shop twice a month to have her hair washed and pressed even though the ladies called him crazy to his face. Some refused to touch Reba more than once at any price, spooked by her unnaturalness.

Sam tried to think of ways to resurrect Reba. To bring her new life. When she drank she went deeper into herself. She drank like no woman he'd ever known. She seemed to hate the taste of alcohol and frowned as she drank it, but drank it seriously, deliberately nonstop, glass after glass, until she passed out.

At those times he tried to prod the whys and hows out of Reba. But she was more stubbornly mute drunk than sober.

Reba did not read. She did not watch television. She did not listen to music. She would not dance. She wandered the streets in a stupor while Sam worked at the service station. Or she sat staring at the walls, going in and out of fits. Sam feared she might kill herself. He tried keeping Reba with him, but she spooked the customers, so he allowed her to stay out in the streets. Nothing ill befell her as if her sheer ungodliness somehow shielded her from incident. After a while, Sam put his worry at bay. Each evening Reba was either home just ahead of him, or came in just behind him as though, despite her apparent numbness, she too needed.

Sam was tireless in his efforts to effect a cure for Reba's illness, an impossibility as he had no clue to its cause. He did the laundry. He cooked the meals. He made her eat, sometimes forcing her. At night he disrobed her and put her to bed. He did and he did. And Sam took his pay in the pleasure of her youthful body though she lay corpse-like during sex. With each passing day, Sam loved Reba more. He wanted to keep her. He made up his mind to marry her.

And so one day, after nearly seven months of caretaking, Sam asked Reba to be his wife. In his proud quiet fashion, he presented her with a band of eighteen carat gold. He held it out to her but she drew back from him and refused to touch it. He stood there, staring at her, his eyes begging her to say yes with all the force of his hunger, his loneliness. At that moment his pain equaled hers. His eyes touched her and triggered in Reba an intolerable wave of hurt.

Reba burst into cries, she shook and she sobbed. She pitched herself to the floor, gurgled and foamed at the mouth. Sam got to his knees and grabbed her, wrestled with her, distraught. He held her still in his arms. She twitched and quivered and began to hiss. He released her, watched her writhing for a few minutes, then went to the kitchen, found the bottle, and gave her a drink to calm her down. She took the gin and in her usual fashion performed her ritual. Sam simmered in his misery and watched her drink. When she passed out, he put her to bed. Sam could not sleep. He sat beside her and studied Reba's every feature, assigning her to memory.

That night Sam prayed. He knew he was going to lose Reba

one way or the other. He asked for guidance, a way to make her stay, and if not stay, a way to cope with her having gone.

In the morning he took himself to work and left her sleeping. All day she tortured his thoughts. When he returned home that night it was with a deep dread. Reba had gone, taking nothing but her favorite housedress, a cloth coat and her purse. On the bedstand he found a letter written simply in her clear hand.

Dear Sweet Sam, I can't make you happy. Find a woman worth your love. I loved a man once. I ran away from home to be with him. I had his baby. The baby was born wrong. When he saw the baby he said it was my fault. He left me and the baby to starve. I couldn't work. I didn't have any money. The baby got sick. One night I had a fit and I smothered the baby. To conceal my crime, I ate my baby. The way a bitch sometimes eats the bad of her litter. It was so tiny I thought I could eat it all. I couldn't. So I buried the rest. They'll find me some day. And justice will be done.

Sam read and reread Reba's letter until darkness fell and he could no longer see her words. He wondered at the truth of them or the lie of them. She needed help, professional help — the provisions of ministerial or medical science — the kind of help he, in all his loving, could not give.

Sam sat in the dark until sunup. Sometimes he trembled, sometimes he sobbed. Sometimes he made a little blues song. Sometimes he yelled out, filling the emptiness with her name. Sometimes he cursed her. Most times he cursed himself. Sam suffered Reba's damnation. For if her missive were the mere rantings of a disarranged soul, he swore he could live with that. Doubly he cursed himself, for if every word were the unholy gospel, he could and would also live with that.

LADIES

AT THE END of the session, Diane stopped Retta and asked her to stay a moment after the other women had gone. She closed her office door and took one of the recently vacated chairs, directly facing the young woman.

"I asked you to stay because I'm concerned about you." Retta lowered owl-like eyes and said nothing.

"Something's going on with you. I've been aware of it for some time, but especially tonight. You were here, but your mind was certainly elsewhere. You hardly spoke a word. That kind of reticence makes the other women feel awkward."

"I'm sorry, Diane." She held her head down and stared at the floor, unwilling to return Diane's open and friendly gaze. Retta twisted in her seat. She looked remarkably childlike and defenseless in her thin pale yellow cotton dress and equally thin gray sweater. She was a small, thin-boned woman with semi-straight shoulder length brown hair that did not require pressing. She wore it in its natural state, lightly oiled for sheen and it complemented her full round face with its diminutive, if definitely negroid, features. Her eyes were brown, veiled by a gray-like film which, in the dim afternoon light, gave Retta a haunted allurement. A decade her senior, Diane was maturely confident, elegantly dressed in a tailored blazer over a silk blouse, belted midi-skirt, and brown calfskin boots. Her pressed hair was severely pulled back from her forehead into a foot-long ponytail, ending in one lovely swirl.

"Retta, I want to help you."

Now Retta looked at Diane fully, eyes moist and struggling off tears. "Nobody can help me. Not nobody."

"Let me try, would you? I mean, I've deeply enjoyed these

sessions. You seem to enjoy them. Look at how the other women have opened up and have taken their problems under control. Our progress has been wonderful. But I sense you're holding back. Would you tell me why?"

Retta sighed and found a spot on the wall to occupy her focus. "Those women, they're nice enough, I guess."

"You guess?"

She looked dead at Diane. "They mainly White and Mexicans. They ain't Black. They problems ain't my problems. Not nearly. I mean, I know how to balance a checkbook. And all that sexual stuff they be talkin'—good sex is the least of my problems. I mean—you know?"

Diane wasn't sure she understood, but knew that Retta expected her to do so innately because Diane was Black also. How did their ethnic similarities enter into this? What was it she felt she could say to Diane that she couldn't say before the others? Diane often had to remind herself that she was not just "another one of the gals," but a paid Health Care Professional. She had graduated from a high-powered eastern university and had held her own successfully in a white-male-dominated field. Her life was a satisfying and productive one. She felt herself fortunate to have done so well in a society where less than three decades earlier the social integration she now engaged in daily was forbidden by all codes, legal and "moral." Diane was grateful and wanted to give something back to the "new society" that had spawned her. The Women's Counseling Service had provided the ideal opportunity.

"Look, I'd like to talk, but I can't stay. It's a long bus ride home."

"Let me drive you. I'd like to."

"Well . . ."

"Please."

"Okay."

"Now tell me, what's wrong."

"That's hard to say. It's jes' that, the things I learn here are interestin' and all. But they jes' don't have much to do with me. I needs to talk about that sometimes. I needs to get into where I'm comin' from."

"How do you—what do you mean, Retta?"

"You don't mind if I be honest?"

"Not at all."

"None of the stuff we talk about helps me deal with my man."

"You're not married."

"Not legally. But that's not it. He's a thug."

"A criminal?"

"Sort of—not exactly."

"I mean, what does he do for a living?"

"I can't say, because I'm not sure. He's never told me."

"Never?" Diane was skeptical.

"He says it's better for me not to know. He keeps me in a little money—enough to keep house, but it's like, this here ain't real, Diane. I'm sorry. But it jes' ain't real." Retta shook her head. A few tears fell.

Diane wasn't sure whether to interpret Retta's words as a denial of her home situation, or of the workshop in contrast to it. Perhaps both.

"Well, I'm real, Retta. And so is my desire to help you." She did her best, speaking softly, to console the young woman. Something nagged at her, but she dismissed it. "Look, what time does your—what is his name?"

"Clevis."

"What time does Clevis get home, as a rule?"

"He don't have no time. He come and go as he please."

Here was a man out of the Stone Ages, Diane thought, looking at her watch. "It's 6:30, now. I've got a couple of hours to spare. Let me drive you home. I'd like to see your situation for myself. That might let me do a better job of helping. We'll try and work out some solution in the long run, okay?"

"I—I don't know."

"Let me. Please."

"You ain't seen where I live."

"Where do you live?"

"Watts."

"I've been to Watts, Retta. I know what poverty is about."

"If you say so," Retta shrugged and smiled a little, wiping her eyes.

"I say so!"

Diane had never gone out of her way to help any of the women outside the workshop but something about Retta compelled her. It nagged her along the drive south as the city's ethnic diversity became less and less apparent and the skins of other drivers and pedestrians browned. She slipped a jazz cassette into her tape deck without thinking, responding to the need to feel upbeat. The cabin filled with lilting strings and cascading guitars.

"Excuse my poor manners, Retta. I forgot to ask if you like jazz? I can play something else if you'd like."

"That's okay. I got nuttin' against jazz, I jes' don't understand it is all."

"What kind of music do you like?"

"Blues, I guess. The popular stuff. Stuff folks dance to."

As they neared Retta's address, the streets rapidly darkened with the night of poverty. Buildings were more frequently vacant — violated by the classless scrawlings of youthful gang members and misfits — in varying degrees of disrepair, some suffering the added bane of old earthquake damage as well as the ravages of age. The streets glittered with the shiny bodies of bottle caps and tabs from beer cans and soft drinks pressed into the asphalt by the persistent pressure of traffic. The trees were overgrown and unkempt. There were fewer luxury cars to be seen, mostly older models maintained for survival's sake. The few new cars she spied were driven by fiery fad-conscious young males, the wickedly mature, or the sedately older and settled, more successful members of a community from which they chose not to venture, having invested their lives into its very heart. Though sympathetic, Diane felt the outsider. She was blessed and knew it.

There was no parking on the streets at that hour even though the location was residential. Diane started to park in the apartment house driveway, but it was so cratered with potholes she feared damage to the underside of her car. She decided to risk the ticket and park on the street.

The neighborhood didn't seem too terrible, Black working and welfare poor. The Pagoda Apartments were painted a ghastly drab olive stucco done in a pseudo-hacienda style of hasty architecture peculiar to the poorer sections of Los Angeles. The so-called security gate, a black iron meshed grate reinforced with bars, stood ajar, obviously dysfunctional for some time. They stepped into an oppressively squat corridor and were greeted on either side by banks of ebony mail boxes, many missing locks, lids askew, the afternoon mail tossed carelessly underneath into the shallow bins for larger packages. What had once been a swimming pool had been filled with cement and reborn as a play area for the children in the compound. School had yet to let out, so the building was relatively tomb-like.

Diane followed Retta upstairs but was suddenly regretting her hasty decision to come. Retta fumbled around in her worn leather bag and came up with keys to the double locks protecting against intruders. Inside it was spare but clean. The furniture was cheap, worn and greasy. The couch seemed to burp and whine at her when Retta extended her brown arm as invitation to sit. Diane hedged.

"I'd prefer a chair. I've got a bad back," she lied, a bit ashamed of herself for doing so.

Retta pulled a chair across the rug from the tiny dining table and set it before the "living room" area coffee table, adjacent to the couch.

"Want a drink?"

"What have you got?" The place was meticulously clean, even the windows — and it was rare that Diane had ever been in any apartment where the windows were freshly washed inside and out. She surmised Retta filled her lonely hours with housekeeping, not that there was much with which to fill so deep a loneliness.

"I gots water, and some orange juice, and I could put on water for some coffee."

"Tea?"

"We don't drink tea."

"Orange juice will be fine." Diane felt her spine stiffening, her pulse increasing in increments. She struggled to conceal her discomfort. There would be no possible communication between them if Retta felt "looked down upon."

Retta poured the orange juice and presented it to Diane in her best glass, an old, rather shapely, peanut butter jar. Diane recognized the brand. She recognized Retta's glass as once having contained a popular brand of strawberry preserves. She took a swallow and accepted the thin colorless napkin held out at her. Retta busied herself putting away the orange juice and Diane busied her eyes with the white apartment walls. Over the dining table, which was flush against the wall, its two remaining metallic chairs looking forlorn, was a portrait of Malcolm X, his forefinger raised prophetically. There was a calendar coughed out by one of the neighborhood liquor marts, and over the couch was framed a huge Bearden-like collage of famous black singers from all eras and styles of music. There was a puny little stereophonic hi-fi rigged a few feet behind Diane, beneath it a couple of dozen long-playing records in the cabinet rack. The floor was covered in a brownish shag save for the kitchen and tiny dining areas which were defined by cheap linoleum cracked by time and infinite scrubbings. As Diane studied the nap of the rug near her chair, she became horribly aware of something alive in it. A huge, glossy black one-inch Japanese beetle was braving its loops and twists, scuttling past her foot. She felt her flesh twinge and go to goosebumps. She dropped her glass and spilled the remainder of the juice onto the rug, jumping up from the chair in order to avoid getting it on her clothes.

"Oh, dear! Oh, Retta—I'm so *sorry!*"

Retta rolled her eyes at her, puzzled by Diane's accident. She was such a soft spoken, composed and "together" woman, clumsiness seemed unlike her. Preoccupied with her own troubles she failed to sense Diane's increasing skittishness. Retta grabbed up a large sponge from the sink, moistened it with cold water and went to Diane's aid, mopping up quickly, thoroughly.

"I—that's not like me to be so messy."

"It's nuttin'. Not dirty as this rug is. What's one more spot."

"Look, let's talk about you—your problem."

"Life is my problem, Diane." She spoke softly, seriously, easing into the couch beneath the loud collage.

"Don't be so pessimistic, Retta! You're poor, yes, but this isn't that bad. You're clean and decent. You want to grow if given the chance. You can and you will."

"It's Clevis. Like I mentioned."

"Your husband."

"I wish. He ain't the marryin' kind. We been livin' together now two years. It was better 'tween us when he worked a regular job. But he fell in with a new crowd about a year ago and he stay in the streets."

"You go with him?"

"Once in a while. But somebody gots to bring in a steady paycheck so I waitress nights. That's how I get to take your workshop."

32

"Oh."

"Then, I usually go to the job afterwards, on the bus, but I took tonight off, called in sick."

"Does Clevis ride the bus too?"

"Oh, no. He got him a brand new car, real nice. In fact, that's kinda why we're so broke, them monthly payments and maintenance and all."

"Can't Clevis pick you up and drop you off at the job?"

"Huh?"

"I mean, he has a car, doesn't he ever use it to help you?"

"He takes me grocery shoppin'. We go out sometimes."

"Doesn't he help you go back and forth from work?"

"No."

"Do you think that's fair?"

"No."

"Have you talked it over with him?"

"I tried."

"What did he say?"

"He don't have the time."

"What? He's not working and he doesn't have the time?"

"Well, he does work — in a way. And we're trying to save up money too — at least I am — to try and get out of this neighborhood."

Diane was pleased that Retta seemed to have her priorities straight. "What's Clevis like?"

"He may come through here in a little while and you can meet him."

"You love him?"

"I'm his woman," Retta spoke nervously, and looked toward the door. "He's a hard man to love."

"How so?"

"He's big and like a bull. He's dangerous. I can make him gentle, but most folks can't. He can be mean like nobody's business."

"Mean?"

"Like I said, he's a thug, Diane. And thugs, they don't listen to what a woman wants. To them, a woman is either a submissive wife, like you always criticize, or a playthang. Not much else. That's what I was tryin' to tell you before. You can't easily reason with a man feelin' cocksure and powerful about himself."

"This is a new age, Retta. A woman is a whole being. Not

an addendum — not an extension of a man. But his partner. You
have rights and they must be respected — by everyone." Diane
bristled with indignation. She was up for the challenge. And
Retta stood to benefit greatly, she thought.

"Clevis got a funny kind of temper. He scares people."

"How?"

"He can be talkin' to you, like if you disagree about
somethin'. Well, he'll tell you that you have a right to your opin-
ion. But at the same time he's saying it, his eyes got an evil glit-
ter in 'em. He might even smile. But you *know* that if you cross
him he'll slit your throat without a second thought. You know?"

"He's threatened you with violence? He's hit you, hasn't he?"

"No, he's not the kind of man that has to beat on a woman.
He considers that unmanly. He's so sure of himself he don't need
a woman's tears to boost himself up. But he'll kill anyone, man,
woman or child, that cross him. And he don't have to say nuttin'. He jes' make it felt when he look at you. And you believe
it too. And — I guess I ain't learned how to deal with that side
of him. Yet."

"You don't want to leave him."

"No. I mean, he's a good man, otherwise. And I don't think
I could ask for a better lover. I'm jes' hopin' I can wait it out
long enough until he quits bein' so wild and kinda settles down.
Then, at least, I'll be a lot happier."

"You're a pretty woman, Retta. You could do a lot better
than this." Her eyes encompassed the whole apartment and Retta's relationship with Clevis.

The door opened and a tall, stocky, honey-colored man
entered by his own key. He was thirty, had a full head of wavy,
marcelled hair and the thick surly features and expression that
made Retta's use of the word "thug" apropos. He was solid and
muscular underneath the shirt opened three buttons down to
reveal curly chest hair. He had been sweating and his shirt was
wet at the armpits. His body odor, mingled with the smell of
alcohol filled the apartment and hushed the two women. He
looked at Retta with a little nod and then cast a blank glare at
Diane. Retta rose hastily from the couch.

"Hi, Sugar. This here is my friendgirl, Diane. She's from
the workshop, you know?"

"She is, huh." He looked her up and down for a moment
as he closed the door behind him. Diane noticed he carried a

mid-sized grocery bag. It gave off a spicy aroma. "I stopped by the Chinese place and got me some shrimp fried rice. Since you wasn't gonna be home to cook supper tonight—I thought." He glared at Diane, and while she could not read it in his eyes she felt a note of hostility. "Ain't you s'pose to be workin' tonight?"

"I—I took sick leave, Clevis. I wasn't feelin' well."

"You felt well enough to go downtown," he again looked at Diane, "apparently."

"Want me to get you some orange juice, Sugar?"

"Naw, I got a couple of beers." He walked around Diane and busied himself over the dining table, setting out his meal. "Don't mind me, *ladies*. Go on about your visit."

Diane looked at her watch. "Well, it's about time for me to be going." An alarm had gone off inside her and she was unable to control her sudden panic. Everything Retta had said about Clevis was frighteningly accurate. He was not the sort of man anyone could readily feel comfortable around. His mere massive presence was a potential threat.

"I don't mean to interrupt. Retta has so few friends and I'd rather her have someone to talk with than to sit up here going stir crazy." He spoke, looking down at the beers, twisting the cap off one proficiently with his thumb and forefinger.

"She was kind enough to give me a lift, since I wasn't feelin' good," Retta sputtered and sat down.

"Yeah? Okay." He prepared his plate and brought it over to the table as Retta moved over and gave him her place on the couch, sitting closer to the door, across from Diane. The women looked at each other. Diane apologized for not being able to stay longer. "Really, I've enjoyed my little visit with Retta, but must be getting home myself."

"Well, I'm glad you stopped by." And then he did something odd, as though suddenly tuning out Diane, expecting her to rise and let herself out as he turned his full attention to his woman.

"You sick, huh? What's wrong with you, Retta? You don't look sick to me."

"I felt bad this morning, but I'm better now."

"How do you mean, sick. Like what?"

"A little nausea."

Diane felt her stomach buck and quiver as she stared

35

helplessly at the couple, feeling trapped in their little domestic drama.

"What else? That ain't enough for anybody to stay home. If I stayed home every time I felt a little something like that I'd never leave the house."

"That's all. Really, Clevis, it's nuttin'."

"If it ain't *nuttin'* then how come I gots to come home and find some busybody social worker sittin' up in my lady's face?"

Diane felt a strong wave of nausea herself as she fought off her shock and anger. He spoke coolly, there was not a hint of nastiness in his tone of voice—he was quite matter-of-fact.

"You been to the doctor, or call him?"

"No, I—"

"Why not?"

"Clevis," she whined his name pathetically, and looked at Diane, who rose and went for the door. Clevis stopped and held her with his blade-like amber eyes.

"Wait a minute. Since you here already, you might as well sit still for the rest of this."

"Clevis, she ain't done nuttin'." Retta interceded.

"She here. She party to it."

"But—"

"Woman, what's wrong with you?"

Retta held her head down. Diane felt for her and tried to transmit strength and courage.

Retta finally came out with it. "We gonna have a baby, Clevis." She looked into his eyes, speaking evenly, searching them, resigned to his power over her/her love for her man. His body hovered tensely over the tiny woman. Diane stood, witnessing, not quite knowing what to do or say, feeling embarrassed for all of them. Retta looked up at her. "I'm sorry." Then at Clevis. "I didn't have the guts to tell you by myself."

"You must think I'm pretty stupid. You're my woman, Retta. Every time you have a period I know because I smell it. That good blood woman smell. But it ain't been on you for two months, now. I've been waiting to see how long it was going to take you to get up your nerve."

Clevis leaned over his plate and resumed eating his shrimp fried rice. "Miss Lady, you can go now. And I don't expect we'll be having the pleasure of your company again anytime soon."

Diane exchanged a fleeting glance with Retta then hurried

36

out the door, down the stairs, past the mailboxes to her car. She stopped in her tracks, caught by the ticket flagged on her windshield. She plucked it from the grasp of the wiper and tucked it into her purse. As she unlocked the door, her eyes were drawn to the building, to Retta's apartment. There at the kitchen window, she saw Retta looking down at her for a moment before dropping the curtain. Spurred, Diane climbed in behind the wheel, started the car, fired the engine and hit the accelerator. As she fled north and west away from the ghetto, she slipped a fresh cassette into the tape deck. She chose a modern piece rampant with angry trombones, turbulent drums, ranting trumpets, and a fiendish bass. She put the volume up loud enough, she hoped, to first drown her thoughts, then blow her brains.

THE SEAMSTRESS

MAMA comes home tired from the sweatshop. She is so tired her body stoops — the weight of slaving on the double-needled power-sewing machine from 7:30 in the morning till 4:20 in the afternoon. So tired she can barely push open the door. So tired we are silenced by the impact of it on her face.

Mama comes home to the imperfect dinner almost ruined by the eleven-year-old anxious to please. To the petulant ten-year-old eager to play outside. To the five-year-old banging on his red fire engine. To the three-year-old crying for lack of attention.

Mama comes home to us so tired she must lay down awhile before she does anything.

So tired, baby, I could cry.

She goes into her room and collapses into the bed. I watch from the hallway. She cries for a few minutes — a soft, plaintive whine. I go and set the table and serve the meal. I fix her a plate and take it to her on a tray. She is too tired to come to the table. *So tired, baby, I could die.*

We eat and my older brother and I do the dishes. Papa has not come home. He calls. I take the phone to her. Her side of the conversation is full of pain, anxiousness and despair. So tired she sounds.

But it's the beginning of the school term. And we need clothes for school. We need. And I watch her rise.

"You know, it was hard today. The white man boss don't want to pay me what I make. I work fast. Faster than the other girls. They get jealous of me. They try and slow me down. My floor lady is an evil witch. She won't give me the good bundles.

39

And she lets some girls take work home to make extra money. But not me.

"I don't care. I'm so fast I do it all right there. And those Mexican girls — they make me so angry. They all the time afraid. Won't speak up for their rights. Take anything they'll give 'em. Even work for less money, which weakens all our purses. We say, 'Hey — don't be afraid.' I don't understand them Mexican girls."

She fills my ears with her days when she comes home from work. I am the one she talks to. There is no one there to listen but me. Sometimes Papa is gone three or four days without word. And my brothers — little boys too impatient for such stuff as what a woman's day is made of. And her few friends — she talks to them by phone now and then. She's too proud to tell them how hard it is for us. And since the hard times, few friends come by.

She goes into the bathroom, washes her face in cold water and dries her eyes. She goes into the front room and sits at the coffee table and slowly, carefully counts out the tickets which will determine her day's wage. I help her make the tally by reading off the numbers aloud. Her eyes are too tired to see them even with glasses. She marks them down on a sheet of paper and adds them up. Satisfied, she gathers them up and binds them with a rubber band.

I bring her fresh water from the kitchen. She drinks it in long, slow swallows, then gets up slowly and goes over to her single-needle power machine, sits and picks up the pieces that will become my new dress. Within the hour I will try it on. She will pin up the hem and then sit in front of the television and stitch it in. And tomorrow the girls at school will again envy the one who always has new clothes.

But now I watch her back curve to the machine. She threads it with quick, dark cedar hands. She switches on the lights and the motor rumbles to life and then roars. *Zip zip zip* — the dress takes shape.

And this tired. I wonder as I watch her. What must it be like? And what makes her battle it so hard and never give in?

40

THE STARE DOWN

"QUIT botherin' me."

"I ain't botherin' you."

"Yeah you is."

"No I ain't."

"You lookin' at me. You got to see everything I do."

"Looks can't hurt nobody."

"If you don't quit lookin' at me I'm gonna put your eyes out."

"I'd like to see you try."

Once upon a time a group of giggling children at play had run past her on the street. She had just been to the beauty parlor. Her black hair was freshly pressed and curled into a crown of sheen.

"You sure are pretty!" they chorused as they ran.

Yes — I must be pretty. I must be. Children that age are brutally honest. I shouldn't be so insecure. If they say I'm pretty I'm pretty.

A group of Lebanese owned a bookstore on north Western Avenue in Hollywood. Shawna had been taking courses at nearby City College. It was the end of the term and she went there to trade-in her books for much needed cash. A number of well-heeled Arab-looking people moved toward the back of the building. The men were suited and wore either a fez or a modified burnoose. The women were veiled. Shawna assumed it was an Islamic holiday as she watched them gather. She stood quietly out of the way, near the cash register, clutching her half dozen books, awaiting service.

A big-chested, befezzed man marshalled up to her. "Are you here for the ceremony?"

"Huh-no." Shawna blushed. "I'm waiting to resell my books."

"You should join us sometime."

"Huh?"

"Of course, you must — uh — dress differently."

"What? Oh, yeah. Of course." She felt conspicuous in her blue jeans, baggy overblouse and sneakers.

"Such a beautiful woman like you, yet so ignorant of the world."

"Huh?"

"You'd be surprised. Many of *your* people are followers of Islam."

"What people?"

"Don't you know what you look like?"

"No."

"You look Egyptian. In fact, many people from the northern part of Africa look as you do. And many of them worship Allah, revere the teachings of Mohammed and study the Koran."

He was interrupted by the clerk who muttered something in Lebanese. He abruptly went to the back room without a further glance at Shawna.

The incident haunted her for weeks. Was it true? Were women of her complexion and facial features considered beautiful in other parts of the world? Or did ugly translate into any language?

A tall caucasian woman came swimming towards her through the tide of flesh that overflowed the interracial party. Shawna had tried to avoid the woman. She didn't feel comfortable around white people and did not know how to talk to them. Whites had such a cold stare down. It was either out of curiosity and/or fear and/or hostility and/or guilt and/or superiority and little else. The very tall, very aggressive woman didn't seem to have a prejudiced air about her as her eyes locked on Shawna.

"I beg your pardon, but what tribe do you belong to?"

"Huh?" Shawna groped for an answer. She'd heard of a black man who had taken on the near impossible task of tracing his lineage back to tribal African origin. Shawna had talked to a few cultural nationalists who claimed Dahomey, Ibo,

42

Ashanti or some other kinship on the superficial basis of physical appearance. The woman read Shawna's surprise and met it with disarming warmth and humor.

"I'm sorry. I don't mean to be rude, and I don't mean to upset you. I'm an anthropologist."

"Oh." That explained almost everything. "Some people tell me I look Egyptian." She was too enthusiastic.

"Nonono. I'm not into *African* tribes. God knows there are enough of us doing *that*. I specialize in Amerindian tribes, especially the Plains, Pueblo and tribal peoples of the southwest."

"Ohhh!" Shawna grinned broadly, then laughed. At a time when her peers were making such a big to-do over how African they were after decades of denial, touting how Indian one was had become passé. That side of her family history was little known and rarely spoken of. Shawna felt too far removed in time and place to consider it significant and found it strange that anyone else would, especially someone white.

"Did I say something funny?" The anthropologist was puzzled by her amusement.

"Excuse me. I've never been asked that by anyone before." She studied the woman, wondering if she were actually white, or passing for white. Her skin had a rich texture to it. Her dark brown hair was pulled back from her full large oval face into a ponytail. Shawna considered herself above average height at five-feet-eight-inches. This woman had two inches on her. Shawna gave up guessing. *White women are such chameleons.*

"Where you from?" Shawna asked.

"I'm from New York. And you?"

"I was born and raised here in Los Angeles."

"I hope my asking you a few questions won't offend you. So many Afro-Americans are in part tribal/indigenous peoples, even though the process of urbanization has removed them from their origins. I'm doing a study of this phenomenon — a book — and I'm desperately seeking blacks who've had recent tribal experience — say, within one or two generations. When I saw you come into the party a few minutes ago I just had to talk to you."

Shawna didn't know how to take this and stared blankly. The woman laughed softly. "It's really not *that* kind of come-on."

"I'm relieved."

"Would you answer my questions now if you don't mind?"

"I don't mind."

"Thank you." She laughed again. "You've got those lovely high cheekbones and they curve out a bit." She quickly worked her hands across Shawna's face before the young woman could draw back. It was the first time in years she'd been touched by a white person who wasn't a school teacher or a physician.

"By the line of your cheeks, I'd say — Cherokee."

Shawna was stung. "That's right. Three generations back on my mother's side. My grandmother's mother. She married great grandad after he made the Oklahoma land rush."

"And by your eyes and the shape of your face — I would also say Sioux — Dakota Sioux."

"Damn. My mother's other grandmother. I don't know as much about her. I seen her in a photograph. A huge woman. She dressed all her kids in braids and them funny little frocks — even the boys. She was a mighty big squaw."

The woman frowned. "Indian women don't like to be called squaws. It's derogatory and a very racist term."

"Oh."

"Is there any other tribal mixing? What about your father's side?"

" 'S mystery to me. My father was very light-skinned in his younger days, now that I think of it. In fact, he was lighter than my mother." She was talking aloud in wonder to herself. "Now he's darker. Hmmm — wonder how *that* happened?"

"Don't you know that blacks darken with age?"

Shawna cocked her head at the woman. *You mean I'm gonna get blacker? Shit. I'm having enough problems as it is.* "What?"

"Yes — it's one of the amazing properties of melanin. That's what causes the pigmentation in skin. It's also an age retardant. It's been researched by gerontologists for years. You blacks are so lucky! You don't wrinkle as badly as we whites do. It also seems to counteract senility."

"What's a gerontologist?"

"Someone who studies the problems associated with aging."

"Oh." Shawna swallowed. She hadn't known there was so much more to being black. "Uh — well — on my father's side I can only go back to my grandmother. He never knew his father. They from Arkansas. That's all I can tell you — if that helps."

"It highlights the problem — yes." She studied Shawna for a speculative moment. "You know, I'm part Cherokee myself, by the way. It's not uncommon to find Cherokee blood among whites as well as blacks. The Cherokees got around."

Shawna's eyes narrowed. She couldn't resist temptation. "You mean we could be kissing cousins?"

The anthropologist's face instantly went blank. "A very slim possibility, but a possibility." She smiled with finality. "Thank you for talking to me.

"And by the way—you are a *very* beautiful young woman. And I'm happily married with two sons nearly your age. So don't get me wrong."

They both chuckled at the implications as the woman disappeared back into the sea of flesh throbbing to acid rock, never to be seen again.

To thine own ugly be true.

Shawna didn't have the nerve to enter the posh celebrity hangout alone so Mari went with her to Scolero's. Mari was a pert, short, dark-skinned woman. They had both dressed fashionably for the rare evening—a sojourn across town into a realm inhabited primarily by whites. First on the agenda had been a movie. Afterwards they made their way to the famous café to see if they could see anyone who was anyone to see.

The two women had counted their pennies and figured they had barely enough between them to go dutch for a two hour hang. No telling what might happen or who they might meet.

The young blonde hostess showed the two goo-goo-eyed women to a nondescript table against the wall in the main room. They wanted to sit in one of the back rooms where all the rumored action took place and where the real celebs were said to anchor. The hostess insisted those rooms were full.

Shawna and Mari accepted this, not sure if the woman was telling the truth or if they were being denied access. Philosophically the disappointed women accepted their nobody status and took the table. Shawna slid into the cushioned seat against the wall. Mari took a chair on Shawna's left. The blond waiter swished over with menus and the two women took them with sighs. At least they could say they had been to the infamous Scolero's.

After minutes of mulling over a selection that wouldn't bankrupt them, they settled on two hard ciders and a cheese and fruit plate, not failing to notice the cash minimum designed to keep out low life. Mari waved their waiter over and he scrawled down their orders with feigned interest and a phoney smile.

The main room was large and airy — thirty-odd tables peppered the space at odd angles. There was a strong buzz of talk, the rattling of silverware, and the clattering of dishes and trays. Under the din a steady stream of pop music hits could be detected between sprinklings of Italian arias. Young, mainly blonde waitresses and waiters clad in black-and-white catered to the needs of an impatient clientele. From where they sat, Mari and Shawna could watch the street traffic outside. As they waited for the cheese plate, they scanned the room.

Shawna was feeling very good about the evening. She felt young, pretty and black. As did Mari — two young soul-sistuhs hanging out in "the Wood."

"So this is Scolero's."

"Yes, isn't it too hip?"

"I guess. It's not as fancy as I thought it would be."

"I heard it's an exact replica of the original restaurant in Italy."

"Really?"

"Oh, yes." Mari, an aspiring songwriter, knew more about these things than Shawna whose only claim to ambition was an inner city secretarial pool and occasional self-improvement courses at City College.

"Looks like we the only two of *us* in the place."

"This ain't exactly *our* style."

"You think we'll see anybody?"

"I don't know. I hope so."

They watched the window. Several luxury cars were parked within view.

"Wish I had me one of *them*."

"If wishes had wheels everybody would drive. What is that one over there, anyway?"

"That's a Stutz. Handcrafted in Italy. Sixty-five thousand. Kidskin seats. And they put your name on it in gold."

"What's that, a BMW?"

"Yeah. Everybody thinks the Mercedes is so hot, but give me a BMW any day of the week, honey."

"What's that new little car they say's hot?"

"The new Jag?"

"No — the Alfa? — hell if I know." Shawna knew very little outside of the auto world within her economic grasp — Ford, Chevy and Japanese imports.

"You know, I once rode in a Rolls Royce."

"Did it feel good, honey?"

"Did he *evah* — and a Silver Shadow at that."

"Impress me some more, girl. Who was he?"

They laughed, and were still laughing when their order arrived on the arms of their harried wage slave. He laid two plain china plates before them, stainless steel service rolled in peach broadcloth napkins, two tall glasses and the abbreviated bottles of hard cider; and enough cheese and fruit to constipate an elephant, then zipped off to take another order.

"I pity the poor cow who gave this up."

"They's got to give you something since they charging you twice what it's worth."

"It sure took 'em long enough to bring it."

"They had to go out and kill it first."

"Service is bad here."

"The in-crowd expects bad service. Ain't you heard?"

Shawna took in the lush mountain of cheeses in assorted sizes and in variations on the theme of yellow. There were also strawberries, melon, a clump of seedless green grapes, slices of apple, banana, oranges, tangerines, and chunks of pineapple. And there was something flat and green, sliced into little wafers. It had black seeds in the center. It was definitely foreign.

"What's that?" Shawna pointed at it.

"Oh, negro *please*. That's kiwi fruit."

"Key what?"

"Kiwi. It's some kind of fruit from New Zealand they startin' to bring in."

"Look at all this cheese. We gonna eat all this?"

"If we can't we can get a doggie bag."

"What is it — foreign or domestic?"

"Looks like some of both. That there is limburger, that's cheddar, that's jack, that's brie, and that one there is edam. That looks like goat cheese — that real dark gold one there."

"Goat cheese?"

"Try it. It's really delicious."

47

"What's this one here with all these blue veins running through it?"

"You can take the spook out the ghetto but you can't take the ghetto out the spook." Mari laughed. "Shawna, chile, *that* is bleu cheese."

"Sure enough—is that what bleu cheese look like?"

"Yes."

"You mean the same stuff that's in bleu cheese salad dressing?"

"Stop it, Shawna, you're killing me."

They laughed at the top of their lungs, but the laughter was swallowed by the din.

"May I join you two young ladies?" Drink in hand, a short tan-skinned man charmingly addressed them. They hadn't noticed his approach. Obviously he had eyes for them. And they needed a third party to help consume the massive cheese plate. Shawna and Mari exchanged a quick affirmative nod and he slid into a chair opposite Shawna. Both women were all-too-single and all-too-available.

"You gals been here long?"

"Long enough to get this."

"You're welcome to it." Shawna eased the plate toward his side of the table. He immediately began helping himself.

"I came in about a half hour ago. I was sitting in the back."

"In the back!" The two women went rigid with keen interest. He smiled.

"There wasn't much happening so I came up here."

"Oh." Mari was disappointed. "I guess this place ain't like it used to be."

"Guess not." He said it between mouthfuls. "But that's how it goes with places like these. I've met some nice people here too. But not very many celebrities."

He took in Shawna's catch potential, then Mari's. His appraisal was diplomatically neutral, not preferring one over the other. Shawna yawned and turned away in deference to Mari. The glib young man was pleasant enough, but not tall enough for her.

"Allow me to introduce myself—by the way—I'm Ted." He spoke to Mari, picking up on Shawna's vibes.

"I'm Mari and this is my friend, Shawna." She liked Ted and appreciated Shawna's deferral, whatever her reasons.

48

"Hi Ted."

"So you come here a lot Ted?"

"A couple of weekends out of the month—off and on the past three or four years. It's still a great place—even if it's got a new owner."

"Oh, so that's what it is?"

"Yeah. The guy who owned this place was in the entertainment industry—so naturally all his friends and their friends supported the place." He was confident and completely at ease with the women.

"What do you do?" Shawna asked.

"I'm a scriptwriter when I can get the work."

"My, my!" Mari was impressed. Shawna began to rue her hasty decision. But she could tell it was too late to change her mind as Mari and Ted drew toward each other. She was consigned to the fringe of their attention. She contented herself by listening to snatches of conversation between the music, munching cheese, sipping her cider, and occasionally scanning the room to see if any more eligible young black men might conceivably stray through the door.

"What do you girls do?"

"Well we're both working at secretarial jobs downtown, but I'm trying to be a songwriter."

"Ah—a kindred creative spirit."

"Yeah."

"What's your sign?"

"Scorpio."

"Whoa! Perfect match. I'm Pisces—the fish." He shook hands with Mari. "Hello Scorpio."

"Shawna's a Leo."

He looked at Shawna and she let out a mock lion's roar. The three of them belly laughed.

"I like a sense of humor in women," Ted said to himself. "Now what you gals drinkin' here?" He examined the bottles briefly. "Hard cider, and just about empty." He turned and snapped his fingers at the same harried young blond man. "Don, please bring us three more ciders." Don nodded and fled before Ted's "Thanks."

Shawna noted the name plate above the waiter's left shirt pocket for the first time. All the waiters wore them. *Writers are so observant.*

"So what brings you ladies here tonight?"

"We went to see *Visions of Paradise* at the Stellardome."

"Great film noir."

"What?" Shawna asked.

"It's a classic."

"Oh."

"Ted," Mari cooed, "have you actually seen your work on the big screen?"

"Remember *The Big Cool?*"

"Came out three years ago?"

"Yeah. That was me."

"That was a really hot movie—wasn't it Shawna?"

Shawna nodded. She didn't want to confess she couldn't afford to see it at the time. And by the time she could, it had disappeared from the circuit. Mari treated Ted to impromptu applause and Shawna joined in, relieved they weren't going to discuss it in detail. Ted rose from his seat and took a series of quick little bows, drawing casual glances from nearby tables. Mari and Shawna broke into whistles and cheers, and Ted joined in with them as he sat.

At that moment Don returned with the ciders and cast a condescending eye on the group that chilled their merriment. "Here's your cider," he sneered, "and the check!" And sped away.

"That honky sonofabitch!" Shawna was instantly irate.

"Don't go off sistuh," Ted cautioned.

"The nerve of these white boys. They got to be superior even when they waitin' on you."

The caustic negative reminder of who they were as blacks in a predominantly white arena cast a pall over the trio. They sat glumly picking at the cheese and fruit.

Shawna selected a creamy white wedge of cheese that had a glossy cast to it. She mated it to an apple slice and took a bite. It had an oddly tart flavor that combined deliciously with the green apple. "Hmmm—this is good. What'd you say this is?"

"Brie," Mari muttered.

Shawna's eyes rolled toward the window. A long black Cadillac limousine was parking outside the restaurant.

"Lookie lookie lookie!"

"What a bad-ass dream machine."

"Dream is right."

The gray uniformed white chauffeur moved quickly to the

50

passenger side to open the doors. The entire room leaned forward to stare out the window. *Somebody* had arrived — at last. The door was opened and out stepped a very tall black woman in her forties. Not a big star, but someone recognizable.

"Who's that?"

"I'm not sure. But I know I saw her on television in something recently."

She stepped aside and a tall black man dressed in a three piece suit climbed out behind her.

"Recognize him?"

"Can't say I do."

"Me neither."

Then a second man, slightly taller, descended. He not only was suited, but sported a flowing black cape and silver crowned cane, his eyes hidden beneath silver-rimmed polaroid-lensed sunglasses.

Ted gasped. "I know who *that* is. That's Lawrence St. Elmo the Fourth! The star of that rave new cop show."

"You mean *Orange Town*?"

"That's it!"

"You're right. That's him. That must be his wife, Helen."

"She's an actress. She does celebrity game show spots."

"Now I remember! That was her I saw on *Hollywood Horizontals!*"

"Who that dude with 'em?"

"Who knows? Never seen him before."

"They look enough alike to be brothers or cousins."

"Sure do."

"Could be they dope dealer."

The three celebrities entered through the door held open by the chauffeur who closed it behind them and hurried back to the luxury car. The hostess leapt across the room at a sprint, her long blonde hair flagging behind her.

"Look at that, will you!"

"Everything but the red carpet."

The hostess escorted them past several tables. None suited them. She disappeared into the back rooms, the flamboyant party trailing behind.

"Goes to show fame and money will break down any prejudice."

"Ain't it God's awful truth."

The trio returned to their munching when the curtains parted and the celebrity party re-entered the main room, led by the apologetic hostess. "I'm so *sorry,* Mr. St. Elmo," she said loudly, "but these are the only other tables we have."

St. Elmo cast a lordly glance at the table adjacent to the trio, barely three yards away. "That will be fine."

"Holy shit—they're sitting next to us!" Nearness reduced their conversation to whispers.

"Try not to stare."

"Should we ask him for his autograph? I sure want to."

"That's strictly gauche. People like that love to be seen and not bothered."

"God, look at those threads. I wish I could afford to style like that."

"Me three, honey."

After an eyeful they turned back to themselves. Mari and Ted cuddled while Shawna peeped the doings at the St. Elmo table.

"Psst—check this out, guys, quick!" she whispered fiercely. Ted quickly rose and situated himself between the two women so he wouldn't have to keep conspicuously turning around. The trio ogled aplenty as the blonde hostess placed three menus on the St. Elmo table then prostrated herself on the floor before him. He bade her rise, then she took his hand, pressed it in hers, spoke words of admiration and kissed it.

"I can't believe my lying eyes!"

"Me neither."

The young woman placed an autograph book before St. Elmo. His wife went into her lovely beaded clutch purse for a pen. St. Elmo took it with a regal flourish, wrote something, signed it and returned the pen to his wife in one swift motion. The hostess read the inscription, clasped the book to her heart and floated off.

"Jeez! Did you see that?"

"Only in Hollywood."

"Disgusting."

The entire event had consumed ten minutes of viewing. Ted glanced at his watch. "You ladies in a hurry?"

"We still got a lot of cheese to eat."

Ted went back to eyeing Mari, openly enjoying her company. The two tuned out Shawna as they explored each other's possibilities. Shawna wistfully turned her attention to the cheese and cider, scoping beyond Ted and Mari to the wall that defined the room. For the first time she noticed a series of pen and ink drawings along the walls a foot above eye level. They were urban scenes in black and white, offered for sale at spectacular prices.

The look suddenly zapped Shawna on the side of her bushy head. She felt St. Elmo's stare. His presence penetrated the opacity of those nightshades and took her by the eyes. Shawna blushed to think she'd be interesting enough to attract the star's gaze. Pleased, she smiled to herself, lowered her eyes, and slightly turned her head in his direction so he could get a full view. Her hands fluttered nervously as she allowed herself to be appreciated.

She took a quick little look at St. Elmo. He caught it, reached upwards and took off his sunglasses. She felt her heart flutter. He was ten times more handsome in person than on television. The camera hardened his face, a wonderfully gentle countenance. He was a lady's man. And he had eyes on Shawna.

Smugly satisfied with herself, she turned her attention to a second wedge of brie.

Ted gently tapped her hand. "Hey, guess who's looking at you, kid?"

"Yes, I know."

Mari smiled. "You've made a conquest, gal."

"Yeah. My luck his wife's with him."

"Maybe they're freaky-deaky. You know — ménage à trois," Ted slurred deliciously.

"Maybe they want a date for Mr. Third Party."

"Yeah. But he ain't lookin' at me. Jes' St. Elmo."

Shawna noticed the other man acutely studying a menu, as was the wife. The hostess returned and they placed their orders.

Shawna was relieved to be free of that stare.

"What you gonna do about it, Shawna?" Mari giggled.

"Nothin' is what I'm gonna do."

"This could be your big chance to be discovered," Ted teased.

"Eat cheese, peasant!" Shawna laughed in spite of the flutter in her stomach.

Two waiters, orchestrated by the hostess, carried in steaming trays while a third busily poured champagne. The St. Elmo table concerned itself with dinner.

"That was quick. They's eatin' already."

"They have what it takes to get good service."

"Speakin' of service, turn the plate this way and let me try some of that goat cheese." Shawna took a bite into her mouth along with a chunk of pineapple. After the brie it was very sweet. "Emmm, this is delicious."

But Ted and Mari paid her no mind, again wrapped up in one another, leaving Shawna to talk to herself.

She was tired of being stared at.

She was tired of being stared at by neighbors the moment she left home.

She was tired of being stared at on the bus. Or while stopped in traffic.

She was tired of being stared at when she walked down the hallway and someone passed her and she could feel their eyes travel up and down her body as they turned and stared.

She was tired of being stared at when she went into a store to buy something and eyes followed her everywhere she went — even into the lavatory.

She was tired of being stared at when she went to museums to try and achieve a bit of solitude and absorb some culture.

She was tired of trying to dress nicely and in a quiet fashion that would not draw undue attention. But that did no good. It was her largeness and the darkness of that largeness that brought the stares.

She was tired of things she felt and read behind those stares. They were doing things to her. They were making her into something she wasn't.

There was no place she could go to get away from probing prying orbs.

"Psst — Shawna, he's looking at you again. Don't look up," Mari whispered.

"Hey, his wife's looking too."

"What they lookin' at? All of us?"

"No. They looking at you."

Shawna turned her head. St. Elmo was staring at her, expressionless. The wife was also staring at her. Mr. Third Party was chewing his last bite and wiping his mouth. As he placed his napkin on the table, he clasped his hands and took up the stare as well. Each set of eyes was trained on Shawna.

"I know I've got a look, but this is ridiculous." Shawna failed to mention she was enjoying the experience, including the concern exhibited by Mari and Ted.

"Do you know them, Shawna?"

"Are you kidding?"

"Maybe you look like someone they once knew. Or know."

"Are you sure they lookin' at me and not just in my direction?"

"I'm sure."

"Maybe they lookin' at the pictures on the wall." The trio turned and looked at the pen and ink drawings. There was one mounted just above Shawna's head. "Maybe that what they starin' at."

"I don't think so. It's you, lady."

"What in heaven's name they want?"

"Maybe it's a new form of mass hypnosis. They'll levitate you and float you over there."

"Maybe they want you to bow down on the floor and beg for an autograph, like the hostess."

"That'll be a cold day."

"What would it hurt?"

"My pride." Shawna was beginning to simmer under the intense focus. It was going on too long. St. Elmo, Helen, and Mr. Third Party, all had their chins sitting comfortably on inverted palms, elbows resting on the hardwood surface of their table.

"Why don't they say something?"

"Maybe they want you to make the first move."

"But why me? Why not you guys too? We're the only other blacks in the place."

"Have you ever heard of anything like this?"

"No. Never."

"I bet they're all coked out."

"Well they was some mighty big eaters for snow folks. I thought cocaine took your appetite.

Maybe they been smokin' some marijuana. That makes you hungry."

"How do you know?"

"Negro — *please.*"

"Whatever they on they need to get off it."

"They must get off on doing this stare-down on people. That's the only way I can figure it."

55

"Why don't we try it on them and see what happens."

The trio turned on the elegant celebrities, eyeballing with all they could muster. As hard as Ted and Mari tried they could not so much as arouse the bat of an eyelash.

Shawna felt the weight of those eyes on her. They were at her soul, draining off her youth. She put up her defenses: *They staring at me cuz I'm beautiful. Beautiful enough to be stared at by the handsomest men, black or white, on the planet. But this business is too cold and too strange. And I ain't interested in a ménage à whatever.*

"The only six niggahs in Hollywood, and we gotta duel."

"We've got to do something to break this up," Ted said.

"What?"

"Here, Shawna—change seats with me." Shawna and Ted got up and scooted around. The St. Elmo party remained unflinchingly zeroed in on Shawna's every move.

"Damn."

"Maybe if you say something to them."

"Say what?"

"Ask 'em what they're lookin' at."

"Be for real!"

"Well?"

"I don't want to sound stupid."

"God forbid."

"Okay, I'll do it. Give me a minute to get my composure."

Ted and Mari exchanged apprehensions as Shawna poured some cider and took a long swallow, settling into a pose, nursing her courage. She took a full three minutes before she finally turned as casually as possible, leaned toward the St. Elmos and spoke in her best would-be-starlet voice.

"I beg your pardon, but do I know you?"

Abruptly and in sync, the St. Elmos turned away without a word. They rose from the table, his elaborate cape flapping with the motion, his silver tipped cane raised like a baton, his wife in his wake. The chauffeur met them at the door and held it open as Mr. Third Party hastily pulled a huge wad of cash from his pocket and dropped several bills on the table then trotted out after them. The three slipped into the mystery of the ebony limousine and within seconds were whisked away.

Ted, Mari and Shawna were struck dumb.

"What was *that* all about?"

"Unbelievable!" Ted shook his head.

They sat in silence for a few minutes of contemplation. Gradually Ted and Mari went back into mutual admiration as Shawna, lost in thought, nibbled at the cheese and fruit, staring into space.

What happened? I don't know. Why did they look at me for so long? I'm no prettier than any other woman in this room. In fact, there's at least a couple who are much better looking. But then, to have a "look" requires something extra — something special. And whatever that is, I guess I got it. At last. Hmph. I hope it's terminal.

And she let out a whoop that caused heads to turn all around the room.

THE SCREAMER

GOODNESS gracious!

Linda looked up from the book. The bizarre scream rode through her on a chill, arousing prickles on the nape of her neck. What was it? Where was it coming from?

She had been hearing it daily for over a week. Sometimes it was so loud it seemed to come from within her.

She set the book open, face down on the cluttered, paint-splotched desk before her. She tilted her bulk over it, and peered out that portion of the plate glass window that was not plastered over with advertisements. There was no one along either side of the long commercial block.

Business in the blackening neighborhood was sparse as the white population fled west, taking economic prosperity with it. This was Linda's first job and she was glad to have it. No one in the real business world was eager to hire an eighteen-year-old high school graduate, black, female and very pregnant. But Mr. Sims had hired her on the spot.

Linda sat all day long. She seldom saw anyone except old man Sims who came in to lock up at the end of the day. Or when he came to pay her the few little dollars he had promised. Or when he came in with nothing but the promise to pay—tomorrow or the day after—or the coming week. And she needed the money—the desperate little money.

She had started her job three months into her pregnancy. It didn't seem very demanding, physically. All she did was sit. Yet each day she found it more and more difficult to motivate herself to get up, get breakfast for her husband, Rupert, get the bus the half mile to the shop, and walk the half block from the bus stop.

59

Her working conditions were not much of an incentive. The shop was musty and stank of old paint. And it was poorly lit.

The nature of her work was boring beyond anything Linda had ever known. She had taken the summer job to get experience as a receptionist. There were always plenty of newspaper want-ads for that calling. But there was rarely anyone in the shop on whom she could ply even that vague trade.

Occasionally the phone rang.

"Hello, may I help you?"

"He isn't in."

"Would you like to leave a message?"

Too frequently the caller was a dunner, angrily demanding payment. Angrily insistent with threats of lawsuits, threats of violence. It upset her, at first, to have to convey these messages to the old man. He took them without a ripple of emotion in his placid chocolate mask, thanked her and said he'd take care of it.

And the dunners would call back even angrier demanding satisfaction from her. She would stammer that she knew nothing. Had no information, could not help them, and would, most certainly, convey the message again. On two occasions the phone service had been terminated due to lack of payment. But in some mysterious way old Mr. Sims managed to come up with the money.

"House painting is a good business," he would say to her occasionally, smiling at her from beneath one of his protective paper caps. "People always need a good house painter." She would watch him drive away alone, the ladders clattering in the rear of his old paint-splotched truck — hardly secured by the threadbare ropes — the multicolored cans of paint sealed tightly, knocking against each other as the truck sputtered off.

Occasionally, for bigger jobs, he took on a helper. Young black men between employments, students, or old ghetto hard-cores — winos and the indigent. She could smell the youth and inexperience on the young ones — their eagerness to learn (like her own); their belief in old man Sims; their desire to help; their gratefulness at a chance to prove and improve themselves. All the more grateful because he too was a black man. And she could smell the destitution and the self-disgust on the others — as aromatic as the stench of the grape. She could also smell their impermanence — all of them moved on — shadows against a

60

darkening vista of white wall. Painted over by pain and disappointment.

I too am a shadow.

Yet she persisted. Time was coming when she'd have to leave the shop. The twinges in her distended belly came more and more frequently. She worried about the effects paint fumes might have on her baby-about-to-be. What would she do if it started to come while she sat there in that cold, dismal, dank little paint shop with its colder, rugless cement floors, and its teensy toilet beyond any possible sanitation no matter how much elbow grease and cleanser she applied? She was so horrified by its nastiness that she held her water as long as possible out of fear of somehow contaminating the fetus.

Now was such a moment. Feeling her bladder about to burst, she bolted the front door and scuttled around back to the hamburger shack next door. There the motherly, sympathetic fry cook allowed her to relieve herself.

"You need to quit that place, chile!" The brown-skinned woman observed, as Linda wobbled out of the restroom. "You 'bout near ready to pop!"

Sometimes the woman would give her a free hamburger, saying "This one here didn't turn out so good. I don't dare serve it to a customer." She had one bagged and ready and gave it to Linda as she left. Linda thanked her timidly, seized the little brown bag, and scurried back to the shop.

She was barely able to keep from gulping down the burger in two ecstatic bites. She never bothered to notice that it was, as always, fast food perfect.

Linda was grateful for any kindness that came her way. She could not afford to buy lunch, and occasionally brought a piece of fruit or a peanut butter and jelly sandwich from home. It was all she and Rupert could afford. And Rupert didn't like her working at all, but his janitor's job barely made rent and utilities. With the baby coming, they needed every cent that could be scrounged.

"Did you tell the old man you leavin'?"

"Not yet."

"When you gonna tell him?"

"I'll tell him Friday, after he pay me."

"Well, he better this time or I'm coming down there and make him."

61

"Don't — I mean — you don't have to. I'll see to it."

"Better. I don't want my baby ruint cause you ain't gettin' proper rest."

She was six months — maybe seven, she guessed. Movement was more and more difficult with each hour, it seemed.

She leaned back in the chair to savor the taste of the hamburger as it lingered in her mouth. She was seized by a sudden and overwhelming nausea. Her head began to throb and her heart jittered fiercely. She sat upright and grabbed hold of the desk, hoping the feeling would pass, leaning into it, fighting off the urge to vomit.

In her struggle to maintain equilibrium, she became aware of that murderous wail. Its shrillness penetrated her discomfort as she clamped her teeth, willing her body to obey. Finally it abated, and the nausea also began to subside.

Linda eased herself out of the chair and walked slowly to the toilet at the back of the shop. She stood in the door of the closet and looked down at the stool blackened with layers of dirt, grease, paint and the remnants of urine and feces. Her head began to ache as the nausea returned. She jerked forward, opening her mouth. Nothing came up except a yellow-green bile-tasting fluid. She spat it into the toilet bowl. She turned to the sink, turned on the cold water tap and ran her cupped hands under the faucet. She rinsed her mouth out and dabbed a little of the tepid liquid on her face. She wished she had something to drink other than the lukewarm water from the sink which was nearly as nasty as the toilet. She stood at the sink taking gasps of stale odorous air until she felt better.

When she returned to her desk, the scream met her, crescendoed, then vanished. This time she was certain it came from outside the building. But from where was still a mystery. She opened the front door and took another, more thorough look. She saw a half dozen passersby, all of them going quite normally about their business.

She eased back into the swivel chair. It groaned under her increasing weight. She was only five-two and the pregnancy had taken her weight up over one-fifty. She was beginning to resemble a gigantic rum ball.

She turned the book face up and yawned. She had found it the day before under a stack of papers at the bottom of one of the desk drawers. Her search had been motivated by stultifying boredom. She had to do *something*—if only read a book. She had discovered it under scores of bounced checks and bank notices demanding coverage. She marveled that the old man had written so much bad paper and yet escaped prosecution.

Again she took up the book. Again she was disturbed by that terrible half screech, half groan. She bounced up from the chair, determined to catch sight of the source. The ungodliness of it left sweat icing on her scalp, beneath her mop of thick kinky brown hair.

But there was no one.

What was it?

She sat down to the book again, forcing herself to focus on it. The story was about a young Englishman on his first holiday "on the Continent" and took place in the late 1800s. His ofay travels and adventures among Europe's wealthy were only a momentary escape. It was a meager getaway, only a bit less numbing than the job. One out of every ten or fifteen words eluded her. A search of the shop had not turned up anything vaguely resembling a dictionary. The French phrases were especially troublesome. She tried to guess meanings by rereading a sentence or paragraph a half dozen times, hoping meaning would somehow jump out at her. It was a tedious process with little success.

And the screamer would not let go of her thoughts.

Who is it? Why that hideous holler? Must be somebody sick—somebody insane. What could've happened to make them banshee so?

She tried to imagine all sorts of horrors. But the limits of her imaginings reflected her avid taste in television: A junky. A spy tortured for information. A cripple maimed by fire. The death of a loved-one in an auto crash. Beyond video banalities she could not conjure. Then the phone rang.

"I told that old cheat he'd better have my money today!"

"He's not in."

"You lyin'."

"Me? No, Sir."

"I'm coming down there and see for myself."

The angry click resonated in her ear. She looked up and was startled to see the old man standing there, his eyes smiling at her.

"Did I get any calls?"

"There," she handed him the neat stack of a dozen little pink slips. "And some man just called real mad. He said he wants his money. He's on his way here."

"Did he leave his name?"

"No."

"Well, I've got to go over to the courthouse, now."

She wondered if this was the right moment and decided there was no better moment under the circumstances.

"Could you pay me today, please, Mister Sims?"

"Of course, Linda. When I get back."

He's not comin' back. He'll expect me to lock up with the spare key in the desk. "Now," she lied. "I wants to run next door and get me some lunch."

"Well — all right."

She watched the dark old man pat his body, searching the paint-stained white coveralls for the wallet hidden in his street clothes underneath. He located it, slowly unzipped the front, reached in across his thick chest, and slipped it out. He opened it and a wad of business cards fell to the floor. He stooped over, slowly picked up the cards, went over to the desk, opened it up in the dimness, and peered into its leathery recesses.

"All I got is this twenty," he pulled out the thin limp bill and waved it toward her reluctantly.

"That's what you owe me for last week."

"Well — all right. Take it." He handed it to her. It smelled of turpentine.

He slipped the wallet back into his coveralls and rezipped them.

"When that guy comes in, get his name."

"I will."

She watched him ease out the back door. Moments later she heard the sputter of the truck backing out the driveway along the side of the building. She listened till the sound of the truck disappeared. Then she examined the twenty and smiled, relieved. She wouldn't go home empty-handed. She reached under the desk where she kept her purse. She plucked out her wallet and laid the twenty in the empty bill section.

You still ain't told him you quittin'.

As she tucked her purse away, the door rattled violently.

A tall, well-dressed, honey-skinned man in his late thirties stomped through it in expensively shod feet. "I called a little while ago!" he announced, surprised to see the young woman so grossly pregnant. He glared uncomfortably at her belly.

"You jes' missed him. I told him you was comin'. You didn't give me your name. He had to go to the courthouse. He said for me to get your name."

"*Hmph!*" He walked past her and went around in the back of the shop to see for himself. He returned to the desk greatly upset. There was a strangely vacant look in his eyes as he turned to her, leaning across the desk.

"Tell him his boy was lookin' for him — the oldest." He turned and stomped out, slamming the door.

At the noise, Linda felt a twinge in her belly. It was so strong she let out a little moan and leaned back in the swivel chair to get her breath. And then she heard it. That resonant agony, laboring in its manifestation. Goose bumps rose on her skin. Hairs tingled at the nape of her neck. She sat still and listened as the scream gradually waned into silence.

Linda bolted upright in the chair, dropped the book, grabbed the message pad and scrawled a note: "Dear Mr. Sims. My husband, Rupert say I have to quit cuz the baby 'bout to come. I left the key with the burger lady next door. Sorry. Linda."

She propped the pad against the phone so he would be sure to see it.

She felt a second twinge as she took the key from the top drawer in the desk, grabbed her purse, and waddled over to the front door and bolted it. She hurried as fast as she could through the shop, past scaffolding, canvas, rolls of poster paper, and old cans of paint and thinner, to the rear door. She pulled it shut behind her and struggled to secure the lock.

There it was again. That scream. She cocked her head and listened. It seemed to surround her. She stood listening until it faded, giving way to the cacophony of traffic and the muffled sounds of the world at work. She clutched the key firmly in her right hand and made her escape.

FAT LENA

SHE RIDING in the car next to her husband he be rubber-
neckin' at all the pretty womens age no object and Fat Lena
feel herself gettin' fatter by the minute wonderin' why he don't
reserve his lust for her cuz they married anyway and she like
to fuck as much as he do even if she new at it and not nearly
as experienced but he want a virgin and that what he got Fat
Lena never had a boy break her cherry till he come along she
had a few hold her hand and squeeze up all around her and
two or three try a kiss and one day Fat Lena go to the liquor
store for her Mama this young man just come up on her and
feel her titty where it ought to be but there's just barely enough
to grab hold to and he tear the button off her jumper and ran
away when she scream in a fear totally new to her not knowing
why she was supposed to be afraid of that skinny little ugly brown
boy so that was when Mama began to explain sex sort of and
Fat Lena married at last and moved out and all day she lay up
and watch television and eat junk and wait for her husband to
come home and maybe they go somewhere and do something
but lately she not so happy as she was cuz he started eyeballing
other womens and not even hiding it from her he whistles and
carries on like she's not there or is just another man and it hurts
her feelings real bad but Fat Lena she don't know how to tell
him and one day he pull up at a stop light and while he lookin'
off in another direction an old man steps off the curb and the
old man catch sight of Lena and he grin a big grin at her and
lick his tongue out at her as he passes in front of the car and
Lena grinned back at him and suddenly she feel good and warm
deep inside like God done told her there's hope for her yet.

LONNIE'S COUSIN

I'M SO GLAD you're home. I was so alone. No one here but me and the baby.

It's okay. I'm back now.

I tried so hard to keep it together. But the neighbors — that Lonnie and his people. They smile and they act nice to you but they ain't your friends and they ain't mine.

What do you mean?

While you were gone they tried to fix me up with their cousin.

What?

I was so stupid. I thought they wanted to be friends — thought they were looking out for me because you were gone.

Uh-huh.

They tried to get me into trouble — to do something I didn't want to do.

What happened?

You know what they think of us, don't you?

What do you mean by that?

They see you got a black wife. And you livin' down here in the ghetto. You got to be pretty stupid for a white man. That's what they think of you. The only reason they pay any attention to me is because I'm with you.

We're friends—Lonnie and me.

You're the manager and they're the tenants. They've been in this building longer than we have. The owner—the only reason he made you manager is because you're the only white face in here. You're cheaper than hiring outside help. And he don't trust nobody black.

What you're saying is really ugly. I don't believe it.

Listen to me. Listen good. They wanted their cousin in my panties. To bring us down. You hear that?

I'm not sure what I'm hearing.

Fool.

Don't cry. Look, honey. I'm willing to listen. Tell me what they did to you.

Okay.
Sunday I was planning to make you some fudge for when you got back. I was getting the cocoa and stuff ready in the kitchen—about eleven o'clock. And the baby woke up and started crying. I had his crib in there in the living room near the stereo, and I'm in the middle of finding out he's wet when the doorbell rings.
So I run to the door. And Lonnie is there grinning all in my face—acting friendly. He sure fools me, talking about why don't I bring the baby and come downstairs and visit with him and his wife. I figure it's safe because he's married. Even though I don't know them, I've seen his wife and she looks like someone I'd like to befriend. But I hesitates because I'm making fudge. But he says to come just a little while because he knows I must be lonely, you being away. Well I was. So I changed the baby,

bundled him up, put a bottle and a couple of diapers in the bag and went downstairs.

See. He was just being neighborly. I knew it.

Hush up and let me tell it.
So when I get down there there's this other couple and they's dancing, smoking and drinking beer and all—having a good time. And then they introduce me to this ugly old man—he's their cousin.

What's his name?

I don't know. I forgets it. But I'll remember him as long as I live.

What did he do to you—if anything?

He put a spell on me. He hexed me.

Come on. Bullshit.

Listen.

He put a spell on you?

Those things happen. Whether you believes or not.

This is the twentieth century.

You gonna hear me out?

Go ahead.

Lonnie's wife, she come up to me cooing about the baby, asking me the usual stuff like she's really interested. She takes the baby and lays him on the loveseat near the door where I can watch him. So that means I got to sit opposite him on the couch next to Lonnie's cousin. I don't think about that. I'm just sitting there. They offer me a beer. I tell 'em I don't drink, 'specially beer because I think it tastes like cow piss. And they laugh. So Lonnie's wife she gets some cherries and she fixes me a drink with lots of cherry juice in it real cold over ice. And it don't taste too bad—like punch with a twang. Lonnie's friend—the other guy—he come over and ask me to dance.

What about the cousin.

I'm getting to that. The friend he asks me to dance. We all up dancing and the friend's lady, she's dancing too, by herself off on the side so she can change the 45s on the stereo.

Then what.

Then I notice his cousin is looking at me. He don't seem to be but I can feel his eyes got feet and they walking all over me. And they strange heavy eyes—got them thick lids. Look like he damn near half asleep or something.

How old a man is he?

I don't know. Forty maybe fifty. Way older than us. One of these country-looking men but he's not. He had on this stingy brim panama and belted slacks *and* suspenders both, like he about to lose his pants. And they was khaki. And he had on a pink shirt.

Did he have an accent?

No. He talked regular like us. And he was *real* dark. Twice—three times my color. Dark as that there fudge I made.

And all he did was look at you.

At first. But after a couple of records Lonnie pushed him up from the couch to dance and I was his partner. But he didn't touch me. We just fast-danced. He just made like he was dancing enough to make us laugh then he sat down again. By that time I was having a good time. And I just naturally was relaxed and started talking to him.

Talking about what?

About stuff. Whatever he asked me or came up. You and me. The weather. Television and movies. Like that. But I felt his eyes pulling at me, drawing me into them. My heart started beating real fast. I felt hot and all sticky under my arms. And I started falling into his eyes. And then I pulled my eyes away but they got stuck on his lips. He had real thick lips. Big, dark and smooth. And he moved closer to me. I scooted back. And he eased still closer to me. And I'm on the couch with no place to go, backed against the arm of it, even leaning backwards. But I'm deeply drawn to him at the same time. I'm not talking anymore. I'm listening. He's telling me I'm beautiful. I don't know how beautiful I am, he says. And he reaches his hand up and brushes my hair back. And a feeling goes through me I've never felt before. He put his spell on me right then.

What kind of feeling was it?

I don't know. Like if I'd've been standing my feet woulda gone out from under me. He took his other hand and stroked my thigh and I almost passed out.

Describe it.

Like electricity near about. I don't know what. But I knew that if he kept touching me like that he was gonna have his way with me. And I wouldn't be able to say no to nothing.

Then what.

He put his arm around my head and kissed me, pulling me in against his chest.

Then what? Come on, tell me what it felt like. Quit crying woman. I'm not angry at you—honey, tell me.

I'm so ashamed.

Don't be. Not at all. I'm here and I'm listening.

He kissed me to my soul. I couldn't break free. I kissed him back. I couldn't help it. I was under his spell. When he

73

let go everybody was looking at me. Lonnie and his wife and the other couple — dead in their tracks — like they were all kissing me. Like voodoo or something. It felt real strange. The strangest feeling I ever felt. I could hear what they was thinking. I came half way to myself. I said how it was getting late and I had to go finish making that fudge I'd promised you. So I scooped up the baby and hurried out of there so fast I forgot his little diapers and stuff. I ran back upstairs here.

And that's all?

He followed me up here after a few minutes. He was carrying the baby's bag.

And you let him in.

I tried not to. But he put that spell on me again — I was still under it. He just reached through the screen door when I grabbed for the bag and caught my hand. And it was his touch — he got a touch like satin and a voice like satin. Black satin. Standing right there in the doorway. Then he pulled me to him and started feeling me all over. Hands and eyes. He lifted me right into him, and I could feel him hard through his trousers. I was lost to him.

You did that?

I didn't know I was so weak. I swear I could not help myself. He had greater powers than I had. Will power don't work against no spell.

Then what?

The baby woke up and started crying. I ran over and got him and put him between us. Then I made him hold the baby while I started making the fudge. He got uneasy and said he was going downstairs and get something to drink so would I please take the baby back. Soon as he left I pulled all the curtains and locked the door. I took the baby into the bedroom here and turned up the television so loud I couldn't hear the doorbell ring when he got back. Later I fixed us dinner. Me and the baby fell asleep in here on the bed. Then you woke us up coming in this morning.

And that's all? That's it?

Ain't that enough?

You're positive you didn't let him fuck you.

I couldn't. I love you, honey. I couldn't do that and live with myself. I know that now. Spell or no spell.

You didn't let him fuck you.

Because of you. You and the baby. Plus I couldn't give Lonnie and his bunch the satisfaction of knowing their cousin got me. The thought of them laughing at us behind our backs really makes me mad. They'd love the chance to run us out of here. That's the kind of low life they are.

Why should I believe you didn't let him fuck you. You wanted it.

I didn't want that ugly old man. He made me want him. That's how a spell works. He was so ugly he was beautiful. He the kinda man Mama Creole used to warn me about. The kind that know women better than women know themselves.

And he touched you — your breasts.

He reached up under the blouse I had on — my little white top with the angel sleeves.

Did he kiss you at the same time?

Yes.

What else did he do?

I don't want to talk about it no more.

But I want to talk about it. I want to hear it again. All of it.

That was all of it.

I have a right to know what he did to you. I'm not sure you're telling everything.

But I said.

That was too general. I want specifics. You said he was darker than you are.

Yes. Almost purple-black. Much darker than Lonnie and his wife. It's hard to believe they're blood kin.

His hands. How big were his hands. Bigger than mine?

Why? You seen him around before?

No. I just want to know.

In case you see him again?

Quit stalling and tell me.

I'm not stalling. I'm just concerned. Yeah—his hands was twice—three times bigger than yours.

And his lips.

Thick. Very.

Did he smell?

Yeah, come to think of it.

Like what?

I hadn't thought till you asked—but he had a real strong funk to him. Like a wino. Only not so bad. Kind of pleasant. But strong and musty.

76

And his eyes. What were they like? What color?

Black-brown. Like big old olives swimmin' round in a yellow dish. You could see the veins in them. They was eyes that's done lots of living.

What was he built like? Was he as tall as me?

By about half a head. And he was lanky. But real strong. Like a man that works the earth.

And he kissed you.

Yes. It made me weak all over when he kissed me. Don't make me keep telling it.

Don't I ever make you feel the way he did?

It's not the same thing. You're my husband. He had me under a spell. I love you and you love me naturally. What he was about was no good.

Tell it to me again. From the beginning. Word-for-word.

No.

Come on. Tell it.

Please don't make me.

Look, honey — relax. I've forgiven you. I believe you. Really, I do understand. Things like that happen.

Do you? Oh, thank you — *thank you.*

Now you said you felt a weakness all over when he touched you.

I was so scared. I was afraid you'd be angry and want to leave me. I was so afraid to tell you. But I had to. You needed to be warned about Lonnie and them in case they try another trick.

77

No, honey, I'm not going to leave you. Not because of something like that. So don't worry. And don't worry about Lonnie. I'll deal with him. Now tell me again, and start at that part about how he made you feel when he first touched you.

I don't want to talk about it no more. I want to forget it ever happened.

That's all right. I want to hear it. From the start. When you first saw him — Lonnie's cousin.

You mean, when he was telling me how beautiful I was, and stroking my hair.

Yeah. Start with that part.

Are you serious?

And then he touched your thigh. Like this?

Near about. But it felt different because I was under the spell, remember.

But what exactly did he do that caused the spell. What did he say?

It wasn't what he said as much as what he didn't say. Why you looking at me so funny like?

It's all right honey. It's really all right. Tell it to me slowly, like it's in slow motion. Close your eyes and tell it to me again. From the start. From feeling so alone — me gone — just you here and the baby — and then Lonnie comes up to the door. And when you get to the part where he touches you, tell it extremely slow. Moment to moment so I can imagine what it felt like.

What?

Come on, honey. Do it for me.

Am I hearing what you're saying?

Don't be hurt. Believe me, baby—believe in me. You believe in spells. Give me your hand. There, now. Feel that. See how hard and good that feels. And it's all yours. And after you finish telling me that story again, I'm gonna give it all to you. But before I do, I want to hear it all one more time. And don't cry when you tell it. Tell it like you enjoyed it.

Tell it just like it happened.

EYES AND TEETH

DAY shimmers aglow with our laughter. Me and my cousin Buzz run through the house, teasing and funning. It is our blackness and our blood that makes us more than kin, be that possible. Be life that deeply sweet.

They've come the long way from the midwest. Along the old Route 66 to Los Angeles to visit Disneyland and Knott's Berry Farm. To walk the glittering avenue of the stars and point to this one and point to that one. To pick citrus wonders in orange groves. To wind and twist along the broad boulevards following outdated maps to the once glamorous homes of movie greats. To baptize themselves in that truly blue Pacific. To rave about mana's fried chicken and macaroni and cheese.

Me and Buzz get along about like always: Him gettin' the best of me even though I'm smarter. Him tickling my feet till my sides ache and I cry "uncle." Buzz and his two brothers crowded in with me and my two brothers in our tiny bedroom. And him scaring me late at night, talking about spooky creatures in the dark, especially that rat just waiting to take a healthy bite out of my big toe.

It is one summer in a cascade of summers. Visits from down home relations coming to see what the city is like, exploring the possibility of permanent uprooting. The small black farmers are disappearing, their lands swallowed up by wealthy white professionals, sold in turn to agricultural giants. It is this move-ment/flow that brings Buzz and his family west to test the climate and get a fix on the lay of urban turf.

Our fathers sit out back most days talking sports and the progress of humankind. His mother and my mother gab hours on end, catching up on old school mates, old flames and old times.

"Remember that ornery old sow we used to tease till one day she up and got loose and chased us cross the south field? Do you ever get over to So-and-So-ville to see Mrs. What-was-her-name, the Sunday School teacher at Such-and-Such A.M.E.?"

We only half-listen, more concerned with bossing our youngers. We're both the eldest, so we eat the most, we're eager to compete, we scrap the loudest, and are first to go running when mothers call.

This summer Buzz seems to have taken on a foreign edginess. Almost a sadness, but not quite. And while we fuss and wrestle, we're older now and I sense he's beginning to regard me as the young woman I'm becoming. But there's something else eating at him. I ask him if something's wrong. He looks at me and I watch his eyes go weepy. Nothing's the matter, he says. And it takes a while, but after a couple of days I provoke him back to mischief and he's more his usual self.

In no time we're roughing and tumbling about the house. This one afternoon me and Buzz are playing hide and seek while our brothers take their naps. I tap Buzz and he's it. He counts slowly to ten as I scout out a place to hide. We've been warned to stay out of the front room, and keep our noise down or suffer a spanking. I'm bold enough to think I can hide right under mama's nose and get away with it.

I tip-toe into the living room, crawl up under the old upright piano, and wedge myself in between it and the cloth covered bench. From where I am, I can overhear our mamas' chit-chat. My mama has the ironing board up in the dining room and is pressing out a week's laundry. His mama is sitting at the table, one of her breasts out, nursin' Buzz's new baby brother. There's a crack between the piano and the adjacent armchair which allows me to watch them without being seen.

Then here comes Buzz. He tip-toes up to the bench. I can see the quick little steps of his worn sneakers. I hold my breath. Next thing I know I'm looking into his eyes and teeth. He's smiling and laughing silently at finding me so quickly. He gets down on all fours and crawls in under the piano and starts tickling the stuffings out of me, daring me to laugh out loud. I hold it in. I don't want my legs tanned with one of them peach tree limbs my mama favors.

Then suddenly something his mama and my mama are sayin' catches our ears and we listen.

82

"I've had my last child," his mama says. "This is it."

"He's such a pretty boy," my mama says.

"He's my favorite of the boys. He's so light-skinned and look at this good straight hair. And lookahere at them gray eyes!"

"He takes after you."

"I'm so glad the other boys didn't turn out dark. But they could stand to be a shade brighter."

My mama made a strange little laugh.

"I'm so glad this baby didn't turn out black and ugly like Buzz. I can't stand to look at nothin' that *black*, and I feel so sorry Buzz is as black as he is—tar black like his granddaddy."

Me and Buzz were staring at one another, our mouths and eyes wide as could be. And I saw hurt, pain and hate flood his face all at once.

I wondered what my aunt thought of me and my brothers. And my father too. We—all of us were only a couple of shades shy of Buzz who was what we called charcoal. At the same time I was filled with a powerful hate for the woman. She thought she was better than us because she was high yellow and closer to being white. My mama had raised us to believe that that way of thinking was sick. And now I was filled with shame. Why wasn't my mother taking her to task?

Maybe she would've if she'd seen the tears burst silently from Buzz's eyes. She didn't see the hardness that took hold of his heart. And she didn't see me reach out my arms, trying to leap beyond my tomboy years to be the mother he lost in that instant.

Buzz crawled out, went to the bathroom and closed the door. He stayed there a long time. I went into the room where the others were napping and thought about it till I couldn't think anymore. We would never speak about it. No one seemed to notice the change in Buzz during the rest of that visit. No one, except me, noticed how sullen, withdrawn and mean-tempered Buzz was becoming. I remember standing just off the hallway, by the piano, watching them leave. His mother reached out to touch Buzz as he was going through the door. He jerked away and she gave him a puzzled look. I took it as a sign. It would be our last time to see each other as children.

When his mother died twenty years later, I did not attend the funeral. Mama went back there to visit, and came home

83

with all manner of family gossip, especially about Buzz. Some said Buzz was gay. Some said he had joined up with a black paramilitary group and was doing all kinds of evil including dope. Then Buzz showed up at the services with a beautiful young wife, two babies and a new car. Seems he's holding his own among the black middle class.

"And you should see Buzz's children," Mama crowed. "They're beautiful! And everyone of them looks like their father."

DREAM 5281

IT WAS Mother's Day—which comes twice a month—when county aid recipients get their stipends. The kids were in school. I had just cashed my check and had picked up my composite photos from the shop—ever aspiring to "make it." I wanted to show off my pictures to Glory. When I caught up with her, she was at the post office fishing missives from her home city, Detroit, out of her P.O. box. She was with a friend I had never met, Minette. She introduced us. I offered them a ride.

Minette seemed nice enough. She struck me as a little *hinkty*. When she walked, her attitude announced: "I'm a lady," and her nose tilted slightly up in the air. She wasn't bad looking, about Glory's same age—almost a decade my senior. But she wore rims—glasses—and a big bushy wig that she'd've looked better without. We were all about the same cocoa brown complexion, except Minette was a little grayer in hue, like she wasn't getting enough sun.

I was full of me that noon, me this and me that. And I guess Minette, not knowing me or knowing much better, got jealous listening to my potential success story. She didn't say much, but I could tell. I suggested we go to my place and critique my modeling portfolio over cold sweet wine.

"Amen to that!" Glory smiled.

But Minette had another idea. "Let's go to my apartment!" she offered in her high altitude voice which matched her attitude.

"Oh yeah, Wanda," Glory agreed, unaware of my growing dislike for her friend, "you've got to see this place to believe it. And for what we pay too, which is amazing—two bedrooms and it looks like *somethin'*—and no pets." By pets she meant roaches and mice.

85

Minette was proud of her walk-up and when we went in I could see why. It was unusually beautiful for a place in our part of South Central. Fully carpeted in the bedrooms and living room, the rest of the floors were solid hardwood except for the kitchen, which was a beautiful lattice work of yellow tiles, and a bathroom done in lavender tiles with walls in matching lilac-patterned wallpaper. There were genuine wood cabinets in the kitchen. The second bedroom was actually a veranda with pseudo Japanese-style windows overlooking the avenue, ideal for watching traffic pass, the sun set, reading or meditation. It was decorated with multi-colored throw rugs and two wicker chairs. Her apartment was a loving space. Minette had furnished it with so much care, I liked her better for having seen how sensitively and tastefully she lived.

And there were lots of books on mahogany book shelves, floor-to-ceiling. Many were black history books and assorted fictions. Minette was that rare find, a black intellectual. But for all her intellect she was little better off than me and Glory. Unlike us she had no children. Like us, she had no man.

The grand tour completed, Minette went to the kitchen to break out the wine, then came scampering out embarrassed because there wasn't any. She had drunk the last of it herself and had forgotten. It was our consensus to leave my car and walk down to the corner store and score a bottle. We all chipped in a few bucks for some fine quality imbibe.

We made light chatter on our way. Minette had a good mind under all her bourgeois pretend. In the store we went for the cream sherry, discovering we were ladies of similar taste. I don't remember much of our conversation while shopping. It is the walk back that vividly glistens word-for-word:

"Damn, Glory—I can use some o' that wine to take the edge off."

"Calm down, Wanda. We know you just got a touch of Hollywood flu. It'll pass."

We all laughed. Even Minette, whose initial jealousy seemed transient. We were feeling especially good in the smoggy spring May sun. We were dressed down in slacks and casual tops, *lookin' good* like three black women on-the-ball. Minette carried the bottle and its accompanying pack of ice as if they were books, clutched mid-torso.

"No—I ain't talkin' 'bout fame—I mean sex. I ain't been

with a man in so long it's makin' me crazy."

"We could all use a little horizontal bop," Glory sniggered and snapped her fingers. Minette remained uncomfortably silent and I sensed our woman-talk embarrassed her.

As if having conjured him up, ahead of us, sitting on the front porch of a single story house, was this muscular mountain of beautiful young black man. His shoulders were naturally broad, his waist and hips narrow as a weight lifter's. He was thinly clad in a black knit stretch tank-top shirt and blue denims held up by a thick black leather belt with a brass horseshoe buckle. He was high yellow and handsome. He certainly caught and held our attention.

As we came nearer he eyed each of us. But when he looked at me, his eyes lingered. I smiled back. He was obviously "street"—maybe a gangster. But I didn't care. All I cared about was that solid build and those chilly gray-brown eyes. He stepped down from the porch and walked over to greet us as we passed.

"Hi," he smiled through big even pearls.

Instinctively, Glory didn't answer his hello. She was old enough to be an aunt if not his mother. She knew who the greeting was intended for—me. But in her visible heat, Minette was not as hip, so her corresponding "Hi," echoed mine. He gave her a brutal glance which stopped us in our tracks. Then he smiled charmingly at me, licking his lips. "Hey, you kinda cute. They call me Rick. What's yo' name?"

That was all he was able to say and I was unable to reply. Minette blew her box at his blatant rejection.

"Look, sucka! Quit *molestin'* that child over there before I call the police. You two-bit hoodlum—you ought to be ashamed of yourself, bothering decent God-fearing women in broad daylight on a public street. If you want *some,* you're lookin' in the wrong place. Try over on Western Avenue where all the whores hang out!"

Hurt and anger uglied his angelic face before it altered into something sinister. Over Minette's barrage of wacky insults, I heard Rick curse, "Stupid bitches," as he turned toward the porch and entered the faded A-frame.

"Hey—jes' a damn minute!" I wanted to beat Minette's sexually repressed ass black and blue then and there. She was carrying propriety too far. Glory, caught between us, grabbed us by the elbows and forcefully dragged us out-of-range. Glory was also upset with Minette.

"Woman, are you crazy? What got into you back there? That poor boy didn't do a damned thing."

"Yes he did. Did you see how he looked at me?"

"It was obvious." Glory was gentle. "He was interested in Wanda. So what's wrong with that?"

Minette struggled to rationalize her feelings of inadequacy. "It's just that he's trouble and I know it. I know his *kind*."

I fumed silently as we walked back to Minette's apartment. I was reluctant to hurt Glory's feelings, but I didn't need Minette's dubious concern for my sexual welfare. I planned to split after a glass or two of wine, go home, exercise for a couple of hours, then soak off my frustration in a tub of hot sudsy water.

Back at her apartment, we made ourselves to home as Minette disappeared into the kitchen with the ice.

"What's with that bitch?" I challenged Glory.

"Beats me. Early menopause. I've never known her to act that way."

And then Minette was back with the glasses. I took out my portfolio and opened it to the first shot. I was sitting on the floor on one end of the coffee table, near the veranda. Glory sat on the couch between us. Minette sat by the ceiling-to-floor bookcase. We poured the sherry and shared a brief toast to our respective futures.

Before consummating the toast, I looked up toward the door. Rick stood there, fists to his hips, eyeing us coolly. He growled, "Stupid bitches!"

Glory and Minette looked up. Minette bristled indignantly, "What are you doing in my house?"

Rick snapped his fingers. Two men snaked quickly up the stairs, into the room and flanked him. They were older, shorter, darker and similarly muscled versions of Rick—brothers, cousins or uncles. Crouched in readiness, one had a clean-shaven head and sported a stubby blade in his right hand. They effectively blocked the only escape, as Minette's apartment, for all its economic beauty, had only one entry and exit.

"It's Mother's Day, girls. And I figure three fine ladies like you gots to have some cash on hand. Like maybe you got those checks this morning?" Rick leered.

Minette, Glory and I were not small or weak women. But

we were no match for the three men. Rick drew his switchblade and the third man, a bowie knife. Terrified, I said nothing and made no sudden move. Minette and Glory sat their glasses on the coffee table and rose slowly from the couch, staring at the men and their knives.

I grabbed my purse from its place beside me on the floor and eased my way to my feet, talking as I reached into my wallet and, regretfully, gave up the dough.

"Here — here's all I got, man — you're welcome to it." Rick took it from me, his hands lingering to stroke mine, smiling faint regret. I prayed they'd just take the cash and leave us alone.

Glory went into her purse and got out her money. Rick took it with a smile, then turned, eyes burning at Minette who stood stonily clutching her purse, her eyes alternately flashing fear and outrage.

"Fork it over, *Godzilla.*" He was all ice.

A peculiar hurt came into Minette's eyes. She dropped her purse and flew into a rage. She grabbed a handful of hardbacks from the shelf and threw them at the two men behind Rick. They ducked. In that split second, she dashed for the stairs and the door below. She boldly pushed the second, darkest man out of her way. He quickly recovered and flicked his bowie knife, catching her arm with its tip. She shrieked and fell back, blood rising from the wound above her elbow. The bald man quickly recovered and grabbed her from behind. The two of them struggled with Minette as she fought, kicking and flailing wildly. They dragged her downstairs out of our line of vision. Glory and I exchanged looks, the certainty that we were next, and that, as witnesses, our lives were zeros. Minette's horrible screams and grunts orchestrated the obvious. They were doing more than killing her. They were raping and torturing first. We would have our turn. We would not get out of Minette's apartment alive.

All the reasons I wanted to live came over me. My kids. My fantasy modeling career. I started talking.

"Hey look, man — we ain't seen *nothin'* — this ain't even our pad. You can have the money and anything else you want. Just don't kill us, man."

Rick looked at me, sizing me up, thinking it over. I read "maybe" in his eyes.

"Hey, man — I've got kids, man — I want to live. I didn't

do you no wrong. We won't even call the cops. We'll just split—disappear."

"Okay, MOTHERFUCKER, *come on!*" It was Glory's throaty roar. To my surprise and dismay, she had come up with her own knife; had probably snuck it out of her purse when she'd gotten her money. She had mad fire in her eyes and was moving into a war dance à la the streets of Detroit. She was going to try and gut Rick. She lunged at him, clearly no match. His arms were so long she couldn't get within stabbing distance. He pushed her into the bookcase, came up on her and rammed his switchblade home three times in rapid succession, just below her stomach, cutting as though she were fabric instead of flesh.

Her blood splattered the open pages of my portfolio.

Glory's head fell back, her mouth agape. She cried my name, "Waaannnda . . ." then came what was not a scream, not a sigh. It was like no other sound. Glory closed her eyes, bent forward and went to the floor.

Rick turned to me, murder fresh, blood in his eyes, on his knife, on his hand. I heard the others coming expectantly upstairs, finished with Minette. And I *knew*.

Not another thought. I ran for the veranda and leapt through the windows. Glass and metal framing bit into my face, arms and torso. Mid-flight I looked down into the astonished brown face of a passerby. He was a black man in his fifties and was deeply shaken by the sight of me crashing through the window, fragments flying.

In the distance I heard Rick's "Man—let's split!"

Something ripped at my shoulder. My arm had hooked around a rigid piece of piping which jutted from the wall a few feet beneath the veranda. It jerked me to a halt, mid-air. "I'll go get help," the passerby stammered and ran off.

Blood streamed down my forehead, into my eyes. I closed them and allowed my body to slump against the siding. The short fall couldn't hurt me much more, but I was afraid to touch ground, afraid Rick and kin were waiting to finish me.

Corpse-like I hung there, pretending death, my mind replaying Glory's end. Again and again Rick's beautiful sleek muscles rippled as he took Glory out. I kept hearing her last word. My name. Wanda. Followed by that utterly final sound.

I was alive. And I woke up to prove it.

90

I was alone in my king-sized bed. I was still dressed in my street clothes. I could hear the elongated beep of the TV set. The room was dark except for the white dot at video center. It blipped and the screen went white then evolved into a test pattern. The announcer interrupted with a sober voice-over:

"Good morning, Los Angeles. This is the beginning of our broadcast day." Then the National Anthem began to play.

I looked at the clock which glowed dimly in the light cast by the television. It was 5 a.m. and the start of a new day.

HAMBURGERS

"WHATCHEW want on it, mahn?"
   "The usual."
   "I's new — donna what yo' usual is."
   "Garbage."
   "Huh?"
   "Everything on it."
   " 'Cludin' onion?"
   "Onion."
   "Some peoples don' like mustard."
   "Mustard."
   "Yo' got it."
   "Extra pickle, too."
   "Yes, suh."
   "And toast the bun."

   "How often dat mahn come here?"
   "Most every day. 6:30 on the dot. Sometimes he skips a day. But you can damned near set your clock by him."
   "He hungry lookin'. Don' he evah order anythin' 'sides a burger and cola?"
   "Occasionally a milkshake. French fries sometimes. Maybe he'll change up and go for onion rings instead. When he's real flush, two cheeseburgers, extra mayo."
   "Yo' jivin' me."
   "Gospel. I swear it."
   "Can't nobody live off a burger a day."
   "He come here, don't he? And you talked to him. You got it from the horse's mouth."
   "I think he's a case."

"I've said that many a time myself."

"You'd thunk a mahn who dresses like dat 'n ride nice like dat'd treat hisself bettah."

"Driven folk do strange thangs."

"Stay the night, James. Please."

"Lorita, I can't."

"Why not. Afraid it'll give me ideas?"

He thought about it. "Great big ideas."

"James David Poke we've been going together two years and I still can't get you to sleep over one night in my bed. This is ridiculous."

"I don't feel right about it, Lorita. I want to do the right thing by you. When I don't believe right about something — I just can't do it."

"Then marry me."

"I can't afford to marry you. And I don't want you paying for the wedding. And I want us to have a house."

"A house! Who's got enough money for that? By the time we save up a down payment, we'll be too old for the honeymoon."

"Not that it's necessary."

She sputtered. "J-James, I swear I don't know what to say to you sometimes. You're the stubbornest man I've met in life."

"And too old to change. It don't make sense to marry now."

"James, it makes perfect sense. We don't have to have a big wedding. I'll settle for a small one. We can live here till we can afford a home — if ever."

"You want a diamond ring, don't you?"

"I'd like one, yes — ."

"That settles it then."

"James Poke, you know you could afford to buy me a diamond ring *and* pay for the wedding too if you didn't insist on driving around town in that *pimpmobile* — I swear!"

"Don't. Just be patient with me, Lorita. I have a plan. And it includes you. But as of the moment it's my money. I earn it. I buy what I want. As long as I'm independent no one tells me what I can and can't have. We'll get married all right. When I'm ready."

"How long do you figure that will be?"

"Be patient, Lorita."

"Patient!" She steamed. "My place is good enough for you to keep clothes here but not good enough to sleep here."

"You can have me like I am or not have me — however, Lorita."

She looked into eyes full of bullheadedness. "Whatever you want, James."

She gave into him as she had many times before. But this time her giving in left her rueful and troubled. As always, James felt utterly in control.

"May I speak to Mr. Temple?"

"Mr. Temple isn't in."

"Could I leave a message?"

"Certainly, sir."

"Tell him James Poke called."

"What's the problem, Mr. Polk?"

"That's Poke. P-O-K-E."

"I'm sorry, Mr. Poke. What's the trouble?"

"Tell him I'll be two-to-three days late with my car note this month. But he'll get it by the end of the week for sure. He'll certainly get it."

"You know our policy, Mr. Polk. I'm sure you wouldn't want your mother to lose her home, would you?"

"Please — just give Mr. Temple my message." He hung up and cursed at the phone, "You fuckin' dog-faced white bitch."

Each time he entered the lush interior it was like his first time. A fresh experience which, like the hamburger, never lost its desirability. Never disappointed him. Even though he knew every nick, crease and do-jigger — there was no tiring of the sumptuous luxury. He had asked the dealer to make some special changes in the model. It was a fabulous piece of technology on which the standard appointments were either extras or unavailable on the average auto. Some things had more to do with time than taste. It had set James back an additional fifteen hundred. And while paying would be a hard road to pave, he planned to enjoy every rock, pot hole and detour.

"Yo' want ketchup with yo' fries?"

"Okay."

"Look, if'n you come back 'fore closin', I can slip yo'

somethin' ex-tra. Eyes be slack 'round here then. Don' nobody be thinkin' 'bout nuthin' but goin' home."

"Why do you want to do me a favor?"

"I jes' like you is all."

"You feel sorry for me."

"No, I ain't."

"I don't need your feel-sorry."

"I'm jes' tryin' to help folks out 's all. What dis white mahn care 'bout food he gonna throw out anyways. You might's well have it. It goin' to waste."

"I don't need charity. Black or white."

"Suit yo'self."

James, James, what's the matter with you? What's the doing that you can't do? You work all day, you worry all night. You do what you can, but what you do ain't right. You get your pay check, you pay Uncle Sam and pride yourself on being a man. You pay your taxes and you pay your bills. You don't smoke or drink and you don't take pills. You go to church when you're sick of soul. You go to the doctor when you got a cold. You love your woman down to the bone. One day you'll marry and never be alone. But James James there's something wrong. There's something missing. There's something gone. I wish you'd tell me cause I want to know. I wish you'd tell me cause I need to know. I wish . . . I wish . . . I wish.

"What's got your dander up?"

"Dat niggah got's nerve."

"What'd he do to you?"

"I try do the mahn a favor. Told him come 'round 'bout closin' I help him out. But he got bad attitude. Talk 'bout wearin' ass-on-shoulders."

"I warned you about him. He's a mental case. Quiet, but a case."

"He need a good woman."

"Are you volunteering?"

"Hell naw, gal. What I's got's ten times bettah and ain't starvin' to death. I swear, dat mahn get skinnier and skinnier."

"Maybe he's got some kind of fatal disease."

"Stupid is fatal. But if'n he do, whatever he got, I gots no mo' worry 'bout it."

96

The rich sound of the music surrounded him. *I get lifted.*
It raised him out of his blues. It sent him into a lovely lassitude.
He snapped his fingers gently to the rhythm as it coursed through
him. He rolled his head side-to-side. He hunched his shoulders
and made like camel's walk. He remembered his daddy and uncle
used to dance that way way back when. It had been such a good
time, peeping the adult action from behind Grandmama Poke's
staircase, spying on the boogie woogie, the lindy hop — moving
away the blues. Snap snap finger-pop.

Who used to call you that? Cousin James Theodore!

The memory made him angry all over again. He relived
his uppity cousin's superior snicker. "Oh, I see you're one of
those finger-poppin' Neegroes."

"And what are you — Neegro? You're damned near as black
as I am. And we both crawled out of the same hole. You think
you're so special."

"It's called good breeding. I'm well bred."

"As far as I'm able to tell we grew up in the exact same
neighborhood."

"I'm in college, J.D. I've got a future."

"Everybody livin' got a future, J.T. Or don't they teach
you common sense in *col*-lege."

A resentment had grown between the two cousins. It fes-
tered in years of silence across tables at family gatherings. It took
the shape of a tightness that ringed James David Poke's heart and
began to squeeze. The tightness found its way into his blood-
stream and traveled to his brain. It was a tightness that hungered
to live, and took shape as stinginess — a pinch penniedness. He
would work hard. He would save his earnings. He would be rich
someday. He would show cousin J.T. who J.D. was. He would get
his car, his woman, his house, his wardrobe — in that vital order.
Then one day he'd look up J.T. and put his eyes out with envy.
He'd show that arrogant clown what a working man could do.

How do you figure it, J.D.? Tell me. What's gone wrong?

At first he fed the stinginess breakfast. He'd eat only lunch
and dinner. But somehow the little money he saved didn't do
much. So he quit eating lunch. It took will power. But he couldn't
stop eating altogether. And he had to have clothes. He figured
rent and utilities were devouring half his income. So he quit
using electricity. And when he started to date Lorita, he found

97

he didn't need gas or water at all. He could at least shower and shave at her place. And sometimes she made dinner for him, but she was barely able to feed herself, and Lorita was not a big eater. Then he had the gas, water and electricity cut off. And since he didn't call anyone but his mother and Lorita, he figured he could do that from a phone booth as well as any place. And he could save that way because he could always call them collect — charges they would eagerly accept out of love. And then he decided he could keep most of his clothes in the car and visit the cleaners whenever he needed. And a set in Lorita's apartment and the rest in his old room at his mother's. He could get along fairly well by sleeping in his car. So he gave up his apartment. But he didn't want his mother or Lorita to know about this *thing* that had seized him. He did not fully understand it himself — just that it had to remain his secret. Between the job, his mother, Lorita and sleeping in the car, he would be able to accumulate greater sums of money until he had enough for the down payment on his dream.

"Oh, James! A Surprise. What is it?"

"A little something." He presented the gift-wrapped box and a bouquet of flowers. "Just to tell you I love you."

"Let me put the daisies in a vase first, before they start to wilt."

They're the cheapest flowers he could find, she thought. Nevertheless, Lorita hurried off and returned with the daisies, heads up, brightening the room. She cut a couple of inches off the stems and arranged them carefully in a yellow and white porcelain vase and placed it on the coffee table before them. Flowers from James — even cheap ones — were so rare — even if only daisies.

She opened the box, eagerly tossing the bright yellow and white paper left and right, parted the white tissue paper and gasped.

"Pot holders!"

"And see — here's a yellow plastic rack. Dish towels and dish cloths — a matched set." He grinned.

"Pot holders?" Lorita was in shock.

James smiled. "I hope you like them."

Lorita rode emotion from anger to sorrow, dizzied by the ride. She struggled for control. "I — I. James, I don't — I mean — James, what are you trying to do to me?"

98

"Nothing—I . . ."

"You won't make a home but you give a homemaking gift. I fail to understand you."

He saw her point. "Oh, I'm sorry. I wanted to give you something nice."

"If I can't have you, James—the way I want and need you, what do I need this for?"

She pushed the box against him and rose from the couch. He clutched it in consternation.

"Don't come back here no more, James. Take your clothes with you. I can't tolerate this another minute."

"Lorita—!"

"Please. Just leave."

She burst into tears. And he knew what he had to say, what he could say, but the tightness took hold of him, strangling the words.

"Everything on it."

"You look terrible, man."

"No fries this time. Just a burger."

"If there's anything I can do. Even if it's just a listen."

"And a cola. Lots of ice."

"You're a hard heart."

"Oh, that burger—some cheese this time."

If he closed his eyes tightly enough he could see himself in the club, the flamboyant male singers strutting in rhythm to their hypnotic harmonics and entrancing bass count as they went from whisper to scream. The waitress scintillated before him, lowering a drink to the table, her shimmering redness a dialogue in sequins and African violet.

Do-wop baby, I need your lovin' got to have it got to got to have all that lovin' . . .

And he could see her smile. "Before you place your order, the management has asked me to inform you that we make the best hamburgers in town."

It's a taste I never tire of. I don't know why.

The two officers approached the luxury car with caution. They had noticed it parked there the night before. And here it was, in the exact same spot, giving off an aura of wrongness. Perhaps it was stolen. Perhaps it had been used in a crime and abandoned. They parked alongside and got out to investigate.

"What is it?"

"Looks like a single occupant—male, black, about forty."

"Drunk?"

"Maybe."

He lay in a bed of music. Its softness was wonderful, but no less wonderful than the crushed leather seats. He could hear the dovetailing moods of rhythm and blues as they moved over and around him.

"Com-fy, Baby?"

She was big-thighed and beautifully brown with the kind of complexion he loved. Like Lorita's.

"Yes. Thank you. I don't know your name."

"What name would you like?"

"What name?"

"Yes. Go ahead. I don't mind. Christen me."

"Hmmm. Let me think."

"How about Lois? Loretta? How about something exotic—Lorita!"

"No, not her name."

"That name is special to you?"

"Yes. I loved a woman by that name. Someday, when I get things right, I'm going to marry her."

"What a lovely thought. But in the meantime, why don't you let me keep you company?"

"You?" He looked at her closely. She was clad in a silk cream-colored teddy. It accented breasts which jutted upward, nipples outlined underneath. She was the glorious sexual animal, a purring, raring engine with unlimited horsepower.

"Me. Would you like a drink to get in the mood?"

"I'm a man. I don't need *nothing* to get in the mood—if I'm of a mind to get in the mood."

"I like you. You know what you want."

James frowned. He felt the frown course through him on a chill. "I thought I did. Once. Now—?"

"Not so sure?"

"She put me down."

"Lorita."

"She told me to get out of her life. I failed her. I was a stubborn fool."

"Go to her. Explain."

"I can't."

"Why not?"

"I guess I'm still a stubborn fool. I guess — I don't know. I just can't face her now. Not until . . ."

"Until what?"

He sat silent, letting the music embrace him, feeling its tug.

"May I confess something?"

"That's what I'm here for."

"I don't know *what* anymore. It doesn't make sense anymore. Not even to myself. I thought having the material things would make me happy. I was certain of it. I staked my life on it. For some strange reason I was never able to acquire all of those things. I was just barely able to keep my ride."

"You made a bad investment. Everyone's entitled to one mistake."

"This one cost me my life. Somehow — something inside me feels it's not fair."

"Who said life's fair?"

He looked at her, at the face which was a mask of unbelievable beauty. She radiated the most blatant lust he'd ever seen in the eyes of a woman. She had the eyes painted on Egyptian temples. She had the eyes of Lorita. She had the eyes of all women. Her eyes were rainbows. Her eyes were tombs.

"Forget it — forget all of it. Be with me for a while. Let me ease your troubled soul."

"What did you say your name was?"

"I didn't say, but you may call me Joy."

"You're a beautiful sight, Joy. You could make a man forget his own name — forget everything."

"Come on, let me soothe you. I promise to be gentle. I promise not to hurt you. Here, we'll start with a little massage. Let me rub your shoulders."

Her hands were narcotic. They freed the tightness around his shoulders. They freed the tightness around his heart. He sighed. "Oh, yes — yes."

Gently she pulled him back against her breasts, turned his head to hers, joined his lips to hers.

"They found him sittin' behind the wheel, elbow on the arm rest, radio blastin'."

"Naw gal, dat weren't no radio. He showed me once."

"A cassette deck?"

"Shit gal, he hadda genuine antique 8-track stereo."

"No jive? You don't see much 8-track anymore."

"The police—so what'd they say about the mahn, gal."

"His girlfriend went down to identify the body. They'd just broken up, too."

"He kill himself. It figures."

"According to the cops he died of malnutrition."

"Malnutrition?"

"He lived out of that ride of his."

"Tain't a wonder. A car like dat runs on blood."

THE FRIDAY NIGHT SHIFT AT THE
TACO HOUSE BLUES (WAH-WAH)

It is 1973 and "we" are low on everything.

DOWN AT the Taco House is where we work, Shurli and me. Shurli's an old timer and was managing the night shift when I first came on the gig. The night shift starts at six in the evening. That's five-forty night people's time. We night folks go by bar time, which in Los Angeles means the clock is always twenty minutes fast. When 2 a.m. rolls around (booze curfew) that's about how long it takes for the customers to finish their drinks, for us to coax the hypes out of the john or jane and sober up the drunks with hot coffee and send them all out into the night and presumably home. Since most waitresses have been barmaids at one time or another, the process is essentially the same. Our night lives — shaped by complete boredom one minute and mayhem and murder (not to mention robbery) the next.

So like, Shurli's been working the Taco House off and on for ten years. Actually, Shurli daylights as a welfare mother supporting six kids, their three fathers (two kids per father, a pretty good ratio), a three-hundred-dollar-a-month car note on her customized Cadillac *Coupe de Ville* and her one-hundred-and-fifty-a-month note on that raggedy-ass crib she calls a house located in the neighborhood about twelve blocks away. Me — I'm just passing through, I hope, on my way to bigger and better things.

I got my eye on a government job — trying to get on as a

receptionist/secretary as they say in the want ads. I struggled awake yesterday morning about ten o'clock just in time to keep my eleven o'clock appointment for the typing, math, memory and the rest of the aptitude tests they give you. Me—I live alone, having no kids. That's one mistake I refuse to make. Not me. I've got to make my fortune first.

The Taco House stays open twenty-four hours in order to catch the night trade. Some are decent folks who work nights. Some are professional hoods, gamblers, pimps, hypes, prosties and shit like that—and of course, the cops, narks and plainclothesmen who are after their asses, and inevitably, the customers they've hooked on one trick or another.

So like, Shurli gets in right at five-forty when Redd completes her run. Redd is a bright-skinned woman who runs the day shift. She's called "red" like most niggahs what got that kind of orangy skin tone and rust colored hair that usually comes from certain black/white combines. She's a good person, everybody likes her, but I don't really know her, with her working the day shift.

Shurli bounces over to the register and takes over as we other girls come in. I say bounce, because Shurli is five feet four and weighs about three hundred pounds. She's got the meatiest forearms—a lot of that just plain muscle. She works the register the way she drives that Caddy, smooth and with profound grace.

As me and the girls come in, Jesus hands us our aprons. There are four of us. Me, Kathy, Li'l Bit and Sharita. Sharita is a tall slender chick whose old man rides with Scarlet Fever, a raunchy all black lightweight version of the Hell's Angels. She thinks she has clout. We don't like each other and I'm waiting for the day when I have to get off into that bitch's ass.

So we check in while Chuck (that's the owner) runs through the one hundred and fifty dollar bank with Shurli. You see, the register always gets a bank. That way the boss knows if you're stealing or not and can gauge his profit and loss margin against the tape. Actually, the money never stays in the register long. Periodically, Shurli removes part of the take, locks it and moves most of the tens, twenties and fifties (we don't change ben franks) to the back where there's a safe built into the floor which is usually hidden under a mat. All the girls work the register.

So like, anyhow, we come in, and Jesus hands us our aprons, and we go in the back, hang up coats and sweaters and

104

then duck our purses under the counter so we can keep our eyes on what few pennies we do have. The set-up here is the usual. Black girls on the counter, Mexicans do the cooking and the owner (who's either white or Jewish as the case may be) rakes in the bread.

Chuck, who speaks Spanish fluently, puts one girl (in this case, Shurli) in charge of the girls, cause he knows that won't no niggah bitch take orders from no Mexican cook. Jesus has two assistants, Don and Herman. They look like Castilians. Don speaks faulty English, and when he does, he talks like us blacks. Herman grins a lot and can only get through the basic hello and good-bye. Jesus speaks both and although his English is usually very simple, I often get the feeling that where he's from in Mexico, he's big shit and can rattle off the King's English as well as any Harvard grad. Of course, just as most of the waitresses (with the exception of myself and Sharita) are welfare mothers, the Latinos are all illegal aliens. But nobody ever says anything and it's cool.

Chuck, the boss man, has a rep for messing around with the girls. Chuck usually hangs around for an hour or so after changeover, then goes home. Shurli tells me that he's slept with everybody except me and Li'l Bit. About herself she don't say. I grunt and shrug. The turkey has pulled at my bra strap a couple of times, but that's as far as it got. He's a family man with one of those pale sickly blonde wives — a classic. And his children are dark haired, slenderer images of himself. I've never seen his son, but his daughter runs through occasionally. Rumor is she's a campus activist and that she and her old man don't get along too well when it comes to politics, but she keeps the books and records and runs that end of the business for him. Shurli says that she's heard 'em arguing a lot about her shacking with some dude he thinks is a shiftless creep. As far as I'm concerned it's their business. I'm just looking forward to the day when I can clear out.

At the changeover, when we hit the counter, business is fairly heavy with the dinner trade. At the Taco House, people have the choice of fast food service in or out. The counter is long and on a curve. The first and the longest arm of the curve is where all the food preparation takes place. The customer can clearly see the de-wormed tomatoes (diced well for color), the week-old onions, the bleached lettuce, pickle, relish, mayonnaise, refried beans, ketchup, hot sauce and chili as we apply it in varying degrees per order. They can even watch as Jesus and the boys fry a barrage of hot dogs, corn tortilla shells (soft, semi-crisp and crunchy), steam buns and flour tortillas, fry hamburger patties, taco meat patties (mainly pork and cereal), toast hot dog buns and boil wieners.

People come and go in a steady stream and then the tide breaks about eight o'clock. Usually things are sporadic during the weekdays. Work is on a six day schedule with alternating days off. All the girls work on Sunday. Days off usually fall on Mondays and Tuesdays. You work half a day on Christmas. On weekends the traffic is killing. The people never stop and periodically Chuck will take on a new girl for the summer just to keep the stream of cash flowing smoothly. But normally, things pick up again about ten o'clock, get spotty, and then around twelve get heavy again for about a half hour. Then from twelve-thirty to two-thirty it's nightmare time. People come and go so fast, time becomes a blur. From two-thirty until five o'clock time comes to a complete halt. It's usually during this period when we girls start to get bitchy with one another. But about five things pick up again, with people coming in for eggs, coffee, donuts and shit. I was surprised to see the number of people who like to eat tacos and stuff for breakfast. The days of ham and eggs are numbered.

I start in filling the orders. We mark abbreviations for each order on each bag, figure the prices and totals in our heads, mark the price on the bag and circle it. We hand the bags to Shurli or whoever's on the register at the moment. She rings it up, takes the cash, makes change and hands the bag to the customer.

So like, this night I'm preparing orders, my hands stinging from continual dippings into the tomatoes. It's cold and the middle of November. Outside, it's crisp and clear and the lights from the bar across the street shine brightly. The juke is blasting rhythm and blues. Shurli is leaning across the counter talking to one of the local dope dealers, trying to score some white folks (bennies) for her and her old man. Li'l Bit and Kathy are feeding their faces on their break, jawing over two plates heaped with burger meat and frijoles (none of the girls will touch the taco meat including me) and gulping down coffee. Sharita has slipped out to turn a trick with a don who stuck twenty dollars in her paw.

I reach for a towel to wipe my hands when a lone customer walks in. He's a tall, lanky guy in his mid-twenties. He's brownskinned, just a shade lighter than me, and has his grayish brown hair cut to a crew cut, a style that spells jerk on the black side of town. He looks like he's safe enough, orders a tostada and a cup of coffee.

I glance at the girls, know I'm elected, and wait as Jesus tosses a tortilla into the fat vat.

K.P. comes in and it's on me to take his order for two chili burgers heavy on the onion. K.P. is one of the regulars. He practically lives here and will come in two or three times a night. Shurli has jammed me that he and a couple of other old cronies are Chuck's paid spies. They give Chuck clandestine reports on the conduct of the girls. And it must be true, because Chuck always knows *everything* that goes down. The Latinos report on the girls, the girls report on the girls and the spies report on everybody.

Another dude comes in. He's dark-skinned, youngish, looks like a thug. He knows the lighter guy and yells, "Hey! Ray, mah man!" They slap hands between placement of his order. After Shurli rings them up, they take their plates and sit at the counter. By now K.P. has joined them and everybody is on the two extreme ends of the counter. I look and decide to join Shurli and the fine piece of meat she's now talking to, K.P. and the two dudes on their end. Everybody's listening to the dude called Ray tell what's apparently an interesting story. I come up and lean against the soda fountain.

"Yeah," Ray is continuing. "She was dead — just like that. I mean, I can't get over it. I went out and went down to Jack's to shoot some pool, hustle up a couple of bucks. She wanted a fifth and neither one of us didn't have no money, man. She hadn't got her check — you know how it is . . ."

He talks like he's high on reds (seconal) slurring his words, stretching each syllable. But I know what that is. That is that high you get — the one I call Pain. Yeah, that's it all *reet*.

"She had come home and washed her hair. You know, she hadn't been feeling good lately and had been complaining a lot — but you know how womens are. Theys always complainin' about one thing or another." The men nod in agreement. Shurli grunts.

"And she was older than me, you know! I don't know how old she was, I guess about forty-five. And I'm only twenty-four, but to me that didn't make no difference. I loved the broad. You know what I mean?"

"Amen," snorts K.P. His crony shakes his head in agreement. I shift my weight to my left leg. Shurli grunts.

"She was good lookin' for her age too, you know how it is with us—we don't age like white peoples do. She had on her favorite wig, a brown one all done up in curls—kind of like yours only shorter." He's speaking to me and everybody turns to look at the wig I'm wearing. A sort of controlled afro.

"I really loved that woman. I mean—I had other girls, you understand me?" Everybody nods. "But she was my wo-man. She was my heart."

"Hey—bring yo' ass over here, Carol."

A shout from Li'l Bit interrupts the bemoaning. I look around to see that fifteen people have suddenly appeared from nowhere, Jesus and his boys are popping at the griddle and Li'l Bit and Kathy are tossing plates, tacos and beans as fast as they can move. I speed to the counter, pencil and bag in hand. "Next, please place your order." Shurli bustles over and helps out. The dude, Ray, and his partner take their plates from the counter and move to a table against the wall in the back. K.P. sips his coffee and picks at his plate, keeping a watch on us and the register.

I work, having trouble keeping the orders in my head as they come rapid-fire. I kind of have my eye on the dude Shurli was talking to. He is real clean cut, wearing a camel hair mack coat and brim to match, clean beige threads underneath. He's built smooth-skinned and muscular on a wiry frame, has even white, pearly teeth and heavy-lidded, sexy brown eyes. I jam Shurli between a chili tamale order and an enchilada plate.

"Who's that—he sho 'nuff fine."

"Oh, Tommy? He's like a baby brother to me. Him and his other brothers are in here all the time."

"Do they all look as good as him?"

She laughs. "Pretty good. I'll introduce you to 'em sometimes. They're nice too—and they all *work* for a livin'."

I look up suddenly and catch his eyes. He smiles slowly, slightly. He knows I'm asking about him. The smile goes through me and straight to my tenderloin. Whoowhee, baby!

"Get that order," Kathy barks and I'm back into the grind.

"Where in the fuck is Sharita?" Li'l Bit pipes.

Kathy sniggers. "That bitch puts a high premium on her pussy."

As if having heard the summons, Sharita shows up through the glass window, footing up the pavement. She pushes the door and enters, throwing off her coat and rushing behind the counter. She glances at K.P. for a second (all of us know Chuck's paid spies) and then slips into the grind.

We're on our feet three hours solid. Seems like a few people did get their county checks and it's Friday night anyhow. Fridays are always busy.

By one o'clock a hundred people have come and gone and we're cranky for another break. Sharita is eyeing my stud who briefly introduced himself to me when I maneuvered service at one of the tables which is strictly Shurli's domain (the tables leave better tips than the counter — sometimes a girl can add ten to fifteen dollars a night to her salary). I catch Sharita eyeing him as he talks to some old man who's taken the stool beside him. Sharita looks dead to me. I stare daggers. She shrugs and backs off.

At one, Tod comes in. Everybody calls Tod crazy.

"Here comes that crazy Tod," Chuck always said whenever he was around and spotted Tod coming in. Tod is a regular. Tale was that he worked for Chuck between jobs and good women. He is supposed to be the best fry cook Chuck has ever had. Everyone is fond of him and regrets the fact that Tod is a Viet Nam veteran.

"He was a fine boy, all right before he went into the Army, I tell you. I don't know what they did to him over there, Viet Nam. Ever since he's been out, he's been crazy like that. He's a good person, but nutty as a fruit cake." Tod won't eat the taco meat either.

Tod's wardrobe is limited (a sign of immense and extreme poverty among blacks) to denim overalls, the remains of his military uniforms replete with ribbons from numerous deeds of heroism and sharp shooting, karate, etc. and a raggedy trench-type overcoat he sports like a private eye. I had seen Tod several times before. He was in at least two or three nights a week on my shift. He knew I was a new girl, and made it a point to get to know me. I kept picking up the vibe that he lusted after me. But I'm ambitious and he doesn't suit my qualifications. The first of which is to have a car and every time I saw him, he was walking, which is a sin in Car City, Los Angeles.

Tod orders his usual, twenty tacos with hamburger meat and fifteen hamburgers. Jesus groans as he always does when Tod places his order. We only charge him half price as is the policy for Chuck's favorites (twenty percent off for the cops from the local precinct and any other officer of the law). Tod is always boozed up, high if not stumbling drunk. His habit is to come in, size up the joint, go out, come back minutes later, order something for himself, eat, go out, come back an hour later, place his big order, which it always takes Jesus an hour to prepare between other orders we take, while Tod cuts the bull with anyone he can find to cut it with, and sometimes comes back just before the shift change for a cup of coffee to sober up and go down to the unemployment office.

I jam Shurli about his order. "He comes in like that all the time. Who's all that stuff for?"

"Oh — that's his mother. She's got twelve kids, girl — still at home. Two girls are married. Tod makes fifteen. Tod's the oldest."

"How old is he?"

"Must be twenty-six by now. All the rest of 'em is still at home. It's pitiful child, pitiful. I ain't never seen folks so poor."

As the lull comes on, I immediately forget about Tod. My eyes go back to Tommy and I can tell he's warming more and more to the idea of waiting out the night and seeing me home after my shift is over. He keeps giving me approving looks as I move back and forth behind the counter. It's rough, trying to be a waitress and look sexy, but most of the girls manage it, me included. It's rough in them white uniforms and white brogans Chuck insists we wear, plus the heavy cloth aprons.

I'm built, no brag. Brothers keep telling me how I've got plenty of butter. A compliment to any black woman — cause our men, for the most part, like their women on the fleshy side. Skinny legs usually get a black gal laughed at although, as Shurli always says, "It ain't the beauty — it's the booty."

The place clears out about a quarter after two and we all settle in for the long haul. The guy whose old lady had died moves back to the counter and perches on a stool one down from my jazzy potential lay. Tod is still sitting on the service end of the room with Sharita and Kathy, cutting the bull and they accommodate him with their laughter. Li'l Bit is jawing with a youngster closer to her own age, which I figure to really be sixteen, although she swears by nineteen and one six-month-old son. Li'l Bit is a green-eyed sandy haired, sweet looking yellow-skinned girl with very small features, except for her eyes. Li'l Bit is married and her old man grumpily picks her up in their 1954 Chevy struggle buggy when shift is over. She doesn't like marriage and wants to leave her child to its grandparents (either set will do) and her old man to the dogs. I notice Li'l Bit is copping something from her friend. Must be some bush (marijuana) or white folks, I figure. But my attention is on my foxy gentleman catch who's listening to Ray talk again, continuing his story which he's managed to tell anyone he can collar.

We check out his loneliness. He just doesn't want to be by himself and we can appreciate his feelings. Tommy, Shurli and me, listening. It gets quieter and quieter, and pretty soon even Crazy Tod, Sharita and Kathy can hear him talking. Jesus has put down the ladle and is leaning against the griddle, listening. His two companeros have gone around back. Li'l Bit is in the jane.

"She bought me a Christmas present, you know? She showed it to me. We had had an argument that morning. She wanted to know what I was gonna get her — her having spent all that bread for me a present. She'll never know how doggish she made me feel. I been trying. I really been tryin'. But like you know how it is with the slump and alls goin' on." Shurli sighs deeply.

"I wanted to get her something. I planned to. I just hadn't figured on what, yet. And there she was, screaming at me and tossing my present around. She had got me a leather coat. It's really beautiful — all lined inside with red fur and got fur on the collar and cuffs. Real natty, you know? She liked to get her shoppin' done early — to avoid the rush. I wasn't even thinkin' 'bout it."

A beat down pause.

"I just can't get over her dying like that. So sudden. So quick. One minute and then — the next."

"Ah mannn, why don't you shut up all that sad talk! Ain't you got nothin' better to do than complain?" It was Tod. We bristle. I get up from the counter as a customer appears.

"Shut up Tod and let the man finish talkin'," Shurli chastises gently.

111

"Finish talkin'? He been talkin' all night and sayin' the same thing over and over again."

"Ah—go on," Shurli comes back. But the guy, Ray, had fallen into silence and is staring down into the coffee he was sipping. He pours sugar into it, takes a spoon and stirs slowly, his head bent. It aggravates all of us. Tommy stares a question at Tod.

A few people are coming in, a group of stragglers from the bar across the street. It is two o'clock. It's enough to keep everyone busy, with me and my man making eyes between orders. Tod catches us, then holds my glance for a second. I was giving the looks he wanted to someone else. He bristles, takes a sharp breath. I signal my intentions and for him to back off. Tod ignores me. He looks at Tommy, then Ray.

Crazy Tod starts pacing, loud talking. "Yeah man, hush up all that whining. Be a man. Shows you a man. I'm a man! One hundred percent man! I don't do no whining, no complaining and no crying." He is pacing the length of the Taco House, going around to Tommy and tapping him on the shoulder at intervals. "Ain't that right, man?" He taps Tommy who smiles, puzzled, but friendly, and nods.

"Can't argue that, brother."

"Shit—a man has got to stand up, show no pain—ain't that right bruh?" He talks to Ray who is shriveled up on his stool.

"I proved I'm a man. See these here ribbons? I got this one for sharp shootin'. I can kill a niggah so dead so quick, quicker than the eye can see! You name it and I can fire it with deadly accuracy. If a man can't defend himself, he ain't a man. And I can always defend myself. I can do that if'n I can't never do nothin' else."

As he talks, Tod paces. His pace gets quicker. He waves his hands and his talk gets louder and louder. He keeps coming over to Tommy and tapping him. We can all see that Tommy don't like what is happening. It's getting on his nerves. He realizes that Tod is a taste unhinged.

"Come on, sit down and have some coffee." Shurli reaches out and grabs Tod by his overcoat, pulling him to her. He about-faces and slams into her huge torso.

"Emmm—Shurli, I loves yah!" Everybody laughs.

"Gimme a cup of coffee, Carol," Shurli orders.

I move to the coffee pot and pour a hot steaming cup, then

slide the cup past Tommy and into Shurli's chunky outstretched hand. "Here, Tod, drink this and come to your senses."

Tod reaches awkwardly for the cup, knocking it out of her hand and into Tommy's lap. "Goddamn!" Tommy yells, jumping up, scalded, hastily brushing coffee from the lap of his fresh beige jumpsuit. "Shit, man — what's wrong with you?" He yells at Tod.

Tod, having gotten the desired response, spins, grabs up a handful of napkins and starts "helping" Tommy clean up.

"Oh, oh, sorry brother. I didn't mean to make a mess!"

Li'l Bit comes out of the jane and walks past the two. "Tod, what you done gone and did now?"

"Hey, man, I can help myself! You've done enough for one night!" Tommy snaps.

"I'm just trying to help." Tod's words are slippery.

"Back off bro-*ther*. You helped enough." We can see Tommy is short tempered and deeply pissed about his clothes. "If you was a man, as you claim you are, you'd offer to pay for my clothes. But that's all right, bro-*ther*, I understands."

"Hey, now — well, wait a minute bruh! I'm just bein' nice."

"Niggah, you can take your being nice 'n shove it!" Tommy's super pissed and moves to the door to leave. My heart does a slow painful sink. I'm getting pissed at Tod also.

Tod moves and halts Tommy at the door, hooking him at the elbow. "Don't run away, bruh! Don't run away from me like that!"

Tommy looks at Tod's hand on his elbow. "Man — is you crazy? What kind of fool is you? Let go of my elbow!"

Tod takes his hand away slowly, stepping back cautiously. "You think you man enough to take me?" Everybody groans. "Huh? You think you *man* enough?" Tod goes into a karate stance. "I gots my piece, man, and, like I say — I gots a deadly aim."

"Oh? You want to duel? I gots my piece too. It's out in the car. I'll be just a minute." He takes off his coat and goes through the door. Shurli turns to me, panic in her eyes.

"Girl, he always carries a .38 in his car. He'll kill Tod. I best go try and stop him." Shurli runs out into the night after Tommy.

Kathy takes her tall dark lithe healthy self and goes up to Tod. "Why don't you behave yourself, crazy, and quit actin' like everybody's a gook? Sit down and drink some coffee, take your order and go home!"

Tod turns to the counter. I hand him another cup of coffee. Shurli and Tommy come back in. She's mollified him, reasoned him down to a simmer.

She seats Tommy at the counter where he's left his coat. "I'll fix you a plate and you eat, okay?" He nods and turns up, spotting me, smiling, remembering our "date." I smile, then turn as another customer straggles through. "I'll get it," Li'l Bit slurs. Humph, I think—red devils.

Tod winds his drunken way over to Tommy, coffee in hand. "Like I said, man—I'm sorry." He stumbles and spills the coffee again. This time on Tommy's shoulder.

"Son-of-a-bitch!" Tommy jumps up screaming. "Sorry! You goddamned right you sorry. Now what you want to *do* sucker? Let's do it now!" Tommy tears off his hat, tossing it into one of the booths, revealing long matted brown hair. "Now do somethin', sucker, do somethin' now!"

"Aw niggah—I'm a black belt in karate. I'll kill your ass, sucker."

"Well, man, you better kill it then!" Tommy raises up his arms in a boxing stance, frustration in his eyes. I can see the thought traveling through his mind—images of being flipped through the plate glass window as he sizes up Tod. They are both about the same height, 6' 1", and frame. Tommy is worried about what his first move might be. He moves to hit Tod. Tod ducks. Tommy reverses, moves and swings again. Tommy misses. Tod grabs his extended arm, raises him up and flings him into the table next to the john. Everybody is out of the kitchen area now, watching. Not a sound but that of the two men fighting.

Tommy struggles up from the floor, beneath the confident Tod. "Get up niggah, get up and come and get me!" Tommy is feeling his way, blinded and dizzy from the impact of his head against the solid edge of the table which is bolted to the floor and the west wall. Tod turns away, mocking him, announcing to us: "That's how a man fights!"

Doggedly, Tommy is half way to his feet, leaning against the table for support, trying to get his focus. His hand brushes against the glass sugar canister. He secures it and pushes forward, stumbling after Tod, catching him by the flapping tail of his overcoat. "Okay, sucker, let's see you karate this!"

Wham, into Tod's skull. The scrunch of glass and blood spurting. Tod spins. Sugar everywhere. He reels under the impact. That is all Tommy needs. He rains blows down on Tod's neck and face. The sound of flesh pounding flesh. Jesus stands, awed. "Hey, man! Somebody call the cops. He's killing that man!" No one moves. Jesus hastily disappears around back to the pay phone.

"You's a man—huh? You's a man—huh?" Tommy screams like a chant. He's on top of Tod, slamming Tod's head into the floor with both of his hands. We all stand, frozen. Shurli finally runs from behind the counter, the unfinished plate still in her grasp. "Jesus is calling the cops. You best get outta here, quick!" She manages to pull him off of Tod with her free hand. Tommy stands, staggering—his eyes glazed, wild. He looks at me, through me, grabs the coat and hat Shurli hastily shoves at him, then stumbles through the door.

Silent, we all turn and look at Tod. He's struggling against the counter, trying to get to his feet. Blood everywhere, mixed with sugar and glass. Blood runs down from the gash in his head, in both directions, down his neck and down the front of his face. One eye seems to be partially out of its socket. His face torn, lumpy and jagged. I look away.

Shurli barks, "Carol—go get some cold wet towels and help me clean him up."

The ambulance and the cops arrive an hour later and Tod is taken away mumbling incoherently on the stretcher. The police sergeant lingers to take testimony, but nobody is talking, not even Jesus. No, we can't identify the assailant. No— we never seen him before. No one got his name.

It's five-thirty and the new shift is coming on in about ten more minutes. Chuck'll probably come in too, if I know K.P. He was sitting at one of the booths on the south wall and saw it all. Shurli and I are sitting at the counter along with Sharita, listening to Ray talk about his wife. He has that look in his eyes, it's fresh strong and sparkles. The one I mentioned at the jump, pain.

"That coat. I got it at the pad. All new and shiny. I just can't bear to go back to that empty room. All her stuff is still there. She'll be buried Sunday. Her sister is takin' over everything. She gave me a week to split."

I nod, trying to keep awake. The ten minutes crawl by. "She tried to tell me, you know? We were arguing and she threw the coat at me, and then clutched her heart sudden like. I asked her what was the matter and she said she was having a heart attack. I thought she was pretending."

Shurli and I look at each other.

It's sunup and Redd hits the door letting in the chilly morning. I reach down under the counter for my purse, go out back and get my jacket.

Outside, Ray is waiting for me. "Say, what's your name?"

"Carol."

"You know, I just can't stand being alone. How about coming over to my place. We'll have a drink, huh?"

I look at him and into Pain. "Thanks—but no thanks."

I turn away and shudder into the moist dawn. My struggle buggy, a tore down '69 Buick is de-icing behind the Taco House.

"Carol, wait up!"

It's Shurli. "I needs a lift, gal. My old man came and took the Cadillac. He has the duplicate keys. Just wait till I get my hands on that son-of-a-gun!"

We get into the car and I crank up. Shurli is grinning like a coon and plowing through that tremendous brown vinyl purse she always carries.

"Looka here what I gots," Shurli chuckles and shows me. It's about three pounds of hamburger meat. "I'm gonna feed my kids!" she announces.

We break into laughter. I neglect to mention the fifty dollar bill in my bra. I wonder what Chuck'll say when he totals up the take this morning.

IN THE CITY OF SLEEP

STILL I look for love. It eludes me. Still I look in this haze/night settling over me . . . ever it eludes in this City of Sleep. There's no love, no hate. Only being and being healed.

There's a war going on. There is so much of everything going on and going and going. My man is a soldier in this war and I was waiting for him to come home so that we could be lovers again. So we could start to build a life together again. That life dismantled by the war in southeast Asia. The yellow war. The war for tungsten. The war I watched take seed after Korea, as a child in my parents' home while looking at the news on television. And at that time I wondered what the war could possibly mean to me. I was only nine years old and had no mind for men or the stuff of men. Laos was a funny word and its pronunciation eluded me.

He looked so tall and sad when we parted at the induction center. I still remember him standing there in his purple jumpsuit—that braid of gold hanging at his chest. God, he was so tall and bronze and *hey good lookin'*. And I had no idea why he was going or where. In a way I thought it was kind of nice—his going. This black man accepted into a military that had rejected my father in '42 as being "ground sick."

"What's ground sickness?"

"Hell if I know." And mother steered me discreetly aside. "They didn't like black men in the service."

And I understood. Somehow my questions to Daddy about what he did during World War II had hurt him. My curiosity had been prompted by the white chemistry teacher at school. He had told the class how he worked on top secret projects in the Army Air Corps and carried on daring correspondence with

117

a Russian chemist. His children were very proud of him. I wanted to be proud of my dad too. Somehow I was denied and didn't understand why. Then I began to reason that perhaps it was a mistake to be proud of men who went to war and built death machines and had clandestine correspondences and killed other men. Men like my father, who didn't qualify for such activities, were superior. And my reasoning made me feel better.

Now my lover was going off to war and I was going to be alone. I feared I couldn't handle the idea that he might never come back to me. Even if he lived to return home I knew he might not be returning to me. That knowledge made our last moments together very poignant. We both knew. It didn't stop me from babbling on about sending him "care packages" of homemade cookies, cigarettes, chocolate bars and stuff. We kept trying to make each other feel there was some possibility. It was possible he'd return home whole; that we'd marry and have children. It was possible we'd buy a home in the suburbs on his G.I. Bill. That he'd get a loan against the home and use it to go into business. It was possible that I'd help him turn that business into a corporation. It was possible that we'd be modestly wealthy. That we'd be able to send our children to good universities. That we would retire early and live comfortably off our earnings, perhaps travel and see the world as we've both longed to see it. It was possible I could be faithful to him every single day he was overseas.

Dear Jane,

You know I don't want to hold you back. And you were such a nice young brown-skinned lady with a big future ahead of you. And I'd hate to be a stumbling block for you. I'd hate to hold you to a promise you made at a weak moment. I'm releasing you from your promise so you can get on with your life. Here is a picture of me with my Vietnamese girlfriend. We have good times together. You should see the insects here — biggest suckers I've ever seen in my life. And you can turn a corner and suddenly you're face-to-face with an elephant. And this heat — this fuckin' heat makes the Mojave feel like a deep freeze. Anyway, this is quite a trip. I just wanted you to know. You are free to be whoever you want to be. And with whoever you want to be.

Goodby. Good luck.

118

Whenever I am hurt I go to the City of Sleep. It is warm and welcoming and I can be there until the pain heals. I lay in the park under the trees that sing. I sit on a couch of stones that surround and soothe me. Or I enter the hushed halls of buildings eager to salve me in solitude. Or I watch the glistening passengerless autos that flow silently along crystal avenues like fish aswim in a stream. I curl up and I go there. Adrift on and above my pain. Until it disappears and is forgotten. Then I return to the world. I wake and go on. Until the next time I'm hurt.

When I was little I always went to the City of Sleep after a spanking. I'd go there until I felt loved again and that I had learned my lesson and that it was understood that I'd never be bad or make that mistake again. I'd sleep through the afternoon or morning. And when I woke mother always had something for me to eat. Or I could go and quietly watch television or play outside, understanding that the crisis had passed. After waking everything bad was gone. It was okay again.

I have thought about taking up permanent residence in that city. It's a wonderful, carefree place. But it's not enough to be free. Mere freedom carries with it the weight of responsibility. To be without care/responsibility/encumbrances. That is the ideal state. I've always thought of it in that way. I could always understand those who had to be free of caring about the world. Free of caring about what goes on in it. Or caring about things like skin color. In caring lies responsibility.

In my City of Sleep the days whiz by if I want them to. And to be free of care is also to be free of worry. I don't worry about what's at the end of my days, for example. I know what's at the end of my days — more sleep. Everlasting sleep. Lasting freedom from care.

When his letter came I read it and went into shock. I was hurt to the bone. I turned on television and curled up in bed and reread his letter, over and over until the pages were damp and I was exhausted with tears. I had to be sure I had read everything — had wrenched from it all possible meaning.

Here is a picture of me with my Vietnamese girlfriend.

Why don't they allow women to go to war? So we can be near our men. So that they won't forget us. So that we won't lose them. So that we can watch over them. So that we can care and feel responsible for them. So that if there's a change we can

119

understand what brought about that change a whole lot better. We don't have to be on the battlefield or get in the way. We can be on the sidelines, nursing, mitigating, observing, rooting them on. . . .

I sound silly. I tend to get silly when I enter the City of Sleep. Things get distorted. Lines are no longer sharp or clear. Colors mute, fade, run into one another. And I have to really concentrate in order to bring objects into focus. Distinctions are blurry on sleepground.

She is a very pretty woman, this new girl, the one in the photograph. Very pretty. She's tiny—a much smaller woman than I am. She has long straight hair that almost reaches her waist. She has on a "Susie Wong" dress of pink satin and there are elaborate stitchings on it in silver thread. And he is sitting there in his camouflage uniform, holding his helmet on one arm and her on the other. There are cards and cigarettes on the table next to them, a bottle and two glasses. It looks like a hut, but it could easily be a club.

I'd hate to hold you to a promise you made at a weak moment.

Was that a weak moment? Was giving myself to him done out of weakness? I had never felt so strong in my life at that moment. I felt I had the power to will away war. I felt my love was so powerful it protected him/would guide him safely through it and bring him back to me unharmed. Was that weakness? At that exact moment, when we lay naked and open to one another I felt armored by our love. When he kissed me I felt my own strength redoubled as his flowed into me on his tongue. And I felt so strong and secure in arousing his nature. Knowing he wanted me, feeling him hard against my thighs. Was that weakness? It's so confusing. When he entered me, that incredible joy I felt as we joined—all of that a weak moment? And as we lay together in the long peace afterwards, curled up and cooing in that delicious stink, clinging to each other as one. That was weakness? How could I mistake weakness for glory?

I'm missing something. What?

I'd hate to be a stumbling block for you.

He means love. Love is a stumbling block. Suppose he fell in love with her and wanted to marry her and bring her home. He knows I'll be here waiting. Or, suppose I met someone else and wanted to marry. I didn't realize it was possible for me to have that kind of joy with anyone else. I guess that's another way in which I'm silly. I believed all that stuff I was taught about love being eternal and unique. That once having loved it could never be the same again with anyone else. I guess I will soon find out. I will be free of caring for one man. Free of responsibility for seeing to one man's happiness. Free of one man's dreams. Our dreams.

In the City of Sleep there are no dreams. Sounds like a contradiction, but it's not. I just sleep. Dreams are full of cares and responsibilities. The City of Sleep is an alternate reality. There is nothing in that city that I don't want. No pain. No heartbreak. No people to involve myself with. Animals are decorative like shadows. They're quiet creatures — cats and birds. They ease round corners and flit from tree to tree. They enhance without creating disturbance. And that's very nice. I don't have to tend to them. They are a part of sleep.

In dreams I'm always busy doing things. My dreams are very exciting; they can be quite compelling — as compelling as reality — so compelling I often confuse the two. But when I don't enjoy the excitement, when I need a rest from them, when they turn into nightmares, I escape into the City of Sleep. The key word is excitement. There is no excitement in the City of Sleep. It is languid and tropical. The sky is forever blue. The houses are of white adobe. The sidewalks are of nephrite and marble. I waft along. I float. I'm just there. I never do anything. And nothing is done around me.

I want to release you from your promise so you can get on with your life.

I was getting on with my life. My life was structured around waiting for him to come back to me. I was making all these plans. He was going to be gone for two years. That's what he said — maybe three. Okay, so what was I going to do? Well, I was going to get a good job and work hard and save up as much money as I could. I was going to buy a new car. In two years, I'd have it just about paid for and it would be mine — ours. And I'd have enough money saved so that when we made the down payment on the house with his G.I. Bill we'd be able to furnish it to our taste. And if we decided to have children within a year or two of that, the money would cushion against my being unable to work while I carried our child. It would also give him enough time to readjust to civilian life. I've always heard that soldiers coming back from war have a difficult time readjusting even

121

under ideal circumstances. And that people who love them never understand. But I would be ready to understand him. I'd spend two years working hard towards that understanding. And while he was going through his adjustment period, I'd still keep working, and be patient and allow him all the time and space he'd need. And then, when he gave word, we'd get married. Of course, I'd set aside a portion of my wages to cover the wedding. I've always wanted a big fantasy wedding, or a traditional church wedding. Or, if he wanted, something small and intimate—it wouldn't matter. Just as long as we married.

I *was* getting on with my life. I had determined to stay so preoccupied in my planning I wouldn't have time to miss him. Why would he say such a cruel thing in his letter. He was my life and I was getting on about him. And now it's all nothing. I certainly don't feel like getting up and going to work—ever again. I want to curl up in bed and sleep.

She's a very pretty girl. She has smooth yellow skin and bright white teeth. I've always heard that women in foreign countries have bad teeth. There's nothing wrong with her teeth. And her lips are very red and glossy. They shine. She looks as happy as I used to feel. Is it my imagination, or is that guilt I see in his eyes? His mouth is smiling. His eyes are not. They're narrowed and looking straight into the camera. He's trying to reach me.

Yeah, she kisses as good as you kiss, Babe. She's different not better. She's here and you're not. You think I'm a sonofabitch. And yes, I know you would have waited for me no matter how many women I had as long as I didn't fall for any of them. You can get past the sex. It's the love that makes you crazy. And you think I don't understand women, don't you, Babe.

I'm getting sleepy. I can hardly keep my eyes open.

Thinking about something too much usually makes me sleepy even when I've had a cup of coffee. But that kind of sleep always brings dreams with it. When I sleep tonight I won't have any dreams.

You are free to be whoever you want to be.

That's outright a lie. I'm not free to be with him in Viet Nam. I'm not free to confront him and his new girlfriend and call her a tramp and call him a dirty lowdown two-timer. I'm not free to make a scene and try and fight her for my man. I'm not free to be his wife. I'm not free to have his child. That is the who I want to be and I'm not free to be any of it.

It hurts and makes me angry—both. Because he's lying to me. This is the first time he's ever lied to me about anything. Why is he lying when this photo makes lying so unnecessary?

I'm going in circles again. It's the sleepiness.

Let's see—how many pills did I take? I can't remember. But I think I took enough. Three and I could sleep through the atomic bomb. And the best thing to do now is sleep.

I wish I could visit my City of Sleep and never return. I wish that. Because if I wake up I'm going to have to do something. And at this moment I don't know what I'm going to do. Now that I'm free to do it. Now that he has freed me.

Upon waking I will have to take responsibility for myself. I will have to care for myself. I will have to find something to do. Damn it. I'll have to mother myself.

Can I?

I'll have to if I wake up. I'll have to.

TAKE IT UP AT THE BRIDGE

THE Club Reverb is open but empty.

A baby grand hungers in the bandstand. A dancer falls by, a blue note seeking metaphor — a way in. She feels out of it, spastic. Her feet itch.

The Professor of Play arrives. He does not see the dancer. His limited idiom allows him to perceive only the piano. He is awed by its line and shape. He mounts the bench. He touches the ivories and his flesh jingles. When he strikes high C the bartender pops up. Glasses rattle and the register sings. And with a copacetic chord in B-flat, the room fills with folks. The Prof finds and fingers a hoodoo rhapsody and the jam jumps off.

A do-wah daddy of dap makes the scene. He spies the dancer and makes his score.

"Hey, sweet mama, turn on the light!"

She smiles, "I can shine for days if the price is right."

"I dig yo' looks and I dig yo' style."

"Come on, daddy — let's rap awhile."

They trip to the floor for fantastic show — a torrid twosome. And suddenly everybody's doin' the do.

The dancer has never felt so viv. Her body extemporizes as it grooves to the syncopations of her too cool dude. He takes off the mute. From the ceiling descends a saxophonist, a drummer and a bassist. They ism rhythm. From behind the bar a vocalist rises out of a vintage bottle of grape. Hers is a lyrical scat that zaps the Prof.

The dancer and her lover note time and density of passion and take five for her place.

The Prof of Play embraces the vocalist with his eyes and every moan that he can improvise. Alas she is jazzed by the bass, the sax and the drum as well. It's all of them or none. the crescendo of their theme starts a fire in the soles of the dancers who jubilate to the frantic friction and go up in smoke.

Without her audience the vocalist goes poof! back to wineland. The combo packs it in. Detroit tomorrow. Another one-nighter. The Professor passes the bar on his way out. He reaches for and caresses the bottle into which the vocalist has vanished. He takes it home and gets royally riffed.

CHUCK AND THE BOSS MAN'S WIFE

SO YOU know how it be for a black man in them days. And them not so long ago. A cracker soon as hang you as look at you. And not all the lynchings be bothered 'bout enough to be reported 'cept amongst us. You know how it be.

So Chuck he kind of got eyes to be sportin' and he went to get him a car. He can jes' imagine himself drivin' up and down them dirt roads his little sweetheart sittin' all up under him. And he be thinkin' 'bout all he can do with his car. So he figure he can get a job workin' evenings after school at old Jack Sark's place. And he figure right.

Chuck he all of sixteen, got a strappin' chest, full grown and feelin' mighty up in his manhood. 'Mongst our menfolk he known not to back down off a fight and can mean swallow lightnin' hot off the still.

Now old man Sark got a wife even prettier in her prime than at her pickin'. Bosom all full and ridin' high on her chest, hips jes' achin' to give up the goody, a walk set fire to the ground. And every man see it and every man's wife see it twice. But Chuck, he so sweet on payin' for his car he can't see nothin' but that little prideful cash money Sark give him to bring home very day.

So like folk start in a teasin' Chuck 'bout old Sark's wife, puttin' evil on his mind, envyin' him his shoes. And he start gettin' nervous cuz he ain't no fool. Chuck he know'd jes' how little a black man's life is worth in them parts if he caught messin' 'round with a white woman of any virtue. And he also start to notice that Sark's wife got a bad itch and she hankering to have him tickle it. Seem every chance she get she all up in his face and with as little on as possible short of being downright

127

indecent. And she take to bendin' over so he can get an eyeful of what she's hung with — in one direction or the other. And right in front of Jack Sark. And Sark he don't see nothin'. Jes' as blind as any man with business foremost in his mind.

But Chuck he's a handlin' it. He figure he only got a few more payments to make on that car and he can clear out. He figure wrong.

One day near 'bout sunset, Jack Sark say he got to make a run across town to take care of some unexpected trouble. Chuck ask if he can help, maybe go along. But Jack he say naw. He gots to take care of it himself — can't nobody help. And Chuck he start sweatin' cuz he hear Sark's wife jes' alistenin'. And he hear Jack Sark in there with her, making his passionate goodby.

Soon as the sound of Jack's old pick-up truck disappear down the road, Chuck know'd his goose is plucked. He start makin' himself busy workin' like the devil in his wake — and he ain't far from the truth. He sweepin', moppin', dustin' and restockin' the shelves, going over the order book — what he did the first time, he do it again double.

Then he hear it. He hear her sweet voice drippin' dew.

"Chuck, honeychile, come here, would you please?"

And what he do? He afraid to obey her. He afraid to disobey her.

"Chuck, come here — *please.*"

He knew how treacherous white womens was. And how that treachery had got many a young black man hung. So he don't know if to run or what. And he curiosity anyway — never mind how dead it killed that ol' cat. So when she call again, he go to her. She in her bedroom and got on one of them fancy silk lounge robes and a slip. And she damn near 'bout to burst out the slip. And she know damn well what she look like got that flaming orange-brown hair and that harlot's face all made up like painted womens do.

And Chuck he be a man. He feelin' his manhood workin' on him. But he also feel that old rope tuggin' at his throat. And he can feel it squeezin' the life out him. And he can see his Mama and his brothers standin' under the hangin' tree come to cut down what the buzzards done left of his corpse.

"Yesss, Ma'am. Can I do somethin' for you, Ma'am?"

"Chuck, I'm so hot and thirsty. Would you bring me a cola

128

out the fridge in the back of the storeroom, please."

And he tore his eyes away and went to the storeroom cursin' her, knowin' she coulda got it easy enough herself.

He brung the cola back to her but found the bedroom door closed again. He knocked on it quiet like.

"Bring it here, chile," she cooed.

And he opened the door real skittish, holdin' the cola with his arm stretched out in front of him as if to ward somethin' off, his head turned away from her, his eyes squinty shut. When she didn't take it, he turned his head to see why. She was standing there naked as judgment day.

Chuck's eyes fell out his head and he started to shake and tremble. She see she got to teach the boy a thing or two. So she took the cola out of his stiff hand and rolled her hips at him.

"Well, honey, don't just stand there. Do what you feel like."

And Chuck's eyes snapped back into his head so hard he fainted dead away.

When Chuck come too, Jack Sark was leaning over him, concern and amusement playin' across his face.

"I swear, the boy worked himself into a snit soon as you left," he could hear Sark's wife sayin'. "I ain't never seen nothing like it."

"The boy's tryin' to pay for that new car of his'n. I guess he might over did it."

Lookin' around, Chuck see he all asprawl in the hallway outside the bedroom. He wonder for a second how he got there, then he know'd it was her what drug him out that bedroom. She musta had a time cuz he was one-eighty soppin'.

Chuck struggled to get on his feet, leaning on Sark's shoulder, clutching at his throat, feelin' to be sure this weren't no hallucination that he was havin' while dangling from a noose.

"Go on home, boy. Go home and get some rest. Here's your pay. We'll see you tomorrow." Sark tucked his day's wage into Chuck's T-shirt pocket. She gone back in the bedroom.

He couldn't see her, but Chuck could feel her listenin'.

That self same night he filled the gas tank of that new car of his. And folks say Chuck lit out for California drivin' as fast as legal limits allowed. Before he left the parish he was doin' a lot of talk 'bout lookin' up a cousin in Los Angeles thereabouts.

129

Maybe get him a job on one of them there movie camera crews. And didn't nobody hear nothin' for two, three months till he sent money to his Mama, enough for her to pay off his car note.

Ain't heard tale of the boy since.

'SHROOMS

DAVID and Rae followed Dingus upstairs. David was anxious to see what was happening, Rae was merely anxious. Their steps were accompanied by some new Reggae sound.

Kit was sprawled along the paisley modular divan. Rae still found it unsettling that this dispassionate odalisque, half a decade her senior, was David's mother.

Kit was a small, acerbic bright-skinned woman, and a heavy smoker. In her youth she had passed for white. Even now, in the eastern light, Kit looked like a white woman. She rolled her enormous sunken eyes at them and put her lit cigarette to her turned-down smile. All that nigger came alive.

"Hi, Mom."

"Hi, Son," she cracked in her raspy contralto. "Hey — Rae."

Rae nodded, preferring to remain mute. Kit and she were on friendly enough terms, but there was a very nasty undercurrent between them yet to erupt.

Rae was beset by strangeness. She was as tall as David and as mahogany as the taller Dingus. David was a carefree male version of his mother. He sported two days of stubble and a mop of wavy brown hair. And he knew, as did Kit, that Rae and Dingus had not too long ago been lovers.

And there they were. The four of them.

It bugged Rae that Dingus and Kit had become a shack-up. How, she wondered, had Dingus come across Kit? Probably at one of the neighborhood counter-culture hangs. Dingus had known Kit was her mother-in-law before he started to date her. Was that Kit's attraction? Was he sniffing up under Rae? Was Kit dogging Rae's trail? Both? Why keep drawing Rae into their

131

circle? She avoided them whenever possible. Rae wouldn't have come if it weren't for David and the mushrooms.

Love on magic *'shrooms* is the most supreme love of all. Sex is unspeakably incredible. Two become one. Some have out-of-the-body experiences. One might see the future. One might talk to God. Enter God. Be God. David had salivated into the receiver when Kit called that morning and told him they were "in pocket." He insisted they share.

Rae kept watching David for any sign of discomfort or jealousy. There was none. He was his usual easy-going self, full of boyish excitement and eagerness.

These mushrooms were supposed to be a *muthafucka*. No ordinary psychedelics—but the tripmaster superb.

"Hey, Dude—let's break out them 'shrooms!"

These were rare tiny "red" mushrooms. Songs, incantations, books and essays had been written about them. The ancient Mayans and Aztecs had used them in sacred rituals. Many a man had lost first mind then soul to them. Occasionally they took a life.

Dingus went to the kitchen and returned with a mason jar of the treasure.

"How'd you score these, man?" David put his chin to the table and studied them.

"I took a trip down to Central America a few months ago. I picked 'em and candied 'em myself."

Dingus' talents always surprised Rae. He was that rare beast—a free spirit—a black hippy/love child; a throwback to "flower power"; a persistent kink that refused to unravel into the social hoi polloi; a man who lived off his cock. Which was why they had gone their separate ways—her slaving paying the bills while he practiced the art of dead beat and fuck around.

"We already tried 'em yesterday," Kit spoke with authority. "It's a fantastic high. Clean. And no gunky after effects like you get on cheap acid. We came down a few hours ago. We've been up most the night."

David picked up the jar and owled it, turning it slowly in the light streaming in from the bay window.

132

"And it don't take long to go up," Dingus spoke from the stereo. He turned the LP over and the air filled with jump-steady. "They actually taste pretty bitter in spite of the syrup. I'll make us some smoothies to down 'em with."

Kit's eyes lit up with exaggerated enthusiasm. "He's really good at that."

"Do you chew 'em?" It was Rae's first mushroom trip. She hoped they wouldn't be ingesting something poisonous and wake up dead. She knew what a jerk Dingus could be. She wondered if Dingus had started giving Kit the bullshit about his being a great undiscovered actor in search of generous patronage.

"You can chew 'em if you can stand 'em. It's faster that way." Kit took another draw. Rae noticed the cigarette was a joint of marijuana. David reached for it, took a hit and pointed it. Rae shook her head.

"No thanks."

"Go ahead, Babe—it's okay."

"I don't feel like it."

David's eyes shifted sharply into blank. Unnerved by his subtle challenge, Rae accepted the joint.

"It's okay to mix it," Kit smirked. "The highs are compatible."

Rae was a novice when it came to dope. A strict Protestant rearing was difficult to dislodge.

"You should have a better trip than the three of us, Rae, because your system is so clean," Kit reassured.

Dingus got in her face and reached for the joint. His Caribbean heritage blessed him with strong African features and laid-back poise. He took it from Rae's fingers making a point to brush her hand suggestively, plumbing her startled eyes with keen amusement. Embarrassed, Rae stood and turned her back on the three. She walked around the divan to the stereo and pretended to be engrossed in the new reggae album jacket. "This is a good group."

Kit had to have seen the exchange between Rae and Dingus. So did David. Why were they so fucking passive? Why wasn't there a scene? Why wasn't David up threatening to mutilate Dingus if he touched Rae again? Why wasn't Kit bristling with wounded ego and indignation?

133

"What's a smoothy, David?" Rae asked pointedly, swallowing her anger, wishing she could dispel the utterly cool atmosphere.

"Ice cream and stuff whipped up in a blender—all thick like a malted. You'll like it." David was abuzz, his tongue fuzzed.

"I make 'em with dates and bananas," Dingus smiled, his tongue fuzzed also. He rose with a list to then fro. "I'll get those smoothies." Dingus made busy in the kitchen, slicing and chopping. The whirrrr of the Osterizer mingled with the music.

David went back to studying the mushrooms. "I've waited years for this. We've had mushrooms before, but not like these."

"They make you feel sooo goood." Kit had held the joint and toked it down to a nubbin. She dropped it into an ashtray atop the coffee table.

"Dingus is really somethin'," she slurred to Rae over her shoulder. "He's so good to me."

"Good, Kit—I'm glad."

David joined Rae at the stereo, making dubbing moves. "Come on, Babe."

She went into the lethargic rhythm, the tilt of her hips mirroring his. He smiled ear-to-ear, eyes glazed. "Relax, Rae. Let's have a good trip."

"Okay," she forced a smile.

Kit fired a regular cigarette and smoked it, watching them dance, working the ashtray.

"You're so good for David, Rae. I'm glad you two hooked up."

Who was she kidding? Straight life was strangling David and everyone knew it. Everyone but Rae. The girl was such a fool. She believed hard work was its own reward; as were goodness, generosity, sincerity; that she'd make it if she kept her proverbial nose to the legendary grindstone. Rae had swallowed the all-American illusion and David was choking on it.

"Come and get down," Dingus cruised toward them with a tray of four monster glasses brimming with viscous nourishment, and four tablespoons. Starting with David, then Rae, Kit and Dingus, each took spoonfuls of mushrooms from the jar, began to chew, then reached for and partook of the smoothies. The ritual took no more than fifteen minutes.

134

They all waited, sitting in silence, exchanging looks. Waiting to go up.

"Yeahhhhhh," David glowed. "Hell, yeah!"

"Me too," Kit gleamed. Her skin had an unusual sheen to it. Dingus wrapped his arms around his head in a whipping motion, elbows flailing, unwrapped them and wrapped them again. His skin also shined.

"How long will it last?" Rae asked, feeling dazzled.

"Eight to twelve hours." Dingus stood and stretched his muscular form. "Just don't waste it by laying up and going to sleep."

Rae didn't hear his advice. Her attention was drawn to the living room wall. There was something come alive in it. Something was that wasn't, wasn't that was. A mouth/void/chasm/consciousness. It spoke.

How do you do.

Hello.

I can tell you what *they* want.

Tell me.

Dingus wants an orgy. He wants to ~~fuck~~ Have you and Kit at the same time. Kit and David will go along with his scheme. David will be content to watch. To what end? To liberate David from your hold. Once you allow Dingus to have you, David is freed to do whatever he damned well pleases. He can have other women and feel no guilt. He will be free to roam the streets again. Free to rob and steal. Free to be all his love for you keeps him from being: liar and thief. Kit won't stop it because she stands to profit. She'll have them both. in control.

And me. What about me?

You will be — whatever you be.

The sound came low at first, a steady pitch — almost a hum. It began to climb. David went rigid beside her. "Babe, are you all right?"

Rae was looking at it. Was in it.

Dingus and Kit became concerned. The sound was increasing in decibels, drowning out the mellow rasta beat — a shrill ahhhhhhhh without undulation.

Rae no longer had it. It had her. It let her into the future. It showed her intolerable loneliness.

You will have to get along without him.

Rae shrieked at the top of her lungs, creating a sobering blast that cut through their highs.

David waved one hand before her eyes.

"Not a blink. She's on a bummer!"

"Oh, shit!" Dingus wrapped and unwrapped his arms around his head in two more rapid sequences.

"David, you better take her home," Kit reached for another cigarette.

And then it was gone. And she saw them staring at her. She stared back.

"We'd better go," David lifted Rae to her feet and pushed her toward the stairs.

"What in hell did she see?" Dingus sniffed at the empty mason jar.

"I don't know," puzzled Kit, "and I don't want to know."

BIG DREAMS

SHADING his eyes from the windshield's glare, the officer took note of the Southern Cal noonday sun. It was a fair late fall day — uncomfortably warm. He noted his earlier chalk mark on the balding right tire of the badly aged gray coupe — indication it had been parked well over the one-hour limit. He scrawled out a parking citation and clipped it under the windshield wiper.

"Hey, Sweet Cakes! What's wrong?"

"I'm in trouble, Rollins."

"You ain't pregnant again is you?"

"Not that kind of trouble, but bad enough."

"Quit cryin' and tell Rollins all about it, Chile."

"I gots a parkin' ticket."

"A parkin' ticket? All this over a parkin' ticket?"

"I'm barely gettin' by on my check. I can't afford no ticket. And I can't afford to be without my car. Not in this man's town. You know how it is. And I gots little kids. I'm tryin' to cut down. I ain't et in two days. I don't watch TV. I sit in the dark to cut down on the 'lectric. I'm down to the bone. Nothin' for me to do but get a job."

"They gonna cut your check," he cautioned.

"I know. I tried to do somethin' on the sly, like waitress. I can't even get past the try-out. They wants girls what's sexy. I ain't qualified."

"Now, now — you're not bad looking, Jo Ann. You're quite an attractive young lady!

I'm too dark. I'm too clumsy — I'm always too somethin'. I can't keep a job long enough to make it count."

"Cryin' don't help."

"It ain't fair. I can't get no breaks at all. I need money, Rollins. If I can't get off'n the county, maybe enough on the sly to make it tolerable."

Rollins thought a moment. "You serious, now, about what you sayin'? About money?"

"As a heart attack."

"There's this fellow come through here a day or two ago say he's lookin' for artist models. Pays seventy-five dollars an hour jes' for sittin' whilst people paint you naked—you know? If you don't mind bein' naked. No experience required for that."

"I don't mind nothin' pay that good. You sure?"

"Sure I'm sure."

"Sounds great. But I don't think I'm what he wants."

"Huh?"

"I gots scars, Rollins. From them babies—the ones I had and the ones I ain't had."

"Don't worry 'bout that. The man's a true artist. Far as he's concerned, marks and scars only make art much more art."

"You think so?"

"I'll prove it to you right now. I'll call and see if I can catch him. Jes' wait there and I'll call you right back, okay?"

"I can't thank you enough."

"No sweat."

"And so I said, 'Look I've got a young lady interested in doin' some modeling. She's a very lovely little bit. But she has some scars—you know, stretch marks. She's had a couple of kids. That make a difference?' And he said, 'No.' So he'll be here at four-thirty. It's almost that now."

Jo Ann shivered in a thin cornflower blue mini-dress, panty hose and high heels which emphasized her maple legs. The blue was sky-bright against her earthen skin. She had wide walnut eyes. Her plain pouty thick lips made a tulip of a mouth. She had a hazel-nut nose, and small ears peaked out from under her bush of kinky, thick, primped reddish-brown hair. She teetered at the edge of the chair next to Rollins' reception desk.

"I'm nervous."

"Don't be, Sweet Cakes! The job's good as got!"

Jo Ann blushed. She wondered at Rollins. He was her play big brother. He was a security guard at the neighborhood check-cashing place. Their nodding acquaintance became platonic

138

friendship the day she lost her wallet on the premises. He returned it, along with advice on what kind of purse it was best to carry. She dropped in on his job from time to time and aired her woes. He was the elder brother she'd never had; the therapist she could not afford.

"I appreciate this, Rollins — so *much*."

"Ah, here comes our man Leroy now!" Rollins peered through the barrier of plate glass armored in black iron bars. Instead of one man, Jo Ann saw two.

They did not look like artists. Jo Ann didn't know what black artists were supposed to look like. She imagined Africanized bohemians, if not flamboyant Afro-culturalists. Leroy and the man who tailed him had the distinct air of street-business about them. They were cleanshaven and ragged in expensive slacks, loafers and silk shirts. Gold and silver accentuated their arms and wrists. At his smooth ebony chest, Leroy sported a gold cross with a diamond at its center. He was very dark-skinned, as dark as the lens of his gold-rimmed shades. The other man also sported sunglasses and busily chewed gum. Leroy and Rollins shook hands warmly.

"Just in time, my man! The little lady is 'bout to jump out her skin."

"I see, I see." Leroy eyed Jo Ann as she timidly rose from the chair. She felt his appraisal beneath the glasses.

"Not bad. She'll do. Quite nicely."

"Sure you don't want a closer look? To be sure?"

Jo Ann blanched, embarrassed by Rollins' hard sell. The two men remained neutral, letting Rollins continue his Samaritan pitch.

"Nobody's here jes' now. There's an empty office you can use. The key's right here." Rollins jangled along his key ring, locating it. The two men looked at one another, shrugged and stepped in behind the reluctant Jo Ann egged along by the eager Rollins.

As he unlocked the door, Rollins took a good hard look at the second man. " 'Scuse me, brutha — what's your name?"

The silent second continued to chew his gum as though he hadn't heard the question. Leroy answered. "Oh — this is my brother, Tom."

"Hi Tom, glad to meet you. Now to business."

139

Rollins hit the light switch, shooting Jo Ann reassurance. The carpeted room filled with phosphorescence. Rollins took her elbow and steered Jo Ann into the center of the large cold space, found a folding chair and placed it close by. Leroy and Tom mutely observed them, hanging back a few feet.

"All right, gents, you're all set!" Rollins gave Jo Ann a wink and tipped out of the room, easing the door shut behind him.

Leroy and Tom seemed as uncomfortable with the situation as Jo Ann. Tom crossed his arms and stood smacking his jaws as Leroy conducted the "interview."

"Yeah—well, peel your dress off, top down."

It was elastic at the top and Jo Ann quickly did as asked, slipping it down around her shoulders, simultaneously removing her panty hose and kicking off her high-heeled shoes. She carefully draped her dress and panty hose over the back of the chair. She wore no brassiere and her small demibreasts stood pert on her chest. They were almost all umber aureolae. In the coolness of the empty room her exposed nipples rose. Her ribs were beginning to show from hunger. Her waist was straight and narrow. Her stomach was lined in satiny light brown striae which curved in toward her kinky patch of dark brown pubic hair. She had "breeder's hips"—disproportionately full, a large derriere jutting off into overly fleshy thighs, tapered into slightly knobby knees and slim bowed legs further tapering into narrow calves, very thin ankles and small angular feet.

"You kinda cute," Leroy snorted after a moment. "Pull your dress back on."

Tom spied a wastebasket in one corner of the room and discharged the wad of gum, allowing Jo Ann a modicum of privacy. But Leroy stood, arms folded, and watched with deliberation. The "interview" struck Jo Ann as somehow not quite right. Leroy's imposing manner made her feel awkward. It was all very peculiar. But since she had no prior experience to measure it against, she dismissed her doubt. She was doing this for money and saw no point in being bashful, having denuded herself before the strangers.

"How much will I make an hour?"

"Seventy-five to start. We pay on a day-to-day basis. No tax deductions or like that. You'll pull down two hundred in no time—easy." Leroy flashed a grin of perfect white ridges that sent a flush of confidence through her.

140

Jo Ann smiled. "When do I start?"

"Tomorrow. We've got a night class going."

"I'm no expert, but ya'll don't look like artists to me," she said, her back to Leroy as she dressed, her skepticism soft, her challenge casual. Leroy didn't miss a beat.

"Actually, I'm not, professionally. I own the studio, I hire the models, I schedule the classes, and I collect the fees. Sometimes I sit in and observe. I try my hand at it. But no, I'm more of an entrepreneur. My art is the business of art." His voice, a frank, soft undulation, gave her goose bumps. Jo Ann was impressed.

"Well, fellas, will she do?" Rollins boisterously re-entered the room, keys jangling, grinning.

Leroy shook his hand. "She's definitely hired, my man."

"Excellent! Excellent." Rollins steered the trio toward the reception area, catching the light on the way out, locking the door behind them, chatty all the while. "Well now, where does she go?"

"We're up in Hollywood."

Jo Ann groaned. It was an hour to two hour's bus ride from Watts, depending upon traffic. And since her last few pennies had been invested in looking pretty, she couldn't afford the fare. Once she had a couple of days' pay behind her, transportation would be no problem. Order of business would be to pay that parking ticket, then fill the gas tank.

"We could pick her up here — if it's okay with you."

"Sure. Whatever else you work out in the meantime!"

"So that's settled."

Glowing gratitude at Rollins, Jo Ann suppressed a squeal.

"You live far from here? We'll drop you off."

"Uh — ." Jo Ann didn't want them coming by her apartment. She was never anxious to reveal the extent of her poverty to anyone. She had left her kids home alone with a TV tray of sandwiches and cookies with a pitcher of orange juice. She allowed them to eat and sleep in her bed before the 19-inch black-and-white television set. It was a risk she had to take in order to try and find work. Before she could formulate an excuse, Rollins interceded.

"Hey, why don't ya'll be sociable. Take the little lady out for a drink to celebrate the start of this new association."

Rollins was carrying things a bit far, but Jo Ann squelched

her protest. It had been well over a year since anyone had taken her out anywhere, if only for business.

Leroy shot another quick little glance at Tom who returned a curt nod of agreement.

"Sounds good to me."

There was *something* about riding in the front seat of a luxury car positioned between two men. Something erotic. Jo Ann caught fire. The fire warmed her thighs and licked her loins. It was the smell of expensive leather, the musk of flesh so close to flesh. It was the throb of soul music filling the cabin. The loneliness and the hunger began to overtake her. She leaned forward and held her face in her palms to fight off a deep wave of nausea.

"Don't get sick in my car—*please*," Leroy snapped.

"Are you all right?" Tom asked softly. Jo Ann sat up assisted by his patient, concerned grasp. It was the first time he'd spoken and his alto was as pleasant and mellow as Leroy's bass.

"I'm sorry. I was just thinkin'."

"Troubles?" Tom was caring.

"Sort of." Her smile was bleak. Her troubles were so basic, so simple, yet so difficult to resolve: enough love, enough money, enough satisfaction with life.

They stopped for gas. Leroy stepped out to monitor the service station attendant, particular about who messed with his machine. Without signal, Tom slipped his arm around Jo Ann's waist. She yielded, her body flooding with want. He lowered his head and nicked her mouth with his. Her head went back with his pushing motion. Tom parted her lips with his tongue and explored her mouth. She tasted the sugary resonance of the chewing gum. Giving in and giving up to this rapid-fire flirtation, she allowed chills a course through her.

Quickly, naughtily, Tom released her as Leroy climbed back into the car. Leroy read the exchange between Jo Ann and Tom. He shot them a jolt of hostile coldness but said nothing as he gunned the accelerator. Rapt in unexpected pleasure, Jo Ann was relieved Tom had made his move. As her new boss, Leroy was tabu.

"You hungry?" Leroy asked no one specifically.

"Like a big dog," Tom answered. "What you got in mind?"

"The Satin Lounge."

"Sure."

Would they treat her to a meal? Jo Ann hoped. Surely she wasn't the only one who could hear the loud grumblings of her stomach.

Leroy swung the Cadillac into a U. In minutes they were outside the stylish South Central night spot frequented only by people-of-color, and, of such, the better heeled.

A valet took the car as Tom possessively squired Jo Ann by her arm. A moody Leroy led the way. Was she unconsciously sparking a case of brother versus brother? The notion flattered her, and she basked in it. Underneath, her pride was slightly pinched by Leroy's fire-and-ice ambivalence.

Pink lighting accented the club's cush interior. The lamé-gowned hostess led them to the main room. Tables arranged in a crescent skirted a half-moon of dance floor and floor-level stage. Two microphones and a suite of instruments — drums, bass, baby grand piano, and saxophone — stood starkly against an orange-gold velvet curtain. They were seated at one of the ringside tables in burgundy leather armchairs.

Jo Ann allowed herself the luxury of feeling extravagant. She had never heard live music at a club. Tom anchored on her left, and Leroy sat across from them to her far right. It was all very new very grand very fast. Her eyes felt too small to encompass it all.

A waitress appeared and lit the brass candle lamp mid-table. Easy jazz dovetailed with soft rhythm-and-blues creating an evocative backdrop. The men were handed menus. Leroy stared openly at the honey-skinned woman. The fleshsome waitress was squeezed into a backless micro-mini dress, revealing a hint of crotch, and all of her lush, chunky legs. Leroy's gaze was one of filthy lucre. His stare triggered an instant replay of her "interview" for Jo Ann.

"See anything you want, Leroy? I'll try the fried chicken," Tom opened.

Jo Ann wanted to share the menu, but the two men talked over her. She shuddered in her sudden invisibility.

"Hmph. Order me a steak sandwich 'n fries." Leroy turned his cold stare on her. "*You* want anything?"

"Uh—I don't have the money." Her pride was transparently false.

"I didn't ask that, Simple." He slammed the menu down with exaggerated disgust and rose. "Tom, get her what she wants. I'll be right back," he snapped and was gone.

In one sentence Leroy reduced her to a child. Could she work for such a man? What was she doing here with him? What was she letting herself in for? Tom took her hand and couched it in both of his, distracting her doubts.

"Don't mind Leroy. He's jealous because you chose me, that's all." His eyes rimmed with desire. She needed that job and the promised money. She needed to believe Tom.

She managed a smile. "Thanks, Tom."

"Now, what *would* you like?"

"I ain't et inna couple of days. If I eat too much I'll get sick."

Tom was sympathy and gentleness. "Tell you what. I'll order the half-chicken plate with extra French fries, and we'll share."

"Thanks."

"Something from the bar?" The waitress was back, poised to jot.

"Gin and tonic for the gentleman sitting there. Scotch on the rocks for me, and the young lady'll have—?"

"A lime soda."

"A what!?"

"I—I don't drink." Again, without quite understanding why, Jo Ann was embarrassed.

"Damn! Leroy's not going to like that!" His unexpected sharpness of tone went through her. She thought she detected fear behind it. Was Tom afraid of Leroy? And if so, why? What kind of man fears his own brother? And what kind of brother is to be feared?

Aware that he had exposed something unintended, Tom's eyes and voice took on cavalier slyness. "Look, why pay a buck-fifty for a glass of soda pop when a real drink costs the same?" His flipflop mystified Jo Ann. She desperately wanted Tom to like her, at least for the one night.

"I—I'll try something—if you want."

He smiled, all charm once more. "Good. Waitress, bring her a sloe gin fizz." He placed the rest of their order and the young woman sped off. "That's sweet, that sloe. You'll like

144

it. It's a good drink for beginners."

Tom cracked open a pack of menthol cigarettes for a smoke and held the pack toward her, one of the cigarettes jutting up for easy access. "I bet you don't smoke either."

She shook her head. "No. I don't."

Jo Ann was distracted by the differences twixt Tom and Leroy. Brothers usually had some kind of resemblance, in mannerisms if not appearance, if only a walk, if only an attitude. They were as unalike in temperament as brothers come. The only things they seemed to have in common were style of dress and taste in jewelry. There wasn't the slightest similarity — in hairline, hair texture, facial features — nothing.

Leroy was a tall, solidly slender, muscular six-footer. His saturnian head was long, narrow of face. He was a very black man, almost Asian about his keen intelligent brown orbs set in yellowed whites with cleanly defined, stern brows. The rich tarriness of his skin was unrelieved by any patches, shadings, or highlights of red or yellow. He was what, in her school days, was degradingly called a "black jap." In those days, any miss above a deep tan was considered too good to date a mister that dark. Now black was so-called beautiful. The blacker the berry the sweeter the wine; although Leroy was decidedly of the bitter cask. His fine thick kinks were trimmed into a modest pomp. He had a high forehead and a widow's peak. His slim hands and pointed fingers were well manicured, unusually long, with clean nails painted in clear enamel. A prideful man, he disdained common labor. His nose was regal and narrow with a slight flatness. There was something exotic about his mouth. He might have been a pharaoh in another life. But what defined him more than any single feature was the repressed rage seething beneath his mandarin cool. It spurted out at odd moments — a cutting, indiscriminatory nastiness. Black would have to be beautiful a long time for Leroy to get over the damage.

In contrast, Tom appeared sensitive and warm. He regarded these traits in himself as undesirable/"sissy." Leroy's coldness was his ideal. Tom's was a postural tightness focal in his hefty chest. He was a slightly taller, more massively fleshy man than Leroy. His well-muscled thighs were almost as thick as Jo Ann's waist. His handsome head was earthy. His face had a boyish openness. One eyebrow permanently tilted upward,

145

giving him impish dash. His cedar skin had a ruddy cast. His "good grade" of dark brown hair had a natural curl, an intermingling of black and amerindian blood. His sharp facial features were thinner, but no less sensual. Impenetrable black eyes were disconcertingly void-like one moment, alarmingly enticing the next. There was something of the joker about him; something of a man going against his nature. *He doesn't like being so black,* Jo Ann guessed. If he had favored the lighter parent over the darker he might have escaped the indignities of blackness.

How each man wore his ethnicity nagged at Jo Ann. She hoped Leroy would understand that her preference for Tom had nothing to do with appearances. She prided herself on her racial consciousness, having no desire to play the skin game. She found them both physically attractive. Personality was another matter.

"You and Leroy don't look like brothers."

"People say that all the time."

"Are you?"

"Not quite. Leroy's the oldest. His father split. Then there were some others. I came along about 4th or 5th. We have the same mother in differing states of untogetherness. We're half brothers. You know how it goes with us." His sarcasm stung her. She lapsed back into her thoughts, wondering how to gracefully extract her foot from her mouth.

Leroy returned to the table as the waitress set fresh drinks before them. Leroy was agitated. "I made a few calls."

"Yeah? Any luck?"

"Hell, no."

Jo Ann interpreted this cryptic exchange as Leroy's frustrated attempt to get a date for the evening. He glared at the two of them and sipped his gin and tonic, dispensing with any toast. Tom cozied his glass to Jo Ann's. With romantic smiles they gently touched rims. She took a dainty swig from the slim red cocktail straw. The drink was almost too sweet, with no hint of alcohol.

"What the hell she's drinkin'?" Leroy grimaced.

"We ordered her a sloe gin fizz. She ain't a heavy drinker."

"She ain't, huh? Well she'll get the knack quick hanging with us." Leroy bottomed up and waved at the waitress, signaling another round of the same.

One by one the expensively suited middle-aged black men took the stage and began to ready their instruments. Jo Ann watched, fascinated at the random noodlings of tunings and warm-up. The piped-in music discreetly ceased and the room bristled with a bluesy upbeat instrumental. There was intermittent applause after each man showcased his virtuosity. This ritual was foreign to Jo Ann and thrilled her to her toes. The right time. The right place. It was all all right.

When the food arrived, Jo Ann helped herself to the leg and thigh Tom set to the side of his plate for her. She nibbled it quickly, polishing the bones and burying them in one of the oversized paper napkins. She reached for a couple of French fries now and again. For the moment, her stomach's hunger was sated. It was the hunger for sex that beset her, amplified by the gin at work in her blood.

The singer arrived on stage, a pink sequined slink of gown praising her Coke-bottle figure. She and the band melded well, old friends exchanging smiles, nods and other subtle indications. Tom and Leroy sat up and leaned forward, uncritically wowed by the fiery beauty. Jo Ann felt inadequate, shrunken into ugliness by the chanteuse's starry presence. Drawing the songbird's sultry eyes, the two men began to tease each other between incantations. It was Jo Ann's first time to hear blatant basic man-talk.

"Shit, man — look at those thighs. How'd you like to crawl into some of that!"

"Looks lip-smackin' good."

"I can damn near feel it."

"Shit, I can damn near *taste* it."

"I know that pussy's as good as it looks. Better."

"And them jugs — lorrrd havvve merrrcy! I could suck me some chocolate milk for a while."

"You on one and me on the other."

"Hell nawww, niggah. I'm a greedy son-of-a-bitch. I wants her all to myself."

Jo Ann retreated into the recesses of petty envy, purpling at no longer being center of attention. The tall radiant performer was more glossy than she could ever hope. When the singer completed her set, Leroy boldly crossed the stage, stepping behind the curtain, hot on her trail. Tom made a sharp little laugh and turned to Jo Ann.

147

"You enjoying the show, Baby?"

"It's very nice." A new warmth underscored her excitement.

"I'm glad."

Leroy zipped out from behind the curtain, his face devoid of enthusiasm. "That's the chilliest bitch I've run across in some time."

"Sorry to hear that, Leroy," Tom was smugly insincere.

"She must be one of them jasper women, is the only way I can figure it."

"It happens."

"It do, don't it."

Leroy killed what remained of his drink and signaled yet another round from the waitress. Jo Ann suspected her growing low was instigated by the sloe. "Uh, no more for me, thanks."

"Did you say somethin'?" Leroy threatened.

"Uh—no. That's okay," Jo Ann backed down. Tom busied himself with a fresh cigarette.

"That's what I thought." Leroy spoke to Jo Ann but his eyes were drawn to another table. A striking, slightly overweight woman in her mid-thirties sat alone. She wasn't as pretty as the singer, but had a similar air of sophisticated unattainability. Leroy took it as a personal challenge. He smiled, "I'll be back shortly," rose and took his drink with him. Tom and Jo Ann watched Leroy zero in on the woman.

Being alone with Tom was much more fun. Jo Ann wanted to be lied to beautifully. She wanted to be the center of his universe, if only for the single evening. She wanted a memory to cherish; there were too few such moments in her life so close to the bone.

"Like your drink?" Tom toyed with the ashtray, tamping out the cigarette.

"Better than I thought."

He shot her a smile. "Good."

"You and Leroy, you work together?"

"I came along for the ride."

"What do you do?"

He sighed, tossed open his palms and closed them around the corners of the ashtray. "Nothin' much. I get by. Let's not talk about me." He radiated interest. "Let's talk about you."

She couldn't remember the last time a man expressed

148

interest in her outside of sex. "I plan to go back to school next summer. Maybe open my own business in a few years, if things go good."

"Yeah? What kind of business?"

"A restaurant."

"You a little skinny to be a chef, ain't you?"

"That don't have nothin' to do with it."

"I thought all women that cooked good was fat," he teased.

"Wait a minute, listen." She laughed.

"Okay, I'm listening."

"I want a real nice restaurant. Here, in our community, where families can go. Ain't a single decent family restaurant in our part of town."

"Now that you mention it."

"This is wonderful, but it's a club, you know?"

"I hear you."

"There's lots of little holes-in-the-wall, and breakfast nooks. But that ain't what'm talkin' 'bout. I'm talkin' 'bout what white peoples got for theyselves. What we got to go way cross town to enjoy."

"Sure, a class joint."

"I'm collectin' recipes for it. I experiments with 'em, which ain't too often, bein' on the county like I am."

"That's quite a leap—from the dole to the executive kitchen."

"I aims to work hard to earn my seed money."

"Big dreams for such a little lady." He kissed at her.

"Big dreams is what it takes."

"Yeah." He began playing with the ashtray again. "I used to have some."

"Really? Tell me about 'em."

"I'd rather not."

"I want to hear them."

"No. 'Sides they's all dead. Let sleepin' dreams die, I say."

"That's lovely. Sad but kinda poetic."

"Yeah. I kinda like to write."

"Really, what?"

"Stuff—sometime. Not much. It's nothing."

"Tell me about it."

"Some other time." He reached for the cigarette pack again and lit another smoke. Their eyes were drawn back to the stage

149

as the stand-up comic closed his set with a light-hearted take-off on a popular old blues.

"Well folks, I'm leaving L.A. on the first thing smokin' tonight. This town has royally whopped my ass! And I can't say I enjoyed it. I'm leavin' here for Chi-ca-go. Goin' to Chicago. Any of you ladies out there want to monkey-up with me?"

There was laughter. "Oh you don't, huh? Well, let me tell you twat is twat . . ."

Jo Ann was relieved by her little communion with Tom. He was a man and she needed a man to talk to. If she could get a night's love out of this, why not? Whose business was it? Not even Leroy's.

As if paged, Leroy slid back into his chair, his eyes misted over in anger, disrupting their rapport.

"So how'd you make out with the dish?"

"That bitch is too uptight, man."

"You sure can pick 'em."

"Tell me about it. She wanted to get to know me first. Who in the fuck's got time for that?"

Jo Ann winced. She felt Tom's arm come suddenly round her shoulders for a comforting hug. "Man, let's clear this joint."

"Give me another minute." Leroy seemed to think of one more method of approach with the woman and decided to try and connect once again. She was just leaving her table, the waitress busily clearing ashes and glass.

"Muthafuck!" Leroy cursed under his breath, and went after her. He was gone less than a minute, and stiffly abrupt on his return. "Yeah, man — we might as well split. Ain't nothin' happenin'."

"Should I get this, Leroy?" Tom went into his slacks pocket and peeped a huge wad of bills. Jo Ann's heart quickened. For a man who did much-of-nothing, Tom did it extremely well.

"No, I've got it." Leroy slipped two twenties from an even bigger wad and slapped them on the table. She was not used to being wined or dined, nor was she used to seeing money flashed in such conspicuous quantities. The business of art paid well.

As she stood, the sloe gin rose with her. Jo Ann tripped against Tom. He grabbed and steadied her.

"Whoa, little lady. Lean on me."

"Oh, my!" Her hands went to her head, but not quickly enough to conceal from her Leroy's contempt.

"If she has to throw up, I'll wait for ya'll outside."

"No — I'm okay, really." The room yawed. Muted lights were suddenly unusually harsh.

"Don't mind him. He's jealous cuz we got each other and he ain't got nobody." Tom frenched her full in the mouth. Leroy fled their public display. When they got to the car, he sat stonily behind the wheel.

In the sedan snugness, Tom nuzzled her neck and ear. Necking so boldly right next to Leroy made Jo Ann uneasy. Their only obstacle to complete intimacy was, in fact, Leroy. When would Tom make his move and have Leroy drop them off at some private cranny? The sizeable wad in Tom's pocket was more than enough for cab fare from anywhere to home.

"We gonna get rid of Big Brutha, Baby, and go to the motel," Tom frenched her again. Jo Ann surrendered her tongue, but felt Tom's eyes on Leroy.

"Don't mind me, ya'll. Jes' act like I ain't here."

Tom teased. "If he's got any sense he'll go home, Jo Ann. Else he'll have to sit tight in the car till we finished. And who knows how long that'll be."

Jo Ann didn't care what Leroy did or didn't do. She was nakedly selfish — one big ache for Tom. His kisses melted her to moans. She prayed he made love as good as he kissed.

The motel was nice and clean and provided radio and television. In their upstairs room there was a dressing table, a chair, a mirror on one wall opposite the bed, and another on the ceiling above. Decorated in sky blue and gold, it smelled of lilac air-freshener. Tom took the enamel pitcher from its tray atop the dressing table and went for ice. Jo Ann went over to the queen-sized bed and bounced on its giving firmness. She could barely control the goodness bursting through her. Love was about to happen.

Starting with his silk shirt, she undressed Tom. Naked, he stepped back and flexed his manliness, indicating he wanted to watch her undress. She did so, slowly, more shyly, repeating her moves from the "interview," trying to put it and Leroy's stare out of her mind. They were soon into one another, twisting

151

across the sheets to the whine of the sax-dominated piped-in jazz. Tom was a big man in length and circumference, and penetration took a bit. She experienced a rush as he entered her.

They had barely started intercourse when there was a polite rap on the door. Tom cursed his annoyance, awkwardly disengaging to get up and answer it butt naked. Dumbfounded, Jo Ann wondered who it could be and why. Seal-like she angled to see. Tom unlocked the door, easing it inward.

There stood Leroy.

The fragments of her pending nightmare whammed into place. She snatched up the top sheet to shield her nakedness. Leroy looked Tom up and down, deliberately not looking at Jo Ann, knowing he would spook her further, having done so sufficiently. He beelined to the television set, flicked it on and turned up the volume as loud as it went, drowning out all music. He took the dressing table chair and straddled it in front of the set, his back to the bed.

Tom watched Jo Ann watch Leroy.

There was nothing in Jo Ann's experience to tell her how to cope with the set-up. In her traumatized arousal, she prayed for Leroy to stay in that chair until she and Tom rejoined and completed their joining. Tom read her play of confusion and question. Her eyes searched his for answers. He radiated his unusual cool, nonjudgmental attitude, untroubled by Leroy's intrusion. Still hard-on, he climbed back into bed.

Jo Ann could no more read Tom than she could read Leroy. She decided his coming back into her arms meant everything was safe; Leroy would be a "good boy" and let them love undisturbed while he stoically kept his eyes on the television and behaved himself. She wanted to believe that. She wanted to believe Tom wanted her to himself; wanted her as badly as she wanted him; that, if flawed, she'd have what remained of the promised night.

"It's okay, Baby," Tom cooed. "Don't panic. Let's try it again." He held her chin, pulling her face towards his, mending with kisses. Tom embraced her. Penetration was easier, more intense. But in her overanxiousness she flailed and shook wildly, her mind divided between fulfillment and flight.

"Hey, Baby—slow it down. Take it easy. I'm not going anywhere. Shine him on. I'm here. That's all that matters." He said it softly, hypnotically. She responded. "That's a girl. Not so wild. Let those hips do the work they were made for."

Frightened, but partly mollified, Jo Ann did as she was told, pleasure nevertheless ebbing from the act. Tom's kisses failed to quell her dread of Leroy.

"You good good pussy, Baby. Come on now. Do it to me. I can't do it alone."

Leroy jumped up from the chair and turned it round, repositioning himself. Jo Ann jumped with his sudden stirring, watching him peripherally. He jumped up and impatiently paced the room. He stopped, hands on hips and watched them. He resumed pacing and after a few steps, plopped back down into the chair to look at more television, but was soon up pacing the floor once more.

Tom's face began to lose its softness. It was becoming clear that in Tom's eyes Leroy could do no wrong. Leroy was his big brother. He looked up to Leroy. His annoyance was not with Leroy, but with her. His charm was fast giving way to mechanical, business-like intensity, focused inwardly on his own gratification, grinding away at her rhythmically, hand on one shoulder, arms circling her head, against the pillow. And now his eyes were on her. Stone cold eyes. There was no reason to keep up the pretense. Jo Ann saw what he saw.

"It's only a game, Jo Ann. Don't fret so."

Leroy was up again. "Hey, man! I'm sick of watchin' TV. I want some of that pussy too!"

His warmth vanished, Tom rolled off of her and sat to his side of the bed, staring at the television set. Leroy took over.

"It's like this, Jo Ann," he smacked his lips as he snaked out of his clothes. "We ain't brothers at all. We's a *brotherhood*. Tom and me—we pimp. Your average run-of-the-mill pimps. And you can't start your job whoring tomorrow night if'n you don't know the ropes. So this here is your apprenticeship. We's breakin' you in."

"What about my kids?" She began crying.

"What about 'em? They'll eat and dress better once you become a skilled *pro*-fessional, Simple." Leroy laughed mockingly. "I bet they's at home alone. Least working for us you'll be able to afford a babysitter. Think of it as an investment in yourself. I mean, the greatest sacrifice a woman can make is

153

givin' up her body to support her children. Or ain't you heard?

"We run this Hollywood pleasure palace. We gots steady-paying clients that craves dark-skinned little what-nots like you. I mean white boys with the long green. They tired of pale pussy. These boys want some freakin' discreet sex with young womens-of-color. The blacker, the better."

Stripped, Leroy crawled into bed on the other side of Jo Ann. He sniffed at her and smiled, making a loud "*Ahhhh.*"

Jo Ann rolled to her opposite side and groaned in passive protest. Leroy winked at Tom, scissored her legs apart, examining her more closely. He let out a piercing whistle.

"Check this out, Tom! She's got quite a clit. Damn near a little dick herself!"

"No jive," Tom leaned over his shoulder.

"Those white boys'll have a field day with that."

"Yeah — and she's tight." Tom smacked his lips. "Got a lot of elasticity in spite of the babies she done had."

Jo Ann trembled, aghast.

Leroy probed between her legs with his tongue. "Shit, yeah. Mighty tasty. Those good old boys'll really go ape for some of this man-size twat. We got us a little gold mine here. Sweet brown sugar. Yes, Suh!"

Leroy mounted and rode her. He rode her good, his long narrow dick tearing at her womb. Rage took hold of Jo Ann. Rage welled up and demanded release. She screamed.

"Oh, shit — bitch! You think somebody's gonna call the police?" Without a break in his fierce stroke, Leroy put a pillow to her face, smothering her. "You on the wrong side of town for rescue."

She struggled against him for air, pushing at his hands, trying to free her face. Leroy could not be budged. Multicolored spots swam in the blackness before her eyes. Jo Ann went slack, giving up resistance. Leroy lifted the pillow, wrenching himself away, dripping wetness onto the sheets. She coughed and sputtered, gasping. She looked toward the door. Leroy followed her eyes and dared her with a smile. "Be my guest, why don't yah?"

Jo Ann shrank back. Where would she run to, assuming she could get to the door without having her neck broken first.

"You've got to know how to fuck, Baby. How to make 'em think it feels good even if it don't." Coolly impersonal, Tom

154

joined the lecture. "These men expect a good show for their money."

"Now let's see you give a blow job."

"What's that?"

"Kkkrist, Simple! Suck dick."

She flushed in terror, shaking her head. She didn't know how. She'd never. She couldn't.

"See how hard you make us? Now get over here and take care of business!" Tom pointed at his crotch, laughing. "This is your grand opportunity. Make all those big dreams come true."

Jo Ann stared blankly, absorbing her circumstance, unmoving.

"Hold her down, man!" Tom commanded. Leroy grabbed and held her while Tom pried her stubborn mouth open. "If you bite me, bitch, I'll knock your teeth out." Tom straddled her. "That's right, gum and tongue."

"Look at those lips work! That looks good. Hurry up, Tom. Give me some of that. Shit, I can't wait. Let me get some of this pussy while you do that."

Both of them were on her at once.

Tom shot off, ramming his powerful hips against her face, her head immobilized in the vice of his hands. "Swallow it, bitch," Tom hissed. "You got to learn to swallow it if you want to get by."

She was afraid to disobey. The smell and sour tang of his cum outraged her. She managed to get it down.

"Now lick it. That's right! Lick it all off. Polish my bone. That's it. Lap it up, Dog."

Her head reeled. She wished for the power to smite. How many hours had it been? Would they ever let her go?

"You think we some mean niggahs, huh. You ain't seen mean yet." Leroy cracked her behind with his open palm. Jo Ann yelped.

Leroy and Tom traded places. "Suck bitch. Mmmm. Good stuff. Yeah." His jerkings and proddings at her throat were more intense than Tom's. His faster, deadlier rhythm, a heat of strokes, blurred into a sweep, keeping her head steadily abob. She was barely aware of Tom's entering and rooting at her below. Her universe was dominated by the blood pressure

155

hardness at her tongue and palate. Several centuries sped by. Leroy began to chant and groan.

"Damn damn damn—fuck me, bitch! Fuck meeee!" He ejaculated, crushing her head to his groin, this time smothering her with his flesh. Jo Ann could not contain the violence of his spew. Vomit ran from her nostrils and mouth, mingled with tears, snot and cum. Her face rang with Leroy's slaps.

"Silly bitch!" He was disgusted by the sloe-red puke in his loins. "Get up Tom and get some towels. Let's teach this fool a lesson."

Tom hurried to the bathroom and returned with a damp white bath towel. They made her clean up the mess, then began discourse and intercourse anew.

"How do you expect to be a good whore, Simple? You got to know what pleases a man."

She cried with the pain. Sex and pain. She was experiencing them together for the first time. They dallied with her, sucking and clawing at her breasts, biting and chewing at her nipples until those nipples stood rigid, raw and exposed.

"Damn, you smell like a fish. Go clean up!" Leroy barked.

Trembling she rose and stumbled to the bathroom door. The knob spun around and around. Her hand chased it, caught it, pulled it forth.

Inside she collapsed onto icy bathroom tiles.

How could two black men be so unfeeling? The only men she'd ever known were black. The only men she'd known had been gentle, loving men. Even if they hadn't stayed. Even if they hadn't claimed her theirs forever. She wanted love and money—enough to get by. Was that such a crime? Demanding such punishment?

She prayed for unconsciousness. If only she could pass out. If only she could get free of her body. They could do what they wanted and she wouldn't have to know.

She closed the bathroom door, blessing the respite. Immediately she was overtaken by shame. She'd never felt such shame—shame to die of. Death was preferable to continued abuse. She rummaged through the tiny drawers seeking a razor blade or knife. They were empty.

Stuff was running down her legs. She could barely see it,

her eyes swollen half shut from tears. She took a white guest towel from one of the racks, ran it under the cold tap water and wrung it out. She took her time. She was not anxious to return to those *things* waiting on the other side of the door. She touched the towel between her legs. A numbing coolness eased the inflammation. She took the towel away and examined it. It was full of bright candied-apple red blood.

"Hey, Simple, what you doin' in here?" The door swung open. Leroy saw the towel. He closed the door.

Jo Ann dragged herself out of the bathroom to meet her Fates. They were watching cartoons. They looked up from the television set.

"Here she comes," Tom observed nastily, "at last." He took Jo Ann by the arm, forcing her to the floor on all fours. "Come on. We got something else to show you." Leroy came up behind her. Sensing their purpose, she shivered.

"No, not there! Please! I'm still virgin there."

"Fuck a virgin!" Leroy parted her buttocks.

The pain split Jo Ann in two. She screamed. Her mind blanked. She went to the floor in a faint. The two men stood over her, shaking their heads.

"Ahw — man. The bitch done conked."

Tom took the pitcher of ice from the dressing table. It had become ice water. He poured it over her head. She bounced upright from the floor, babbling and crying. "I can't take that! I can't take that! Please! No more. Leave me alone — please!"

Tom discussed it with Leroy. "What are we going to do with this dumb cunt? She's gonna have to take *that*. We can't have her actin' silly like this with a customer, Leroy."

"You're right, Tom." Leroy kicked her. She contorted in pain. "Get up! You gonna get this shit down. We need you, Simple. You got good pussy. Too good for us to let it get away."

"Don't fight us. Jes' enjoy it. Get up on them haunches," Tom commanded.

Jo Ann rose to her knees, trembling in pain — pain becoming a thing apart. Pain become a *living* thing. Physical pain so intense it eased her deeper, spiritual pain/shame; diminished it. This aspect of pain was new — a thing beyond her.

Tom gripped her head, invading her mouth and throat. Leroy resumed his attack at her rear. Pain took her as well.

157

Pain tore at her. Jo Ann struggled for resolve. Pain took hold of her heart and refused to let go. Pain shook her beyond fear, beyond fury. Pain became the universe. And in pain she found another part of herself—a strength she did not immediately recognize as hers. A strength roaring toward unspeakable release.

It freed her.

Oh yes, Baby. That's a good hard cum. That's what you're made for. Yes, Lord yes. Take it, Baby—take it like a woman.

And she did.

THE HABIT

SHE LAY there in the dark forever awaiting his return from work.

She heard the door open and close very softly. She heard it only because she was listening for it/him. He was the quietest man she had ever known, barely ever making a sound. Most times she loved the silences they spent together. Simply sitting or laying around doing nothing. Sometimes listening to music. Sometimes sharing a smoke. High. Before and after love came down.

But of late she was beginning to wonder about these episodes. She wanted him to talk to her. Something was wrong. Something foreign had entered them. And she was yet to name it.

Words would not come.

Was it her? Was it not having enough of anything? She tried not to put pressure on him. The day had been hell. But thoughts of loving him got her through the job. Even with two pay checks ends refused to meet. What could she do about it? Was it her? Her blackness? His blackness? A surfeit of melo-drama/melanin? And the eyes of others/strangers telling them over and over they were a doomed coupling.

She heard him reach the top of the stairs. The banister made a little squeak as his right hand instinctively supported his weight on that last step up. *Now he'll start down the hall towards me.*

But he didn't. She heard him go into the bathroom. She heard the door close behind him. Her sigh was involuntary.

He spent so much time in the bathroom lately. Could

159

something be wrong with his kidneys? He did seem thinner. And more listless in his silences. Distanced. At night he tossed and sweated and sometimes sat up and shouted in fear.

Babe I need you. Come to bed why don't you.

She leaned out of bed and peered down the hallway. A blade of light glared at the base of the door. She saw no flits of shadow in it. No indications of movement. Then there was a sudden whoosh and the rattle of the toilet's flush. The glub-glub of water from the faucet followed.

She lay back and waited.

She heard the light scrape of his white sneakers against the worn carpet. His knees turned outward when he walked. He walked on the lateral borders of his feet, his lean body gone into a glide — almost a float. She loved to watch the way he walked. She imagined him walking hungrily toward her.

He was in the bedroom doorway now. She could feel him feel her eyes and her anxiousness.

Oh. You're still up.

I was waiting for you.

He began to undress. He stepped out of his pants.

How'd it go tonight?

Slow. It took me a while to lock up.

He slid into the sheets beside her. His body chilled her nakedness.

Tired?

Beat.

I miss you.

She embraced him. He responded with a soft flat little kiss to her lips. She touched him to let him know.

I can't, Babe. I'm tired.

She couldn't think of anything to say. She let one hand move to his chest and nest there. She tucked the other under her chin. She stared up at the ceiling above their bed. It was a sea of thick layers of peeling white paint. Globules of light danced on the surface from the street lamp outside their apartment building.

Babe?

Huh?

I love you, Babe.

I love you too. Sorry.

This time the silence hurt.

THE BIG LITTLE GANG

3 VIGNETTES

THE DAY was warm and green in Inglewood. Sally had finally gotten Curt to get off his lazy behind and take her to the races. She searched around in her purse for her lipstick, pulled down the car mirror and looked, dabbing on a bit so her lips looked fresh and moist. Curt was slowing the car at a stop light. He turned and looked at her.

"Why don't you save the money? Suppose you lose? Then what are you gonna do for food stamps?"

"I'm not gonna lose. Don't even say that. I'm gonna win. I know I am. Daisy over to the beauty shop gave me some good tips. She been playing the horses for years."

"Then how come she's still working in a beauty shop?" Sally eyed him.

Curt turned to the wheel as the light changed. It didn't make any sense. He wondered how he had managed to hook up with the woman. Looking at her, she was pretty and all of that, had wide hips and wider thighs. And her tits. *Wow, those tits!* Sally was going through her purse again. She came up with a wad of bills. Curt glanced and saw the money.

"Where'd you get all that?"

"I didn't get it from you so don' worry 'bout it."

Curt could feel the anger coming on. Was this bitch out fucking another niggah, and him not knowing it? He didn't know why he fooled with her. She was a dumb tramp, just a dumb black tramp.

Sally smirked; she read his mood.

"If you wanna know, it's my savings." Sally knew he was

161

pissed. She liked to piss Curt off. He deserved it. He had a job and everything, but he never wanted to contribute to her support, nor the kids. He didn't mind coming around laying up to fuck, trying to make babies, but when the bills were due at the first of the month, he never offered to help pay them. About the only time she could count on seeing the chump was when he wanted to eat, screw and watch television.

"You know, you're a sorry ass nigger, Curt. I mean, really sorry."

"Look mama, this is my car and your ass will hit the pavement and bounce if you keep runnin' off at the mouth."

They were going through the ritual of their daily argument. Curt was too deep into it to notice the kids standing there. They were bunched up on the corner. About four of them. They were standing there, waiting. A bunch of ragged looking little black kids with big hungry staring eyes. The oldest couldn't have been more than eleven. He didn't see them watching as he eased the car to a halt at the stop light. He and Sally were still arguing. She was shouting now, telling him to take her home.

Suddenly the door on Sally's side of the car opened, a small hand reached in, snatching the gaping purse and money from Sally's lap. It happened so quickly they both sat stunned for a second. Curt looked up to see the kids darting off around the corner, behind the service station. Other motorists were stopping to look, having seen what happened. Curt left the motor idling, jumped out of his side of the car and ran around it to chase the little thieves, yelling his lungs off. When he got around the corner, there was no one there. They had disappeared. In broad daylight. The nerve.

As he got back to the car, he looked at Sally. Some people were asking her questions. Sally was crying. All she kept saying was, "They took my money. They took my money! How am I gonna buy food for the kids?"

Curt snorted. She was a damned good actress.

2

The Reverend Willis felt his pocket. The gun was still there. It gave him a sense of confidence. He gripped the handle of the attache case at his side, tighter. A month's rent from the five apartment buildings he owned. He knew he was going to have to break down and find another way to collect the monies. Maybe hire someone to do it. But that was the problem. He couldn't trust anyone, not even the managers. So many times he'd caught people stealing. It was such an ungodly feeling. One should be able to trust one's fellows. But here he was, ready to kill, on the nervous edge of violence, just to protect his own life. Turn the other cheek? he thought. Not where money was concerned and especially when it was his money. Close to ten thousand dollars.

The eyes watched the Reverend as he came slowly down the stairs. They blinked dimly in the shadows surrounding the Reverend's new Lincoln Continental.

The Reverend walked slowly, listening. He was sure he'd heard something. No — it's just his nerves. That new diet Mrs. Willis had him on. What he needed was a late hot supper when he got home to take the sting out of the day. Yes, so he could relax and —

The eyes darted in front of him.

"What — ? Oh!" He got hold of himself as he saw the little boy standing there. Just kids. Damned kids. Ain't got no place to go and nothing to do. But this kid — he was standing there staring at the Reverend. Reverend Willis tried to ignore him, turning to the car, feeling in his left pocket for his keys. But there was something about this youngster. He could feel his eyes through his back. Damned kid, why don't he go home or go somewhere. He felt guilty at the thought and turned around to say a few words to the youngster. Why miss a chance to offer up a little wisdom and the words of the Lord? It was well into evening and the children should be home eating their suppers and getting ready for school.

He turned and took in the others. There were four of them. They were all staring. All looking at him and the briefcase. *The briefcase!*

Reverend Willis fumbled for the gun, but it was too late. The kids were on him, silently beating the Reverend, who poorly fended them off, afraid one of the quick little bastards would seize the briefcase and run off with it. They were kicking, hitting, stomping. The sudden attack took his breath away. He gave no thought to the gun. They were just kids. He doubled over in pain, unable to cry for help, feeling his years. All he could think about was the money — *the money!* He couldn't let them have the money. One of the kids picked up a pipe, the cast out remains of someone's domestic repairs. As the others stepped back, the youngster slammed the top of Reverend Willis' skull. Blood shot out and the kids squealed as it dotted their arms and shirts.

"Get the case!" shouted the oldest. "Get the case."

The Reverend collapsed, releasing his hold. It was heavy, but two of them managed to lug it swiftly off down the alley, synchronizing their steps. The others followed.

Upstairs, a light went on and one of the tenants looked out.

"Hey — Rev. Willis look like he in trouble!"

"What's happened?"

"He's laying out there on the ground next to his car."

"I knew that ol' joker was gonna get robbed sooner or later. I bet that's what happened. I only wish I had had the nerve to rob him myself. In fact, you better call the cops or else they be accusing one of us!"

3

Cold night in Watts. Windy, chilly. Ol' man Cook stumbled down the avenue behind the supermarket at 108th and Broadway. The rag man was drunk again. He had pinched pennies for over a decade, recycling the city's discards. He had amassed a small fortune in limp one hundred dollar bills stashed into his stingy wallet. And on top of that he still collected from the State. Just got his social security check, bought just enough food to get him through a week or so, bought a bottle of wine — just enough to get him out of his troubles and away from the memories of down home — the memories of his dead mother and all the other deaths haunting him. And he stowed the rest away. And nobody knew he had it.

He moved, faltered, picked himself up, moved on, slowly, unconcerned. He hummed a little blues. Gut bucket. Stopped to cough, nasty — he spat up a wad from his lungs, moved on toward the alley.

The eyes were there. Watchful, alert eyes. Hostile eyes, more. Eyes that were young, cold, estranged. They were waiting for old man Cook. He came this way regularly each Saturday night at about two in the morning. Just about the time when all the clubs let out and the liquor stores closed. Just about the

164

time when all the cops were running around town hassling the grown folk. Just about the time when people closed their curtains for the night and started taking care of serious fucking.

He was coming. The old man was coming. His footsteps grew loud, dragging. The eyes turned, widened. Tension between the four young boys.

Ol' man Cook felt ill. He stumbled, turned to the wall. Maybe he could find a place to vomit. He wanted to vomit. He wanted. . . .

The kids were there. He caught sight of them, quick — moving, darting shadows. Damned kids, he thought. Through his haze, he watched as they watched him. They were coming very close to him. They were looking rather strange — they were after him! He stopped, looked desperately for a place to run to. As he turned he saw he was trapped by the sub-men.

One pulled a blade. "Where's your money, Pops? We know you got some. Give it up!"

"W-why you — you little punks! You little black ass punk!"

They didn't wait for him to say more. One threw the first blow, catching the old man in his ribs. Blows, the old man was suddenly in a shower of them. He lost his balance, falling. His body curling up on the pavement. Blows, becoming kicks. They stood around the old man, kicking, kicking, kicking. The oldest started kicking at his head. Soon they were all kicking his head. They kept kicking his head. Blood came out of his nose. Ran down his mouth. Another kick and blood spurted from his teeth and gums. Ol' man Cook let out a muffled cry and a groan. The old man tried to shield his body. They stood there — the four boys over the old man, like some grotesque ritual. All kicking. Legs aswing until suddenly the leader stopped, went into the old man's coat and came up with the wallet.

"Let's go."

They scattered into the darkness, running at first. Running as hard as possible to get away from the dead old man in the alley. They were certain he was dead. They ran for blocks. They ran until their chests heaved and they felt like they were about to burst. Then they slowed into a rhythmic skip. And then they began to walk. And then they started to strut.

A WAR OF EYES

"THIS afternoon," she tells us, "you are going to have a war—a war of eyes."

Blue-Eyed Soul-Mama speaks in her customary softness with a slight rasp at its edge. She is a white woman who screams often and intensely. Primal screams that shake the center. And because she takes us all to our centers we love her selflessly.

Half of us are black, half of us white. She has handpicked us for an artistic statement on racial harmony. But even as we move toward that day of completion—a theatrical performance —things come up and out. Our hatreds, our frustrations, our deep inner madnesses. And sometimes they overwhelm us, threaten to devour everyone. But Blue-Eyed Soul-Mama keeps us collected.

"You will seek out your enemy, move in and destroy that enemy. You may form alliances if you like, across boundaries of race and sex. There are only two laws. No one may speak. No sounds. Not even a hum. And no one may touch. You absolutely *must not touch!*"

Thus war is declared. A combat sans words, sans physical violence? We look at each other and wonder.

The room in which we work is lined with full-length mirrors and exercise bars along the west wall. The ceiling is up two stories where a skylight provides a diffuse northern light. Blue-Eyed Soul-Mama dislikes anything artificial; we work in available light and, if necessary, candlelight. On the upper west wall there's a small balcony perfect for spectators; the walls are of a beautiful, cool, highly glossed wood, as are the floors. The room is bare except for the permanent fixture of a huge combination heater and air conditioner on the east wall. Two beautifully handcrafted conga drums perch majestically on the small stage. On the step at the foot of the stage, we place our towels, candles and personal miscellanies before each day's workout.

"This," she says, "is no-man's land."

War. What is it for me? How will I wage it? Does Blue-Eyed Soul-Mama know me? Her big Black Doña? Her one-hundred-and-sixty-pounds of molten maroon, six feet in stockings? No. She does not. She casts me in the role of Earthmother for the entire experimental ensemble. And I am always more than willing to go along with her script. Now, at last, she provides the opportunity for me to experience myself as I truly am: the consummate woman warrior. Ready to die at peak battle if not to emerge victorious. Now I will be free to unchain my war lust—my fantasy. To be a splendid fighting animal; the ebony Amazon, subservient to none. Free of historical chains. Free, in that room, as never before. Unleashed.

And so the others—male and female, black and white, each in their own self-image, assume various positions about the room, clad in leotards and body stockings of black, navy, burgundy, gray and green; armed with their youth and physical dynamism. Otherwise we are spiritually naked to one another as the communal nature of our workshop demands.

Blue-Eyed Soul-Mama retires to the northwest corner of the room. "You may begin—now!"

I assume a position slightly off the center of the room. I work best passively, from odd angles. From sitting positions we snake slowly across the floor, dipping and crouching, swaying in our reconnoiter. Some of us on all fours, some of us on our haunches; we rise and lower in imitation of one predator or another. A panther here, an eagle there. The congas thump and trump. The hands of White Drummer and the hands of Black Drummer read our rhythms, enhancing, translating. White Drummer uses traditional beats, steady pulses and takes on more sophistication only when he's fully "on." Black Drummer is more experienced, more a showman and speaks several tongues interwoven into his Afro-Cuban dialect. He hums and sings with his hands, trails in and out, encompasses all White Drummer can give; inspires it, fuels it, educates it, then returns to his own persistent rhythms in dialog with White Drummer, counter to, but never contrary.

168

I determine my first move — to stake out my territory and issue a challenge to anyone who'd dare violate it. I've concealed my optimum strength from the white members of our group. They have little understanding of strong black women. Nevertheless my prowess had revealed itself inadvertently on two occasions.

During a standing movement exercise, I suddenly whirled Black Ronnie off his feet and swung him full circle. It was simple acrobatics, but so unexpected it brought a simultaneous gasp from the entire group. Black Ronnie and I were approximately the same height and weight. When I lowered him carefully to his feet, he was stunned, his eyes glazed over with love.

A second time occurred at the start of one of our usual ten-hour workouts. White Nick was the largest man in the group, a strapping red-haired mix of Irish and German. He stood two inches over me and out-weighed me by thirty-five pounds. We were instinctively enemies. This was expressed by mutual indifference. He went his way, I mine. We never touched unless proximity required it.

That morning Nick was moody and difficult. He couldn't get into the exercise routine. I noticed he and Blue-Eyed Soul-Mama huddled together in a corner of the room. She was talking to him, hard and fast. He was sullen and kept shaking his head, "no." He turned and fled the room, our stares after him. Blue-Eyed Soul-Mama pulled me aside.

"Doña, Nick is leaving the group."

"Why?"

"He's upset. He doesn't like to work with the smaller women. He's fearful he may hurt them. He's unable to obtain physical release. It's too great a pressure for him." She wrung her hands nervously. It was the first time I'd ever seen her so anxious. All of the women in our group, including Blue-Eyed Soul-Mama, were five-feet-six-inches or shorter, averaging one-hundred-and-twenty pounds. I was, by far, the largest as well as the darkest. I appreciated his problem. It was similar to my own. The other men were reluctant to lift me during many of the exercises. They were afraid they'd hurt themselves and preferred to work with the smaller women. I understood. No one wants a hernia.

"Doña, please do me a favor. If I can convince Nick to give it one more chance, will you work with him?"

169

"Sure."

Blue-Eyed Soul-Mama returned minutes later with the reluctant Nick. She began instructing the group on a series of lifting and touching exercises. We were slow and awkward at first, still "enemies." As we worked, the intimacies of sweat and smell unraveled tension. By the end of the day we knew each other as well as it is possible to know another's body sans sexual intercourse. Long after the others had finished we continued working, transfixed in the joy of our mutual release. We lifted, moved, swung and balanced each other without fear of harm. Finally we sat and hugged and hugged. I held him, rocked him. We cried and laughed and clung to one another. Afterwards he told Blue-Eyed Soul-Mama he'd stay.

But neither Nick nor Blue-Eyed Soul-Mama have any idea of the power I keep painfully in check. I inherited it as a gift upon birth from my father. Even he hates it in me. I am doomed to a world in which women of such stuff are anathema; must learn to tolerate an endless assault against being. Until this afternoon I have lived life believing I'd die without fulfillment. Without having my chance at true battle. Without ever having had my taste.

Some of the men, aware of my potential, start to take me on. But I see they can't take war with a "girl" seriously. It is, after all, an exercise. The sexual "thing" is also too strong as I project it. Black Sam kisses and falls away. White Richard kisses and falls away. Black Ronnie kisses and falls away. They all fall away. And White Nick is particularly docile, averse to the very idea of violence against a woman. And there is the specialness between us. He kisses and rolls away.

The women, black and white alike are up for conflict. But when I increase my transmission even slightly, they retreat from my line of fire, singed. I pick up a few willing allies, but do not need them. They flank themselves to my queenly rear as we leap and spin about, dip and weave, crawl and prowl, a skirmish here and there between different individuals. And while I wound and maim, I take no kills. We are two dozen warriors engaged in psychological warfare, the men resolutely among themselves; and of the women I haven't encountered a worthy enemy. I am hungry for a kill.

Disappointed, I survey the room, watch the others in their respective aggressions. Already some have begun to tire, or met

170

an early and final defeat. They retreat to the sidelines, at the lordly foot of Blue-Eyed Soul-Mama who observes us with unprecedented interest.

Ah, I find my target. White Deborah. She is the "princess," a spoiled, wealthy, snotty bitch. Of all the white women, the blacks in our group dislike her most because of her arrogance and reserve. Her femaleness is all that we hate in life; all our society has made us suffer. I will seek revenge. I will war upon this opposite of myself: blue-gray eyes, hip-length blonde-brown hair, her fine-boned "daintiness." She is all I hate. I will obliterate her. I will slay and dance a ritual in her blood.

As I fix my eyes upon her, a jolt of psychic electricity travels the room. All eyes follow mine to settle upon my victim. Deborah reads me and stiffens. Two of her white female lieutenants flank her at once, Cheryl and Margo. I sense a disturbance to my own rear. My black lieutenants, Ronnie and Sam, desert and go to her aid. I take immediate offense and blast them without mercy. *How dare they betray me?* I zero in on White Cheryl and White Margo, the beauty in their supple paleness; arms and dark hair fly as they bob heads and hands, choreographing Deborah's defense, attempting to shield her eyes from mine. I am momentarily touched by their devotion and sacrifice, noble traits in warriors. But they are short work as I banish them to defeat.

The room is cleared. Only the two of us remain locked in combat: Black Doña and White Deborah.

We are soaked. Deborah's long hair is matted and clings in bizarre fingers to her delicate face and soft white shoulders. My bushy black crown has shrunk to an unruly patch of jagged kinks. My maroon skin glistens with silver rivulets running from my scalp, stinging my eyes, along my high cheek bones, down my nape and broad shoulders. Deborah wears turquoise, I wear black.

I cast umber eyes upon her. She struggles. I see she is not the Iron Maiden she pretends to be, that I'd hoped she'd be — my psychic equal. She is as puny as the others. Contempt washes over me, mingles with surprise and disappointment. Her determination falls way to surrender. She is willing to cede.

I don't want her peace offering. I want war. Win, lose, draw, but war. I see she does not have power enough to wage it. Well, then, I will accept her surrender but on my terms. I

171

will make her pay homage. The image mollifies me. She will give herself to me as I command. I will spare her, but take her as a slave. I will take her mind as generations of my people have had their minds taken. As delicious a victory as I can imagine.

Pleased with my militant superiority, I preen under the intense gaze, all eyes upon us. There is the flutter of faint movement behind us, but so distant and dream-like, neither Deborah nor I pay it mind.

It is necessary that Deborah come to me. I rise from the floor and my eyes take her with me; she rises. Standing doubles my hold. I loom above her. With my eyes I push her back against the south wall, stagger her. *Wonderful.* She waits. I move her along the wall parallel to my own movement to my left. Her steps are the sluggish stumblings of a somnambulist. I bring her to rest in the southeast corner. She stands, unblinking, her eyes locked in mine.

Now — come to me. Come, Deborah.

She moves toward me, slowly, something inside vaguely resistant. She puts her arms before her and paws the wall with each tiny step forward.

Come, Deborah. You want to come to me, don't you?

I become aware of the drums. They have been present all along, but so much of how we are as to be unnoticed. Now White Drummer and Black Drummer orchestrate a frenzy, reach climax.

You are mine, Deborah. My slave.

The drums shatter and cease. Her trance is complete. She lowers her arms. The walls sing with the resonance of rhythms and the crosscurrent of labored breathing. She inches toward me, less than two feet of space remains.

Come, here, Deborah. The deadly calm of my eyes. The fierce welcome.

With lightning grace, Black Johnny rises from his lotus on the floor at the rim of the outer circle and gently strokes Deborah's hair. He runs his hand the length of her back. My hold snaps. She slumps against him, freed.

I turn on Johnny, a fury eyes only and condemn him to hell. *How dare you betray me, nigger — you gutless aberration of human flesh.* Stunned, he freezes, his hand rigid mid-stroke.

Instantly I feel the gentle caress of White Nick as he surrounds me in a lover's embrace from behind. I cry out, a murderous howl. I turn into him, attack him, clawing his arms, chest and face. Of greater strength he holds me, my torso pinned to his, his face expressionless. I fight, kicking and clawing until exhausted. Spent, I lower my arms. Dutifully he releases me. I drop to the floor, gasping. Black Ronnie and White Cheryl rush over to us with a bowl of water and clean towels. They hastily tend to Nick's wounds. I have drawn blood.

I half crouch, dazed in the silence, under a shower of eyes that soothe me, stroke me, forgive. I am enraged. I rebuff them.

Deborah comes to herself and pushes Black Johnny away. She walks the outer rim of the circle around Blue-Eyed Soul-Mama. I get up on all fours and enter the circle as the others part, making way for me. My eyes seek out Black Johnny who has also re-entered the circle. He hides, his back to me. I spot him and my eyes slice through his skull. He leaps up immediately and flees the room. With a sweeping gesture, Blue-Eyed Soul-Mama sends White Margo after him. My vengefulness upsets her.

"War is over!" she announces loudly, absolutely. There will be no usual discussion of the day's events.

"We'll reassemble at ten in the morning."

But no one moves. We sit in silence, eyes roving back and forth between the three of us women. Blue-Eyed Soul-Mama locks eyes with Deborah, brims with unreserved love and deep concern tinged with fear.

And then she casts eyes upon me. *I am ruler here.*

It was she who sent Black Johnny to rescue Deborah, and White Nick as consolation to me. And in her eyes I read another, more basic sort of fear — something primal — a constriction and a great sorrow.

We watch as Blue-Eyed Soul-Mama rises from her throne and leaves the room. I am flush with anger and resentment. In my heart I know my siege against her daughter will never be forgotten. That the real war will be fought on other ground.

LICKETY-SPLIT

JANICE hit the pavement about four p.m. on Friday and bounced. Another screamer with Frank and he threw her out of the house again. She went because Frank was too big, too black, and too burly for her to even consider putting up a fight; the kind of man only a bullet could stop—maybe.

There was a drought in the southwest. It was a hundred degree swelter and no shade in sight. Janice was broke and didn't even have bus fare. Where would she go and what would she do when she got there? She had to find some place to hide for a couple of days. She'd call about the baby late Sunday night. Frank would plead for her to come back. Then early Monday morning she'd show up looking forsaken, and he'd rush to her, go to his knees and beg forgiveness. All in time for Frank to crawl between her legs, shower and get to work. It had happened too many times before. It was becoming a ritual.

She had tried to get Frank to see a psychiatrist but he refused. He even refused to see a marriage counselor.

The heat was punishment on top of punishment. Combined with the inner city smog it was intensified/had more burning power; was an ugly burn that not only ate away layers of skin like acid, but worked at the mind and the spirit as well. Janice sizzled.

What had happened to them? Where had their newly married happiness gone?

Two years into connubial bliss and six months after the baby arrived, Frank began to insist their sex life needed spicing up. Perhaps he'd read too many porno novels during those final months of Janice's pregnancy. Perhaps prolonged masturbation does affect the brain. Suddenly Frank was interested in

175

having other women outside wedlock. But he felt it wasn't fair to indulge his lust without granting Janice equal opportunity. He maintained he still loved her and didn't want to be selfish. Frank's only stipulation was that none of their extramarital affairs become serious.

Hurt and angered, Janice refused to go along at first. She thought Frank might be suffering an acute case of womb-envy. Then he gave her the ultimatum: he would do what he wanted and she had the option of either joining the fun or watching from the sidelines. Besides, he insisted, sex with her had become dull. It was like eating hamburger for dinner every night. He wanted steak now and then. This vulgar analogy stung Janice into submission.

The sun was burning through the thin leather of her cheap high-heeled sandals. Her walk was the lethargic saunter of *de zombie*. And she felt half dead, drained by the strain of argument, vaguely ill at ease. But it was all Frank's fault.

After several adventures, he got scared and reneged. Janice would come in after an afternoon or weekend just a little too happy and a little too smugly satisfied. This was much too much for Frank to manage. He began to question her closely and suspiciously as she came and went. Janice exhibited no such curiosity about *his* comings and goings; acting as though she didn't care was bittersweet revenge.

At first Frank responded to this by trying to compete with her new lovers. This translated into increased frequency of intercourse for Janice, which she thoroughly enjoyed. But as soon as she began to get a real thrill out of her new lifestyle, Frank became extremely jealous. She was spending more and more time away from him and the baby. Frank feared she'd eventually find someone better than he'd been at his best. Someone who'd want her as much as he wanted her. Someone who wouldn't want to share her. Now Frank wanted the marriage closed.

Janice could feel sweat rising in her scalp. Shortly it would start to run from the top of her head, down the back of her neck, into her face, stinging her eyes, turning her freshly pressed hair into a matted cap of snaking tangles. She could feel a heat rash threatening to break out where the bra was too tight against her breasts. It was hot enough to fry fish on her forehead.

So their little stint at so-called free love had backfired. Frank

176

had developed a case of premature ejaculation. He became so uptight during foreplay he shot off as soon as he stuck it in, leaving her cranky and dissatisfied. And lately Frank had started trying hard to bring Janice off, head and tongue laboring overtime between her sepia thighs. But the art of oral sex eluded him. After weeks of Frank's frantic fruitless gropings, suckings and slurpings, Janice was tearing out her pubic hair.

Without realizing it, Janice felt liberated for the first time in her life. And she was reluctant to give up her new found sexual freedom. She had known nothing about other men. Frank had been her first, and until he had irrevocably altered the possibility, Janice had planned for him to be her last. She confessed all of this to Frank. Shortly after that he started with the terrible arguments, sometimes bordering on violence. After weeks of confusion, Janice quickly learned to use these arguments to her advantage. Sometimes she deliberately provoked him, then fled the house in a well-acted rage for a prearranged rendezvous. She'd indulge herself for two or three days, then hurry home.

But this time Frank had started the argument.

She imagined poor Frank sitting there roasting in that crackerjack box, half crazed with the fear of never seeing her again; driven half mad by the baby's screaming; overcome by the rancid stink of soaking soiled diapers. Of course she'd come back. She always came back. If only because of the baby. And she still loved her husband.

The blocks ahead were interminably long and seemed to lengthen with each step. Cement, stucco and steel baked in the afternoon sun aflame over the Pacific Ocean. It cast an orange glow over the city, creating an illusion that the concrete was alive and crackling with fire. Steam rose from its surface.

Yes. Yes. This is it. This is hell — the real deal — the hell folks always talk about going straight to when they die. And I'm in it up to my funky behind. If only Frank could get himself together.

Janice was tired of the game. Where would she go? With whom? Another casual pick-up? They were lucky Frank was only suffering a minor sexual dysfunction. They would both be writhing in pus and agony from who knows how many venereal diseases if they kept this up.

The sidewalk throbbed and wept in the heat. It cracked, blistered and bubbled around her. She grew faint and dizzy.

177

It quaked beneath her feet. The flames licked up around her calves. Between sun and emotion it was too damned hot. Way too hot to be on the streets. She had to find some way to escape. She was starting to melt.

She could go back to Frank. She could beg him to see a doctor. She could promise him she'd never let another man touch her again. It would be an easy promise to keep because she never wanted that in the first place. This time she would be more patient with Frank. She'd love him stronger somehow. He'd feel that stronger love and he would have to respond. She made her decision, spun about and quickly headed back to the apartment.

When she got to the door, she held her breath and wiped the sweat from her brow. She pushed the door inward. There was no one in the front room. The electric fan was full blast, furiously circulating the warm soggy air. She went towards the bedroom.

The baby was asleep on the bed in her spot. Frank was sitting at the foot of the bed, stripped to his shorts, in front of the television watching baseball. He had a giant bowl of popcorn in his lap. He was stuffing it into his mouth by the handsful and washing it down with a bucket of beer and ice. Someone hit a home run and Frank cheered along with the roaring TV crowd. Then he looked up and saw Janice wilting in the doorway, looking more than slightly dazed.

"Back so soon?" he asked.

WORD MONKEY

"SHAME—a body like this has to get old and ugly."

She laughed at him. Ruthie was pleased with Joe Martin Smart's pride in her.

"I got to start breakfast. The kids—it's almost time for school."

"Sure," he watched her dress, basking in gratified lust. His haphazard life had finally screeched to a positive stop. He flexed wiry muscled arms, not failing to notice the linear ghosts of his renegade past.

Ain't touched the needle in a year now. And that was a chip. As was the time before that—after I swore off.

Now things were taking shape. He'd successfully authored seven books—the seven little literary sons of the seventh son of a New Orleans high-yellow, high steppin' Baptist preacher.

Joe Martin Smart was the purveyor of a truth—a living, breathing marketable truth affording every middle class housewife from Seattle to Savannah a look at the intimate lifestyle of a dedicated full-time black pimp and sometime junky. Black product had a limited market. There was no place to go if you didn't have a Ph.D. behind your name. His first novel was published by a black and white outfit and had out-sold all previous works by any other black man in history. He'd figured out, after the contract was signed, that the white guy was really the man who ran it. His black "partner" was a front, bait to reel in colored chumps with stories for sale. They sold cheaply in haste/desperation. And the would-be best sellers were all afraid to look too deeply into that pocket bearing cash. Afraid the promised money would vanish, and with it, their shots at immortality. So they accepted the best offers made and swallowed the rip-off.

But not Joe Martin Smart. He hustled. He wrote more books. He convinced them to see his value as a writer; enough to put him under contract and pay a few royalties because there was a big demand for his "mack." And he was a handsome *brutha*, a high-tan lover to the bone. And when all those lonely ladies got a "whiff" of his curly brown locks off the back of those book jackets, they were inevitably hooked.

When you gonna realize you ain't a bona fide writer, Joe. You just a man of many words. A glorified storyteller. A con who steals the truth and distorts it. You can't keep givin' up game — puttin' bad folks' business in the streets. Don't they call that a snitch? Cop to it, man. You didn't know you could write till they told you you could write. Admit it, man. The thrill of seeing your name in print is the biggest and best cum you've ever had. Ain't a woman born whose jellyjam can match it. And the dope ain't been found could take you higher. Which is what keeps you off the smack, Jack.

And you've got to have it. Got to have that adventure. When was the last time you done some wrong brother-man — to tell about? You wouldn't mind gettin' arrested if the bail and attorney fees weren't eatin' up the story money as soon as you brung it in. The cops are in your ass every time you wear a short-sleeved shirt. And don't dare scratch your armpits, sucka.

Pretty man got all the pussy he can eat but it's that bitchin' print he's jonesed for. Word junky. Got a word monkey.

So now. Like you said after the last one and the one before that. This is the *one* and the one you'll be able to kick with.

Tell me, pretty man, Joe Martin Smart.

And so life became sweeter still. Leaving his wife Stella for love with a lot less mileage.

And now it was breakfast time in Big Town and a new manuscript half finished. A new excitement. This was going to be the one to catapult his waning book sales. This was going to be the one to prove to his publishers that even though he was run dry he had the limitless ability to cleverly disguise truth as fiction, and make more than a passable living at it.

"It's ready," Ruthie winked at him from the doorway and blew him a kiss. She was young and fresh, convinced that all

180

the other mistakes in her short, torrid life would be absolved in her love for and with Joe Martin Smart.

Her Cree cheek bones, two generations removed; her plump, lovely breasts via that heathen Shaker woman great grandad rescued from destitution just before "the war"; and that tight, bumptious behind, the spit image of a youthful tar-skinned strumpet who'd given birth to her mother despite the best efforts of a Cajun witch woman; and those white man's cool gray eyes still lustin' after all those decades.

"Be right there, Honey! I want to make a couple of notes on that chapter I finished last night."

Stella had become the supreme bitch. She saw through you but it took her three babies and damned near a decade. Stella got quickly old. Your tenacious laze grayed her. Her eyes shadowed and recessed until whenever your eyes met hers, you had the eerie feeling she was looking at you from a universe away, like Goddess in merciless judgment of a cockroach before lowering Her foot.

You had to get away from those eyes, those mudholes sucking you into who knows what accusation. She gave you every chance to prove her right. You shriveled under that gaze. You shriveled up so small Tyou were able to walk into the hypodermic from the tip end.

Joe Martin Smart, you hear me?

Yes, Stella. Loudly. Clearly. Irrevocably.

"Who is she?"
"You don't know her. It just happened."
"Do you love her?"
"I'm a lover. You know that."
"And what about me?"
"What about you?"
"Joe Martin Smart, you know the sacrifices I've made!"
"The sacrifices?"
"Yes. The sacrifices. Me working all these years; working my youth; working my ambition; working into fat and discontent so's you could write. And all you been doin' is fuckin' around."
"Stella—"
"You writin' the wrong *thang*—all this romantic bullshit

181

about pimps and whores. You need to be writin' them sex books. Cuz pussyfyin' is all you expert at. Using women. Makin' 'em love you and have babies by you. Ain't got guts enough to be a genuine pimp. You too yellow for that. Too lazy. Cuz pimpin's a man's work. You a boy—hidin' from the world under Mama's skirt—sniffin' up there and wonderin' why you ain't got a hole like she got!"

And he struck her, indifferently watching her head jerk back and her eyes swell and close tight as his fists. His pulse calmed to a whisper, singing just beneath the rhythm of his blows, stealing her consciousness. And he left her, taking nothing but the clothes he wore and the change in his pockets.

There had been no divorce. Why hadn't they divorced? He never wanted to marry again, and Stella provided the sure enough stopgap. She was waiting for him to grow up and come back home, a man.

"Yeah, Uncle Jake?"

"Joe boy, let me tell you about lockin' a woman's mind. Build a dream. Keep that dream in front of her. Keep remindin' her about the possibilities. It don't matter that the dream can't come true. It's the dream itself. Make that dream vivid. Breathe life into it. So that when you standin' there, and she looks at you, she sees that dream livin' and breathin' before her eyes. And if you do it like you s'pose to, she'll see it right there in front of her—even when you're not there. And when you out doin' wrong, and she know you doin' wrong, she'll cling to that dream. She'll be convinced that you'll straighten up and do right by her because it's your dream too. She won't realize that the dream is somethin' you've created jes' for her. She'll be so blinded by the beauty of it—if you do your dream buildin' right—that she'll swear by all that's holy that that's what you really want. When all the time the only thing you want is to lay up a little while and enjoy the fruits of her garden. You understand, boy?"

"I think so, Uncle Jake."

"You a smart boy, Joe. Wish your Mama'd named you after me."

Leona was the most uppity brown-skinned woman he'd ever met. But Baby Jake knew he had what it takes to bust her down to size. It didn't matter that he was five years her junior. He had her figured just right. No sudden moves. She was the type to bolt. He'd compliment her intelligence—prove his respect. And once she bit, he'd put both feet up her ass and make her like every inch. Make her beg for more.

She was due home from the office. Her sometime lover was going to be an unlucky man tonight. He watched her mount the stairs to her tiny apartment on the second floor. She fished into her coat pocket for the keys (description here—give her a brick shithouse figure). He was up behind her quickly and catlike before she saw him.

"Hi, Leona." He used a very low tone with a slight grittiness to it. He had a good voice and used it. He had long since understood its effect on women.

"Oh! Baby Jake. What are you doin' here?"

"I need to talk to you about—something. I need some advice." His voice was soft; he let her misinterpret that as shyness.

She smiled, knowingly, big sisterly. "Oh, you mean about a woman?"

He flashed all boyish thirty-two from ear-to-ear, and let out an exuberant, "Exxxactly!"

Note: When Baby Jake sees Leona in the doorway, have him stub out his cigarette. The fire at the tip end would reveal his presence in that particular darkness. And he wants to violate her mind. Have to work that out in dialog on page 210.

The smells of coffee and bacon; the hum of electricity and gas as she did her stuff; eggs and toast, the clatter of plates, knives and forks.

Robert was nine and Rhonda was seven. The youngsters eagerly helped set the table—chocolate darlings quietly murmuring to themselves, playful teasings; creating the sound of morning and one big happiness: Ruthie, her children, and the man of her hopes—Joe Martin Smart, black author extraordinaire.

"Hurry, before it gets cold!"

183

All that warmth coming at him, sweeter than any drug had ever been — at last. On the right track — the right kind of track. He congratulated himself.

"In a minute!"

p. 317

"All right nigger, what is it you want?"

"I'm a niggah all right and I wants to be your niggah."

Detective Baxter stared so evilly hard at him, Baby Jake felt an itch behind his head.

"I don't need another nigger. I got plenty. Niggers come cheap." Baxter's voice dripped more venom than a whole cotton field of Ku Klux cross-burners. Jake was not dissuaded. He met Baxter blow for blow.

"I'm about to take your main man for a fall."

"What's that bull turd about?"

"History. And Presidential campaigns."

"Spill it."

"Seems like a certain very very rich and important white man was raised by a woman who had a Southern Belle complex."

"Keep it short."

"He was raised by a succession of high-busted black mammies. Seems that fucked with his head — severely."

"So what. He can't get it up unless he's with a nigger whore. You're telling me."

"More than that. He has to be humiliated and dominated. Here." Baby Jake handed him the photos. "There's plenty more. And worse."

Baxter shuffled through the sordid scenes of denigration. His face froze over with disgust. "You sick sonofabitch."

"Doin' my civic duty, with national pride."

"What do you want!"

"Your main niggah's turf. I want him on ice and I want Downtown."

"You've got it, scum."

"Thank you. And give the Senator my regards."

Baxter lurched and popped Baby Jake across the face. Baby Jake flinched and his head drew back sharply. A little blood trickled into his mouth from his lip now sporting a small split. He

184

went into his pocket for a kerchief and held it to his swelling mouth.

Baxter was bursting with rage. "Look, nigger — I'll swallow your shit, but no law on Earth says I've got to like it."

"White boy — let me hip you. What you got there is just the tip of a very ugly iceberg. I got enough shit to bring this whole bloodyfuckin' town down around your head. So you better learn some manners — Chapter I — how to be cool with niggahs. Read that for a start."

Baxter slipped the photos into his inner breast pocket, then hit the ignition. "Get out. Get out before I kill you with my bare hands." From this big beef of a man it was no idle threat.

"I got one more photo for you — before you go, Baxter." Jake opened his palm like a magician revealing something mysterious. It was another photo, face down. Baxter stared at it coldly, took it by the edges and flipped it over. He let out a gasp, snatched it from Baby Jake's palm and began to tremble.

"She wanted you to know what she really likes. She's so afraid of you she's never had nerve to tell you to your face."

Baxter was riveted to the photo, eyes aflame.

"So," Baby Jake spoke with unmitigated confidence and authority, "when my whores are working the neighborhood, I'll expect them to go unmolested. You dig? And that heroin concession — see to it."

Baxter nodded numbly.

"Why, thank you, Chief Baxter."

Baxter glared at him, dazed and confused in his shock. "I — I'm not Chief yet."

"You will be. It's all in the game plan."

Eggs scrambled easy. The toast perfect. The bacon crisp. Ruthie is a striver. Always at her best to please. He is foremost on her mind. It trims the years off; makes him young buck sure. There's nothing evil between them.

"Can we watch cartoons, Mama?"

Robert and Rhonda crowd the couch, laugh and elbow for the best eye's view.

"When I finish this, we'll go back to Oakland, get a house and settle, Ruthie. I'm ready to settle. I've had enough of being pimped. I've got another publisher interested. It means real money. I'm sick of this chump change."

185

"If you're sure, I'm sure."

"I figure I can kick back—get a regular stint. Something menial and not too demanding, leaving me plenty of time to coast. Write when I feel like it. No pressures to cannibalize. I can't keep thievin' stories. I don't feel good about it."

"Nobody knows it's you. There's no photo on the jacket and you're using an alias."

"I don't want it to go sour. It's so sweet now. Just like I like it."

Coffee cooled to medium hot. Two drops of evaporated milk, a half teaspoon of sugar. She set it before him on the kitchenette table.

"Are you going to see *those men* today?"

"Why?"

"I wish you wouldn't hang out with those thugs. They scare me."

"I have to. They're my material—and our ticket to all the things we want in life. Just one more book and I'm quits. With these bloodsuckers, anyhow."

"When did I hear that last, Mister J. Martin Smart?"

"This one will put me over, and that is a *promise* promise!"

Ruthie turned away from him with loving acceptance, and went to the stove to start a pot of black-eyed peas for supper. In the skillet, she prepared the base. A delicious steam of fatback worked away at the onions, doing a scrumptious sizzle.

Joe Martin took a deep breath and the aroma took him ·home.

The door opened inwardly, quietly jimmied.

Two men entered at a catwalk.

They ignored the boy and girl on the couch. The children stared in open-eyed curiosity, blind terror, then shock. The men carried guns—.357 magnums. Wordlessly Ruthie turned and saw the two men. She backed away from the skillet.

The bullet took her scream mid-throat. Another jolted her lovely left breast, knocking her back from the stove. She crumpled to the ashen gray tile of floor, speckled with her blood. The air was charged with gurgles as life escaped her.

Joe Martin Smart went rigid. His eyes bucked. He was frozen to the dining chair, the cup trembling in his grasp. He knew his killers. He had written their stories. He groped for

186

the words to save himself, knowing Ruthie's death was prelude to his own. His tongue thickened with fear.

"We want you to know why. You're such a big man with words. You tell too much. We ain't as stupid as you think. We can read good enough to know who wrote them books under that phoney name."

"Yeah, Mister big shit novelist."

The first slug ripped through Joe's hand, shattering the cup of coffee.

I'll never type again.

A second bullet sent a scream into his shoulder.

God — God!

He fell forward, toward the table, struggling for consciousness, struggling against the third bullet and its fire consuming his abdomen — struggling to spit out the blood which gushed up into his mouth; struggling to quell the thunder of his heart as it burst through his ear drums; unable to move, unable to utter a sound — yet noting every detail: the bizarre cackle of tiny cartoon characters clucking cheerily against the awed stillness, the horrified silence of the stunned children staring at their murdered mother and dying stepfather asprawl in blood.

Images flooded in on Joe Martin Smart as his well-trained writer's eye rolled around in his skull to witness the elegant tailored lines of the slacks worn by the killers, taking note not of their pugnacious faces but of their shiny mahogany brogues as the men fled from the room.

He could hear the scream and cries of the children. Through his audial haze they sounded like the distant chimes of cathedral bells. Smoke began to fill the room with the choking stink of burning fatback and onions. There were the muffled anxious footfalls of running neighbors.

The light sliced across the lower half of the open door caught in Joe's dying gaze. It was quickly becoming brighter and brighter until there was nothing but light consuming his ebbing consciousness, whiting out all possibilities.

If only he could somehow live to write it down.

WITHOUT VISIBLE MEANS

YOU NEED, Baby. You need a lot. You too needy. I can't deal with it.

Baby, you've got everything any one man could want in a woman — looks, personality and sexual overdrive.

But you're poor.

Your poor is too big. I can't fill it. What you crave is beyond me. I can't satisfy it. I mean, ambition is one thing. But you want one hundred per cent and I've only got forty.

Cold part is I know what you need. And I'd like to be able to give it to you. But what I'd like to do and what I can do are two different thangs. As much of a provider as I'd like to be, what little I can squeeze out of the white rock will *nevah* do the j-o-b. Consequently every little thing is a crisis. Every little thing is a melodrama. It's too much.

If this were my world I'd give it to you on a platinum platter — never mind the silver. But this *iszant* my world. It's theirs. They mean to see that you and me don't amount to diddlysquat in it. And diddlysquat plus diddlysquat is nothing more.

Understand me?

The Parrr-taayyy was going on long before we showed on the set. It's nobody's fault — least nobody I can *see*. It's hardly more than I can do to wipe my own ass.

Understand me?

What's a niggah to do? Dream?

If you're dreaming you're sleeping, and both of my eyes are wide open. I'm woke. And I'm sorry to say I can't see no future for you and me. None-at-all.

It's not like that. They don't come sweeter than you. One look and you bring my nature to a rise. I mean, I'm hot for you. Since that first time we hooked up—you know—that was a righteous thrill. I say, you thrilled me! The way we do the slow dance? I couldn't get enough then, can't get enough now—of you. But there's more to a happy ending than sex, Baby. Sweet as it is it don't keep Goldie Locks in wolf pelts.

Baabee, don't be like that! You know I love you. I know you love me. But we can't use love as collateral. This *iszant* real estate. You can't build on it.

No, I'm no materialist. Let's not start calling folk out of their name. I'm not hung up on material things—so don't *mistake* me. Please see me for the man I am. I could lay up here and lay around and run you into the ground. But I'm not like that. Credit where credit is due. I'm being realistic. I'm seeing our situation—*what it is*. The things you want I can't give you no matter what. I don't have the power. And knowing that hurts, Baby. It hurts real bad. So that's why I'm leaving. That's why I've got to go. I've got no say-so. And I'm doing this for you. Why? Because—because, after a while, you yourself will ask me to leave. You yourself will put me out because I will not be living up to what you expect of me and I will not be giving you what you need.

So that's why this has to stop now.

It's best this way. For both of us. I'm saving us both a lot of pain and ugliness.

Don't cry, Baby. Wipe those weepy eyes. Come on—courage, now. Put your hands on your hips and let your backbone slip. Smile, Baby. Smile through those tears. Give a taste of those salty lips. Give a little kiss. It'll ease the pain.

There. See there?

And please, please do me one favor. Do one big thing for me. Will you? Sure you will. Just don't ever change. Be sure and stay as sweet as you are.

This is not like "goodby forever." I'll be in the neighborhood from time-to-time. And I'll drop by to check up on you, to see how you've been getting along in this world.

Remember. You'll always be in my Top Forty, Baby. Always.

There, now. Don't that make you feel better?

BUYING PRIMO TIME

"THE Life Security Assurance Council has reviewed your application thoroughly, Miss Niobe. I'm afraid we can't help you. Loans of this nature—well, I'm sure you understand."

The man was a beet-red Benjamin Franklin clone in 21st Century garb. Della understood all too well. She felt that mid-gut gnawing again. The statuesque cocoa-skinned woman struggled to control her feelings. Control meant the difference between life and death—a lesson she was continually relearning.

"Secretary Decius, my potential as a painter merits this loan. I've so much to give mankind, I assure you." Her smile was suggestive. Women are always reduced to using their bodily charms with these kinds of men. Della Niobe figured she might as well shoot her best shot. There was everything to lose.

"The amount of this loan—it's far from staggering, but—." He eyed her openly, lightly drumming his fingers against the fiberglass desk top. He could find no reason to equivocate. She had nice, if bowed, legs.

"When you balance that against what it costs the Government to raise my four children, I'm sure you can see the State would be ahead in the game," she appealed. A woman had to use every means available. Della had banked on it with her first pregnancy out of wedlock.

"Your argument is reasonable." Decius wondered when the Feds would finally get hip to the ploys afester in the subculture.

"And look at it this way, you'll have four additional citizens, well-raised, who'll also be of great social merit and creative genetic coding." That expensive course in Rhetorical Logic had more than paid for itself.

191

"I find it impossible to agree with you. All of this is beyond my area of expertise."

She had him.

"Consider this: Would you prefer my children as artists giving to society? Or as criminals taking from it?"

"Artists — of course!"

He visualized himself being mugged. Rather than decrease under the Population Control Amendment, crime had tripled. To every reasonable man this was deplorable.

"Then you must concede there's something to be said for the artist in society."

"That has always gone without saying!"

"Secretary Decius, history doesn't support the assertion."

Decius fluttered his eyes briefly. He reached for the elegant gold cigarette case Della extended to him across the desk. He sniffed the aromatic fag and fired it, inhaling with much pleasure.

"Hemp?"

"Quite. Black market."

She lit one for herself. Della was grateful, at such moments, that marijuana had finally been legalized. Unfortunately Federal regulations and taxes kept it out of reach of most of the poor. Underground production was still a viable enterprise. She returned the case to her purse.

"Secretary Decius, I want the Council to reconsider my loan." Della managed to maintain her stony, unconcerned expression. Her stomach churned.

"I must admit, purchasing one's life one year, one month, one day at a time is extremely difficult. But it's the supreme sacrifice we all make for a better world."

"Not all. Just those of us unlucky enough to be born in the lower classes, and who haven't yet achieved upper class status."

"How many days do you have left?"

"A total of two months, give or take a day."

"There are many miserably more qualified than you, Miss Niobe. Some down to a matter of hours and can't raise the money. It's a dastardly situation, isn't it?" What a shame, he thought, all that delicious black cunt going to waste. She knew full well the closer the deadline the more impossible obtaining funds became. One was labeled a loser. It was an insidiously delicious catch.

192

"Well, I'm sure all of those who voted for the Population Control Amendment are enjoying it. And I bet you did, didn't you?" Della delivered her bitterness with a salacious smile.

"Vote for it? I authored the Amendment, Miss Niobe, so don't expect sympathy from me. The upper classes have never had it so good. And they control legislation. Besides, we all benefit in the long run. Each individual must do their maximum best to stay alive. By the end of the 22nd Century we'll be a world of geniuses. A perfect world in perfect balance."

A silence came over them. Decius thoughtfully dropped his ash into the Mexican onyx ashtray. Della crossed her legs, uncrossed and crossed them again, then stubbed out her smoke impatiently. "Look, will you at least examine this additional case material?" She went into her attaché case and took out the sheaf of papers. "I made four photocopies as per your original specifications." She handed them to him.

"Hmmm. Very nicely typed." He looked at her legs again. He tamped out his cigarette and reached into his slacks and began to finger his cock.

"I process a hundred and fifty words per minute — if you're looking for an Information Engineer." She noted his degree of intense arousal. She went into her purse for the condom. He took it from her and watched as she lifted her skirt and slipped out of her panties.

"Well, if I can personally be of help. You understand I only make recommendations to the Council. Indeed, I'll do my best. Although a salary from us would provide you with only half. You'd still need the loan."

She went around the desk and assisted him in positioning the condom. It was French ribbed.

"No matter. I've worked as many as four jobs when the situation demanded."

"Amazing. You must be a superwoman. No wonder you've managed to last as long as you have." He meant it.

"What a lovely compliment." She meant it.

He stood ready. She balanced her butt solidly on his desk, raised her legs and circled his hips. He entered her, rooting in rhythmically, kneading her healthy brown rear with his broad soft blushing hands. It took a full twenty minutes. He gasped and fell into her, hugging her for a few seconds' recovery. She reached for the tissue box on the desk. He withdrew slowly, then quickly disposed of the condom in his office waste basket. Then he smiled, smugly officious.

"Frankly, Miss Niobe, your civilized manner has convinced me you deserve help. A mature colored person of your decorum and ability is rare — indeed." He seldom encountered blacks in her age bracket doing so well. It was a sad thing so many of them continued to remain at the bottom of the official economic indicator.

"You're too generous!" She deftly replaced her panties.

"Not generous enough. Let me do you a favor. There's a man I'm acquainted with — Jake Zeno. He's very powerful. Here's his card. Go to him and tell him Mr. D. sent you — D. for Decius." He laughed at his own jerkoffishness. "You know, I love those — what do you call them?"

"Monikers."

"Yes. Tell Jake Zeno I said you're a good risk. He'll call me if he needs confirmation. In the meantime, I'll bring this addition to your application before the Council. I'll do my best. In any event, this gentleman will be a help."

"Thank you, Secretary Decius. I am eternally grateful."

"Good day, Della Niobe. Good luck."

"So like what's Mr. D. say your chances are for the Council to change their decision?" Jake Zeno believed in dark colors and expensive things. He was particularly turned on by Della's large, shapely rear. He knew Decius was an old fuck and had to have scored a taste.

"Excellent. But I don't want to take any chances. So he sent me to you." Della couldn't keep her hands off the mahogany desk. He smiled, amused, as she ran admiring hands over the cool surface of the wood, thrilling to its elemental beauty. Rare woods — not much of anything was made of genuine wood anymore. She sighed.

"You wouldn't believe how much this desk set me back. A person could buy themselves half a decade of primo time. Now what can I do for you, Miss Niobe?"

"I need money." She had heard of Jake Zeno, a good looking man of outlaw status. She'd heard he was into whips and chains on the serious side. She had no love of pain, the spiritual or the physical. But business was business.

"Everyone needs money. Especially the poor."

194

"I'm an artist. I'm also working class poor. We're a deter-mined class. And we'd all be dead if it weren't for the underground economy."

"And gentlemen like myself . . ."

"Yes, gentlemen like yourself, Mister Zeno."

"Then you consider me a gentleman."

"I'd rather consider you a lifesaver."

"Then to business." He liked her looks and her indepen-dent air. He had a thing for reducing strong women into sub-mision and then hard-dicking them senseless.

"The Government is charging me an additional five hun-dred a month because of my A-5 rating."

"A-5? That's a new one." She was class A-1 in the exotic erotica department, he thought.

"Artist, fifth rank. I do have a few shows scheduled in the latter part of the year that are guaranteed to pull me up to an A-4 rank and reduce my monthly Breathing Permit Charge to half, if I live long enough. My children will receive any posthumous monies in the event that I—"

"Hmmm. You're not doing too badly." The thought of her pleading to be freed from his frantic clutch gave him a hard-on. He'd love to put the handcuffs on her.

"That's the idea. I'm not just 'some people.' "

She radiated a sultry beauty. He felt a wetness in his jock.

"I'm taking on a third job, Mr. Zeno. Just in case my ap-peal to the Council fails. Mr. Decius will do his best, but . . ."

"Better to be safe."

"You sound like a supporter of Population Control."

" 'Deed I am. I'm in a very lucrative profession because of it. Time Brokerage is as sure as death and taxes. It's the sweetest set-up in the world. You charge low-ranking people between twenty-five and sixty for the right to live. Give 'em a head start—enough time to finish college, get established, marry and start a family. Then you've got 'em. Fear of having their children raised in a Government youth camp keeps them hus-tling and society benefits. They *want* to live. But to live is to pay the State. And if you can't earn enough legitimately, that means taking risks—going into crime, going to the Council, or alternative freebooters like me. To fail to support yourself means execution by the State. Believe me, Miss Niobe, I'll kill you a lot more humanely than the Feds. With me you keep your dignity."

"I'll bear that in mind."

"How much do you need?"

"Five thousand."

"There's a five hundred handling charge payable in advance." He smiled and went into this desk for the money. He slid an envelope across the surface to her. She swiftly counted out the bills, then slipped it into her purse. She took out a condom.

"Forget it. I like authenticity. Why don't we step into my inner office."

"What do you have in there?"

"A bed of nails." He rose to escort her through the door which opened on a room that was a virtual museum of sado-maso paraphernalia.

Well, Della observed philosophically, another dollar, another day. She laughed softly at the thought.

"What's so funny?" Jake asked as he locked the door behind them.

"That," smiled Della, "is a private joke."

THE TWINIGHT OF
REVEREND JONES

WHAT don't you see?

You don't see the eyes cupped in puckered flesh, sinking in on themselves, descending into that knobby cranium. You don't see the cheeks slackened and hollowed with mal-diet, a lack of proper home cooking. You don't see that suit which hangs and bags as if two sizes too big cutting the figure of an undertaker — *yeah* — the corpse itself. You are oblivious to those ears standing out as if tiny angel wings awaiting flight, almost smothered by the dapper black derby. You don't see those silvering sideburns or that smile revealing that cavernous edentulous maw. Or that lengthening bullet of a proboscis with its snarling nares curled into a tight prolonged sniff. You don't see that chin honed bone-tight, jutting upward in conflict with gravity.

What don't you see? You don't see the years, the failure, the disappointments, the denied opportunities; and you don't see any hate. He's past that now. He's past hating *them* — the ones who manufactured his plight. He is past knowing them. Who are they to know? No ones. Not a one. And he is beyond knowing you. You don't see this shadow that assumes its stance to go one more round. To duke out another dream — that wisp easily carried off by an above average breeze. You don't see any of that.

Do you?

The house is dark. There were no children. He did not have time or the patience for children. And Regina had never insisted. She had never much complained. She followed him in his service to the Lord — the pulpit — and contented herself in Sunday School classes, socials, weddings, funerals, the rituals of community life as they encountered them at Bethel Baptist. She budded, bloomed, bled and was finally buried in the blessed light of a devoted congregation. She had sheltered them; loved them unreservedly, without judgment. She had softened the wrath of his hellifications, recriminations, tirades and damnations; of his Behemoths and Goliaths. She had complemented her man, and when he began to lose his grasp on this side of Jordan, she salved him with her dreams and thoughts of making passage to the other shore.

But she embarked before him.

Alone, he lost leverage. Bethel Baptist slipped from his clutch as a younger, more capable minister was hastened in by the Bishop in response to the frantic pleas of a congregation frightened and befuddled by Reverend Jones' accelerating confusion. And they spoke gently to him about moving toward modernization/toward progress. And he made his resignation but remained among them.

That he had once been a man of The Gloves became legend with the membership. He had fought many contenders and had lost few bouts. Tiger Man had made his way up the fisticuff rungs toward growing renown. And then there was the one-too-many. Kid Samson crowned his head in resounding thunder; caught him off rhythm and sent him asprawl to the mat, a startled uncomprehending muddle.

As they carted him from the ring, he spoke in tongues. Interspersed between disjointed ramblings was the unmistakably clear and distinct name of one better known as The Son of God.

Mister Jones had heard the call.

He slugged his way into grace with monies earned as a sparring partner for prize-fighters ascending and descending pugilistic heights. As long as he possessed the stamina and the will — as long as he was able. But in his twenty-ninth year he abandoned active participation in the sport.

I saw him fight way back in forty-three. He took Rock Liver Brown in two by a knock-out. It was one of the most memorably brutal fights I ever saw. Brown had all the money behind him. But I put my faith

198

in Tiger Man Jones. He was definite champeen material. Never known to throw a fight. Whatever happened to him?

Feint to the right. Jab with your left. Peek-a-boo.

There were the long mornings rising before six, climbing into those jogging duds, hitting the bricks to pace out two to three hours—as much as Lord and ligament allowed. It took a long time to break the habit of jumping rope for thirty minutes or so an hour after breakfast. It took even less time to give up those one-hundred push-ups that steadily and persistently dwindled to the mere passing thought of getting back into shape someday—just to stay fit.

And there were the long nights, longer and more sleepless, reliving those unsettling bouts; those angers pushed under and asurge beneath scripture. His handler who couldn't seem to get him the fights he needed. His too casual trainer. No one to take real interest. Waking to the loud reverberating clang or in a sweat anticipating that final stinging blow. They wrote it up in the papers:

Tiger Man Jones Throws In Towel and Picks Up The Cross.

He went down to the recruiting office. It was in the white part of town but that didn't matter to Jones. He'd been there before as someone known and to know. It was over on Detroit Street near the gym. And he wanted his old cronies to see and know he still had fight in him. He loud-talked and joked with the men who recognized "The Tiger."

So you want to be a soldier.

You got that right. Let me at those Japs and those Jerries. I want to do my part for Uncle Sam.

Well, I tell you, ain't too many of you colored fellows sent overseas. But we damn sure can use you for kitchen duty. And I ain't met a white boy yet who could beat you niggers cleaning latrines.

Something snapped. He came out of his corner throwing combination after combination, his opponent helpless under the unexpected assault. Tiger Jones made hamburger meat. It took damn near half a dozen men to pull him off the senseless recruitment sergeant. Jones was classified loony and certified punch-drunk. He was harmless enough. But they locked him up for a few weeks of observation to ensure his violent outburst was aberrant and not a permanent state. And everybody in town knew it.

199

Crazed Bomber Hits Below Belt.

And she came to get him, with family and friends. And her father, the elderly Minister of Bethel Baptist gave oath to take this man, still so full in his prime, shelter him, and turn him into an upstanding member of the community; a black man no white man need ever again fear.

They took him home.

"Yes, Robert Lee Jones, I'll wed you."

Regina was dark sisal. Hers were the borderless eyes of love. She had waited patiently for him. She knew he would ask. And he did — the future she had prayed for nightly, silently was hers. But not all of her prayers were answered. She was small and frail. Not the breeding kind. She would grow sad for that but never bitter. For she had so much to do and more. She would be his helpmate. She would fill the spaces created by the beatings he'd taken, as well as given. She'd keep him whole.

"Regina, I can only promise to do right by you. Give you the best I've got to give."

"Oh, Robert Lee — that's more than any woman could ask of a man."

"Then we'll talk to your father."

"He'll want to perform the service."

"Fine by me. I — I'm happy. Very. You sure you don't mind having a pug-ugly for a husband?"

"Shush your lying mouth, Robert Lee Jones! I'll have you know I'm giving my hand to the Deacon of Bethel Baptist Church, no less. He's a proud, hard-working handyman, able to fix most anything needs fixing like magic."

"I guess you've made a passable choice."

"I've made a wonderful choice."

The fix-it business grew and prospered, mainly through the utilitarian support of church members. Between that and the fraction of what came to him out of the collection plate and Regina's popular bake sales they managed to buy a home — free of the tithes of parenthood. Thus he took pride in keeping a new car yearly, dressing better than the average black man, and, once in a while, taking in the Saturday night fights.

"Who's that at the door?"

"It's Reverend Jones, Mama."

"That old stumble bum — what he want?"

"He's lookin' for Papa."

"Well for heaven's sake don't let him in."

"I already did."

"Ruth, I just stopped by to see if Jack was home."

"He had to work late tonight, Reverend."

"Well, tell him I was by."

"Right will, Reverend."

"It does my heart good to know he's working so hard to keep his family. Jack is a very lucky man. And you're a lucky woman, Ruth. 'For would not our sufferings be lessened by the laughter of children?' First Corinthians, Chapter Four, Verse Five."

"Amen, Reverend Jones."

" 'For the seed that springeth from the loin of a man and his wife contains the abundance of the Lord.' Hebrews, Chapter Eight, Verse Ten."

"Yes — yes."

"Well, Ruth — I just stopped by to see Jack. So I guess I'll be gettin' on."

"I'll be sure and tell him you were by."

And she took hold of the door knob, pushing the door gently toward him to sweep him out with the motion of it. But he would not be moved.

"You know, once Jack and I did a little sparring together down in Tijuana."

She knew. She had heard the story just a week ago. And a week before that. And a week or two before that. She had heard it with increased frequency since he'd gotten into his habit of dropping by to catch Jack at home. Both men were sentimental about their abbreviated boxing careers. Jack genuinely enjoyed old Tiger Man and his disjointed romantic congress. But Ruth had no such empathy. She stood the man as much as she could out of respect for The Cloth.

Before she could shoo him off with her usual barrage of good-bys, he made his way into the living room and stood before the full-length mirror on the door leading to their tiny hallway and bedrooms beyond.

She agonized as he went into his stance, psyching out his imaginary opponent, drawn to that mirror and the momentary glory it refracted through his senility. Had the door been closed, as it sometimes was, he would have boxed his shadow as cast by the living room light. Now he bobbed, now he weaved, his still flawless ancient footing defining a spot of wear on her expensive wall-to-wall carpeting.

He turned toward Ruth, eyes rolled back in his head, with an upper-cut followed by a combination. "One-two-one-two." Coming inches within her face, she jumped back as those fists threatened to lay her flat. Ruth struggled for control. A good-sized, hefty woman, she was as artful wielding a fry-pan as the Reverend was with his mitts.

"Jack, you've got to do something about Reverend Jones. I can't take it no more. That old fool got in here last night and damned near knocked me for a loop—shadow boxing at who-knows-what."

"What'd you say to get him going, Ruth?"

"I ain't said nothing. That's just it. Rita Mae let him in after I done told her a thousand times not to let that man through the door. I told him you were out but it did no good. He insisted upon waiting around. That's a crazy man."

"He's not crazy, just lonely."

"Whatever he is, I don't like him comin' by when you're gone."

"I'll talk to him, Ruth."

"Please. He had me so scared I started to get the mop and go upside his head with it."

Rita Mae fell from her choice spot on the arm of the couch in front of the television set, and rolled around on the floor, convulsed in giggles.

"Shut up, Rita Mae, 'fore I get that mop and bury it in your behind."

Reverend Jones made his way hurriedly through the streets at late evening. Jack could use the extra piping for something. Reverend Jones knew that for certain. Perhaps he could use it on that new room he and Ruth were adding on to the house. He didn't need it himself, and it was a shame for such costly piping to go to waste.

As he walked, it did not occur to him that he struck such an odd figure. That he looked at all displaced; pant cuffs too high off his shoes; white socks pooked out, and that wrinkled black suit, looking as if it walked by itself, swallowing the lankiness that propelled it onward. His was a loping, gliding stride, a walk apace with his pinging thoughts. He was leading so far in front with his jaw as to make himself appear headless, the derby seemingly perched on his stiff white collar.

It did not register, the potential threat that lay in the elongated pipes he toted under his arm, butt ends wrapped in brown paper, as squarish as the butt of a rifle, the stems of pipe extended before him, snaking languidly like the stems of daisies in a brisk breeze.

The apparition of Tiger Man Jones inspired turning heads and curious stares. Intent on his purpose he was rapt in his thoughts of Jack, Ruth and the pipes; those torrid bouts in the summer's heat of Tijuana; that Mexican girl showing them how one drinks tequila; that shifty shady promoter who vanished with the purse; sending home for bus fare.

Jack was a good man. A man to be envied his good fortune. To have a loving wife. To be blessed with healthy children. To have a home.

"Hey, Mister—you there! Stop, turn around slowly, and put your hands up!"

"Keep your eyes on him—that piece he's got is damn near big as an elephant gun. Could take your head off."

"Why don't you get out over there and give me some back-up."

"I'm on my way."

"Hey, Mister—are you deaf or something? I said turn around and put your hands up!"

And come out boxing.

It is hot under the lights. But he hears them out there—his fans are cheering. Tiger Man Jones. And he roars and claws at the air with his gloves. And they cheer louder.

And now they boo. The boos tell him his opponent is entering the ring. Some young beefsteak they're touting out of Chicago. Grooming him for the belt. An experienced old tough like Jones is the man they need to make the youngster look good.

A victory would bring him that much closer to the title match.

And come out boxing.

He hears them quieting down. He hears them holding their breaths as the two contenders move toward the center of the ring. The referee jumps back as they bump gloves and go to their corners. The bell signals the start of round one.

What do you see?

Life spilled out along that broad, star-lit boulevard. The two officers search dejectedly for the rifle they thought they saw, shocked and angry. This nigger was now a blot on otherwise spotless records — a blot pending investigation.

What is there for you to see but a nondescript headline in 9-point type in the last column at the bottom of a page:

Ex-fighter Slain in Accidental Officer-Involved Shooting.

The Reverend Jones turned abruptly, the piping swinging out toward the two officers, startling them. They were already afraid of the black man. Afraid he was some kind of mean nigger — the kind that took great pleasure in catching cops off guard. They simply drew their weapons and fired automatically. It was the sanctioned art of public self-defense. This was a madman. An inescapable deduction. They had seen so many drug-crazed black men.

"Holy shit, this creep was some kind of preacher."

The sound came out of nowhere. Was it the parting of that Red Sea? Was it the quaking walls of Jericho as they tumbled? Perhaps the rush of wings as an archangel descended through the manna to carry forth some work of the Almighty?

Tiger Man Jones never knew what hit him. He went down for the count.

"Regina, is that you? Have you come back to me? Will we be together again?"

"Oh, Robert Lee. Sometimes you make me feel so sad."

"Don't leave me, Regina. I'm sorry we can't have children. It's as much my fault as yours."

"We have each other. Let us enrich ourselves in that. We have each other."

STASHED

"HEY-Y-Y — Mozell, what's happenin' my man?"

It was Shake. It was late afternoon and I was slidin' through the Ace-Hi Billiards Emporium to shoot a few games solo over a beer, maybe three. Nuthin' ferocious. Then maybe fall by Dee's for eats, a little TV and a climb between her big juicy thighs before going back to the crib—if that. Dee always begged me to stay over. But runnin' into Shake was enough to make me change my plans.

Me and Shake went back over a trey and a deuce runnin' head medicine for Dr. John. The Doc was a dope dealer long established in the game before it became a popular side-line for pros. He was called Doctor cuz he was, in actuality, a bona fide M.D. Me and Shake we had a mutual partner, Foster. Independently of one another we'd both hit Foster up for where the fast action was goin' down. He told us to call Dr. John and set up an appointment, and to be sure and wear a jacket when we went.

There was we, two healthy niggahs sittin' up there between all them womens and babies and all of 'em screamin'. So like we get to talkin' a little and come to recognize we brothers of the same scheme. No coincidence us both wearin' jackets. We agreed to hang, as we righteously dug one another's company.

Shake went in and did his do and said he'd wait for me outside. Then I went in to do mine. This Dr. John was a righteously smooth muthafucka. He runs it down how I'm s'pose to unload a kilo a week — more if I can handle it, otherwise he can't use me. I'm unsure as to how much I can move, but I act confident and very next thing I'm jawin' it over with Shake — both us nervous about the bricks of high-grade sans wrapped

in tin foil, plastic wrap and newspaper knockin' around inside
our togs. Jes' the thought of it accidentally droppin' out has us
'bout to pee.

The short of it is we bumped heads figuring two could get
rich quicker than one. So Shake and me — we teamed up and
rented a nice house over in the jungle. Life was a *parrr-tay*. I
mean to tell you! Our action was so hellishly mean Doc started
cuttin' us in on some of the heavy white folks action. You
remember when *'ludes* was hot for a minute? So we started
workin' that little taste. Every now and then Doc would have
us run a little pharmaceutical crystal up into Beverly Hills. We'd
dress up like delivery boys or somethin' and pull up just as big
in a van and drop a load worth four or five bills. Everything
was everything — most cool. And it would've stayed that way.
But I had to go fall in love. And not with no mortal woman,
neither. She was Shake's baby sister, Vonnie — no less.

She was the loveliest thing I've seen in life, Vonnie was.
She had a real dark skin and big, big doll-baby eyes. And let
me tell you she was a stone fox and a stone freak. And she wore
her hair in one of these wild-woman styles with diamond stud
earrings. And everything the little woman wore was completely *sassy*. I damned near popped out my socks first I lay eyes on
her. It took a while to realize Shake had been deliberately holdin'
out on me.

"Moz, Vonnie's goin' to college. She's gonna be somethin'
'sides your toy or your whore — any man's." That's what Shake
said after Vonnie told him I'd made my play. My feelings was
real hurt. Now here's a dude and we be *parrrdners* and he's doin'
the same dirt I'm doin', but my hands ain't clean enough to touch
his little sister. And it mighta come to nuthin' 'ceptin' Vonnie
was feelin' the same about me. Can you dig it?

Shake couldn't stop us. Vonnie and I hooked up in a big
way. And it was sweet for a moment. But only a moment. The
little broad had a bad temper — I mean fierce — and we was con-
stantly clashing. And you know how some of us gets behind a
little booklearnin' — uppity ain't the word for it. I tried my best
to get her under control, but it was one thing after another, with
Shake instigatin'. We had our own soap opera goin'. When we
finally busted up it damned near killed me. Vonnie went off
to college like Shake dictated, but not without first takin' a detour
to abort our mistake.

Me and Shake couldn't see eye-to-eye on *nuthin'* after that. So I threw in my hand and faded before it got too deep and me or Shake ended up seriously assaultin' one another, or one of us dead.

Now after all this time, here's me and Shake crossin' paths at the Ace-Hi. And I'm feelin' downright strange behind it, but he's warm and friendly like nuthin' ever went wrong between us. I was truly weak to see my old ace boon. And even though a part of me was doubtful for a second, I dismissed it.

"So how's tricks, Moz?"

"I's through with tricks these days, Shake. I'm strictly playin' it straight. How's yourself?"

He frowned. "You ain't heard. They busted the Doc."

"No, man — you jive!" I was genuinely shocked. I thought Doc John would never take a fall. A man with his smarts? I definitely thought he was too slick to ever be caught and said as much.

"It happens, Moz. He went down for five in Sing-Sing. I been kickin' around loose since — a nickel here, a dime there."

He must've felt how hard I was watchin' him. He musta known where my head was at. I had to ask it. "How's Vonnie these days?"

He smiled. "She's fine. Graduated college with full honors. Got one of those scholarships where they go to Europe to finish studyin' and all *that*."

"I'm real happy for Vonnie. Honest." I meant it, but couldn't help wonderin' if she ever asked about me. I couldn't bring myself to ask. I was relieved he thought what I was thinkin'.

"She asks about you now and then."

Hearin' that pleased me. Shake asked what I was doing to stay alive and I ran down how I had a seasonal gig in construction and was working part-time on the side doin' security. How I was pullin' down enough steady ready cash to keep a crib, cover car maintenance and, after all my expenses, still manage to salt a little somethin' away. I wasn't doing too bad for the average ghetto grad.

"And I'm clean these days, Shake. Don't get higher than a couple of drinks or a joint now and again. Got the sweetest woman a man could want."

Then Shake took my hand and gave me a buddy hug and

told me it was good to see me again and hear I was doin' so well. That damned near made me cry. And then he asked if I could do him a favor and run him across town to Hollywood. He had a little business to take care of and his car was in the shop. I'd never known Shake to be without wheels for any reason. And always brand new. By that I figured things couldn't be going well for Shake and that he'd been reduced to frontin' off. So I felt for the man — took pity on him — and told him it would be no trouble at all to take him any place he wanted to go.

So we jumped into my Fix-Or-Repair-Daily and headed northeast to Hollywood. The place he was headed for was up in them hills. I started havin' a nicotine fit, so on the way I ran into a liquor store to get me some cigarettes.

I mean them Hollywood Hills are somethin' beau-ti-ful. Shake didn't appear to be in too big a hurry, so we cruised takin' in the scenery. It was the kinda territory we mighta worked our way into if we hadn't fell out over Vonnie.

Shake fired up a joint and we shared it, mellowing out to some sound as we drove along street after windin' street. It was beautiful but unfamiliar turf. Finally Shake tells me to pull over and park and scrambles out the car. "I'll be a minute."

Shake hurried up to this house what looked more like Castle Dracula, went along a walk and disappeared behind some bushes. I fired one of my smokes and kicked back. I was on a righteous high and it was more than that joint. The fact that I seemed to be back in Shake's good graces gave me the buzz. Cuz I had always figured that as impossible. And, to cap it off, it was late afternoon in movieland and the sun was startin' to set on them hills — the sky all done up in reds and golds.

Fifteen minutes passed and Shake failed to show. I started feeling uncomfortable. I didn't know what was goin' on. I had been so thrown off guard by our reunion I had neglected to find out why Shake wanted to make this run to the 'Wood. I'd assumed he'd come up there to score. That can be sticky too 'specially if you dealin' with some whiteboy don't know you too well. I started wonderin' maybe somethin' funky jumped off, Shake gettin' the worst of it.

I got out of the car and walked up the way I saw him go. Wasn't a soul around. There was this narrow path long side the house so I went thataway till it was cut off by the bushes I saw Shake disappear behind. There was a fence and a gate and I started to go through it when some monster dog on the other side damn near took my hand off, snarlin' and carryin' on.

I beat it to the car and put a five minute limit on Shake. Shake was a no show. I took off, deciding to resume my previous plans. I felt real weird drivin' off and leavin' him. I also felt foolish bein' left in the car all that time. I was a bit pissed about it too, but unsure as to how pissed I should be since I didn't know if Shake was righteously off into some deep shit or not. If we were s'pose to be on good terms again, I was s'pose to feel uneasy.

I coasted down street after windin' street of green trees, luxury cribs and outrageous rides, tryin' to keep my mind off Shake and all the million questions jumpin' around in my head as to what had happened.

I finally made it to the bottom of the hills and was crossin' this big intersection when I saw the red lights flashin' in my rearview. I cursed and pulled over, not particularly worried. The marijuana smell was long gone and I was otherwise clean. I had nuthin' to fear, far as I was concerned. I'd paid all my parkin' tickets. I sat there coolly waitin' for the officers. You shoulda seen them studs. They came on like John Wayne and Clint Eastwood, guns drawn — one on the driver's side and the other on the passenger's side. I was surrounded.

"Let's see your license."

"Yes, officer." I handed it over, carefully, makin' no sudden moves.

"And the registration."

"Excuse me, officer, but would you mind tellin' me what this is about?"

"We received a report on a burglary. The description of the suspect and the suspect's vehicle matches you and yours. The registration please."

Upset to say the least, I reached over and flipped open the glove compartment. This foil wrapped packet fell out. Them two police got so excited they damn near came. They knew they had me dead to rights. The one on the passenger's side, he snatched the door open, grabbed it up and opened it. My stomach did cartwheels.

"What is it?"

"Rock — cocaine."

"Okay, Mister, step out."

I was lookin' down the barrel of that police special sweatin' blood, my head about to burst. Shake had set me up. That dirty double crossin' sonofabitch.

"Up against the car."

People were drivin' past starin', watchin' 'em pat me down. And all I could do is think about Shake. Where was Shake? Was he out there somewhere watching and crackin' his sides?

"I'm innocent, officer!" I knew better than to talk, but my mouth wouldn't stay shut. I was totally shook. Shake had sacrificed his coke stash to get even with me, stowing it in the glove compartment while I was scoring smokes at the L.I.Q. He probably tipped off the cops while I was coolin' my ass and worryin' 'bout his whereabouts.

"I was set up, officer. I mean, check it out! If I knew that was there would I have opened it like that? It don't even make sense!"

"You niggers are shot so full of shit none of you make sense anymore. Now shut the fuck up!"

He was goin' for the cuffs. I panicked.

"Officer, please!"

We started to scuffle. It was quite a scene. Then, either him or his partner cold-cocked me with a stick or the butt of they gun. I couldn't tell who or which. Next thing I know'd I'm seein' stars. And they was definitely not the kind you find on Hollywood Boulevard.

GAMBLERS

THERE was a dare in the walk of the man entering the Club Hobart. Sam Clark took it up.

He squinted, but did not recognize the stranger. Sam knew every regular patron; was one himself. He had occupied the same stool for many years. His name had finally been affixed to it as a token of fiscal appreciation. Sam studied the stranger, radiating a benign curiosity and a friendly willingness.

The stranger leaned into the counter as his eyes adjusted to the winelight black and red interior. Short of stature and honey-skinned, he was shabbily togged in worn, dark olive workman's coveralls, black leather boots, and a black stingy-brimmed hat cocked over a very egg-shaped cranium. His full beard and brush of eyebrows were lightly grayed. The maverick quality of his facial hair told Sam the man was mixed blood—a Jew or an Irishman somewhere in that "ol' woodpile." He noticed the man's arms were disproportionately short for his build. Were his truncated extremities a birth defect? Sam generously "felt" for the man. It was hard enough—life—as a black man. And being a poor black man made it significantly more difficult. A physical handicap had to make it screaming hell.

Reading Sam's attitude, the man cocked his head and shot Sam a look. Those narrowed eyes were serpentine and penetrating, set in yellow. Embarrassed, but further piqued, Sam was compelled to speak first. "Good afternoon to you." His reedy alto was as good natured as he could make himself sound.

The stranger gave a quick little smile and nodded. His "good afternoon" was more a comment than response, in a rich bass vibrato. A big voice in a small man.

Sam scanned the room for the bartender. He was anchored

by elbow on the far end of the room, making soft small talk with a new barmaid.

"Hey, Umberto! We got a customer!" Sam barked.

Umberto jerked to attention and hopped toward them. The stranger made note of the nameplate on Sam's stool. "Are you the owner of this establishment?"

"Uh — no," Sam blanched. He knew the impression he gave. "I'm jes' a very old and very reliable customer." He chuckled immodestly modest. Sam's springy black hair was neatly trimmed to a conservative afro. He had a broad forehead remarkably smooth for a man of his fifty-odd years. His nose was broad and flat, even the nares. His brown eagle-eyes had a disarming simplicity to them. His skin had the texture and richness of cedar. He was casually dressed in expensive clothes: loafers, slacks, a pullover — tastefully accented in gold jewelry — a wedding band, a chain bracelet and wristwatch.

"Samuel Clark," the stranger nodded, reading the name on the stool, which was a glorified director's chair.

"Call me Sam." Sam eased down from the stool and extended his grasp across the yard that separated them. The stranger did likewise. Sam had nearly two heads on the man and forty pounds. But the bantam fellow radiated something that made him seem equal in height.

"Pleased to make your acquaintance. We have the exact same surname — an accident of birth and/or history — to be redundant. I'm also a Clark. William Clark at your service. Call me Will."

Sam concentrated on Will's quiet rap far more than was his habit with strangers. There was something distinct about Will that grabbed and held him. It was not his voice, but his particular enunciation. It brought back school day memories of authoritarian Caucasian English teachers droning, "Howww nowww brrrowwwnnn cowww."

Umberto, left pending, cleared his throat loudly.

"Whiskey sour," Will ordered and Umberto went immediately into the mechanics of creative libations.

"Give me another of my usual, Umberto. This one is on me." Sam quick-drawed into his slacks pocket and pulled out a fistful of crumpled singles. He hastily pressed out several with his palm against the counter as Umberto set the drinks before them.

212

"Whiskey sour, bourbon and water."

"Thanks, Umberto." Sam pushed the stack of wrinkled bills toward him. The two Clarks watched as Umberto hastily rang up the tab and hurried back to continue his discourse with the pretty chestnut-colored woman. The silence between them made Sam uneasy. Will was indifferent to it, bathed in it.

Another, rather obese umber man came in and sat expectantly near them. He was down in spirit and anxious to involve anyone in conversation. Both men picked up on but ignored the vibrations.

"Uh, why don't we go over to one of the tables and talk." Sam spoke softly, with an unfamiliar formalism, made conscious of, and struggling with, his own articulation. Will was obviously well educated. Much brighter than the kind of men who ran in Sam's usual circle. Sam wondered why he was dressed so tackily and chose to hang in a club known for its black middle class clientele.

Will selected a booth across the empty room and moved to it. Sam followed and slid in at the mouth of the horseshoe, opposite Will. The cushion was soft and Will sank into the red leather. He took a quick sip of his drink and set it on the table before him, his arms clasped upward. Sam felt as though Will peered up at him from an abyss.

"So, Sam—what do you do if you're not the owner?"

"Oh—this," Sam smiled, extending his arms into the void and bringing them back down on the table. "I'm early retired. Used to work for the County—years and years. The wife did too. We salted away a little sumptin' and sunk it into some income property. So now I'm fairly independent. I do a little yard work and upkeep—collect the rents. Otherwise, I'm bird free."

Will gave a quirky smile and repeated the expression. "Bird free."

"Heh—heh. That's it. It's rare *we* can be our own man—if you know what I mean."

"I know too well." Will leaned back into the redness, his eyes opaqued. His mind was clearly elsewhere.

"So what do you do, Will?"

"Nothing at this very moment. I've done many things in the past. I'm of mind to find something I might do tomorrow, or the next day. But at this moment—nothing."

"You're an educated man."

213

Again Will's quick, penetrating smile. "I have a Ph.D., Sam—in stupology."

"Tell me about it."

"I'm an ex-convict. A former jailbird—quite recently released into the population."

Sam's mouth fell open, then snappily closed. "I—I'm sorry to hear that." Sam had never spent a day of his life behind bars and knew he never would.

"Don't be, Sam. I was guilty."

"Oh, man. What'd you do?"

"Seven years. I killed my wife. Same old same old."

"Cheating."

"Yes. I strangled her." Sam looked at Will's hands. They too were small, with fingers broad and spatulate. He could see the strength potential.

"I know. I'm much stronger than I look. There isn't much to do in the joint but lift weights."

Sam shook his head. "My Martha's not a fox, but she's no dog. I've been luckier than most men I know." He went into his wallet and pulled out a series of snapshots. Martha, a plain, but well-endowed, yellow-skinned woman, smiled up from hugging positions alongside Sam. "No children. We never had the time, trying to keep a roof over our heads. After a while we decided we were too set in our ways. Too selfish to take time, I guess. Martha's a good church-goin' woman and has always kept her marriage vows."

"You're a lucky man, Sam, Very lucky."

"Yeah, well—" Sam took a sip of his drink and felt the warmth invade his tightness. He was starting to relax. The sketchy revelation of Will's tragedy somehow made them friends. "Where'd they send you, Will?"

"Folsom. A little time at Soledad. Mainly Folsom."

"Whew! I hear that's—what they call it, maximum security—the slams? Yeah, like in the movies."

"It was hard time. But I did it. The crime and the time."

"You're lookin' for a job, then."

"Perhaps. It depends. I'm not in too big a hurry. I'd like to have a little fun before I re-enter the labor force."

"I can understand a man wantin' to take care of all those—urges. Once he's out."

"Definitely."

The two men laughed warmly.

"My Martha is so churchified, I sometimes think if I couldn't get down here for a little outside stimu—uh—excitement, I'd go off my nut." His laugh was selfconsciously loud. Sam downed his bourbon and water and waved to Umberto, who sent the new waitress sashaying over with two fresh drinks. Sam watched Will's eyes travel up her bronze miniskirted allure.

"Nice," Sam held up his glass for a toast as they watched her return to her station.

"Very."

A silence settled between them. Will finished his first drink and set the glass aside to start the second. Sam broke the silence on a conspiratorial note. "Know what I do for kicks, Will?"

"I could guess, but tell me."

"I *gamble*."

"Oh?"

"Man's got to do something for kicks. Man needs a little risk in life to remind him it's worth the effort."

Again they laughed softly.

"The biggest thrill I get from it, is not in the winnin' or losin' itself. Martha don't know a good goddamn about it. That's my biggest thrill."

Will cast interested, introspective eyes on Sam, radiating empathy.

"I swear, Will—and I'm sure you can recall your own marriage—wedlock is a prison. It's tolerable when you ain't itchin' to get out. But when you itch, it's hell."

Will thought the metaphor a grossly poor one, but let it pass. "Why not leave?"

"No—no. I'd never leave Martha. I love her and all that. It's jes'—sometimes."

"Sometimes. Yes."

They laughed quietly.

"So what's your game, Will?"

"My game? You mean card game."

"Precisely." Sam aped Will's inflection and they laughed again.

"Poker, rummy, cooncan, tonk . . ."

"Now tonk—that's my game. That's a *nigger* game, and my favorite. Best gamblin' game there is. Damn near impossible

215

to cheat at." Sam said this by way of invitation, which is how Will heard it.

"Well, Sam — I don't know."

Sam looked at his watch. "My wife's out to choir rehearsal till eleven. Come on by the house. We'll have some real relaxation."

"Sam, are you sure about this? I'm not very well-fixed."

"If it's money you're worried about, we can play for pennies. Martha keeps a jar of 'em on the mantle."

The beer was imported and ice cold. Sam uncapped the bottle and handed one to Will. Will bottle-upped a long swallow. Sam seized any opportunity to play and enjoyed his rituals mightily. It did something for him to have someone, even a stranger, with whom to share his larceny.

They sat at the lacy cloth-covered oak dining table in Sam's modest, comfortable home. Sam derived abiding satisfaction in his residency in the ebony middle class.

"May I smoke?"

"Sure."

Sam retrieved an ashtray from the coffee table. Will went into the breast pocket of his coveralls for a pack of cigarettes and offered Sam one. "No thanks," Sam declined with a shake of his head. "We don't smoke. Martha keeps ashtrays for folks who do. Would you like some eats? There's some of Martha's killer fried chicken in the fridge."

"Thank you no."

"Say, I bet we could be cousins — second or third! My people are from Boley. Boley, Oklahoma — yes 'em. Still got family there. Course, I was born and raised up here. But still it's like home. I even takes Martha with me when I goes back for the annual family holler. Where your people from?"

"Florida. Mississippi. Thereabouts. I grew up quick and left early. So home is anywhere I set foot. Home was that Big House for seven years." He took another swallow, removed his hat and placed it on the table. His sandy hair was shaved to the scalp.

"Yeah, well — look — let's get to the business of havin' fun!"

Sam left Will to relax and scurried to the rear of the house.

Will's eyes recorded the living and dining rooms with pedestrian weariness. The walls were matte white. A half dozen

216

paintings broke it up — seascapes, pastorals. A kitschy felt portrait of Martin Luther King, Junior hung above the mantle, staring into infinity over the inscription, "I have a dream." There was a navy blue sofa with matching loveseat, a white recliner chair, oak coffee table with matching end tables and designer lamps, all laid against a field of navy blue wall-to-wall carpet. There was a breakfront filled with china, glass and silver services. A bookshelf crammed with Book-of-the-Month selections stood on one wall; and a tiny bar signified drink as pastime and not pursuit. Indeed, there was a jar on the mantle brimming with pennies.

Will hadn't been in a home like Sam's for years. Yet it was familiar. He wondered if there was something known to interior decorators as American Negro Modern?

Will mulled over his new buddy. Sam was well off but not wealthy, aware yet lacking. And Sam hungered for something. More than friendship. Prison had taught Will to distrust anyone who confessed too readily to anything.

Sam returned to the dining room, carrying a shoe box under his arm and two fresh decks of cards. He set the box down on the table and removed the lid, pulling out a wad of bills — a thousand dollars in twenties.

Will's pulse soared. Eyes riveted to the cash, he jumped up from his chair, shaken.

"Look, man — maybe we ought to call it a night."

"No — no. Don't get uptight, man. This is my *fun*. You know — *mad* money! Martha, she don't even know I got it. I won it all in games like this. Friendly games."

"I told you. I don't have *that* kind of money."

"Aw, come on. You got at least one twenty, don't you?"

"One twenty. Yes."

"Then that's good enough for a start. Or don't you play good enough?"

"That's just it, Sam. I've had seven years of practice. I play too damn good."

"Just the words I want to hear. Now, here — have another beer and sit down."

Will took the fresh beer and sat. He gingerly rolled up the too-long sleeves of his coveralls to reveal thick veiny muscular arms.

Sam placed the stack of bills on the table next to the box,

flicking several twenties off the top for easy handling. He opened up the first fresh deck and shuffled the cards, spreading them expertly, Vegas style, for the cut. Will waved, indicating he was satisfied with the shuffle and had no desire to cut the deck. Sam dealt five cards each and turned up the starter.

"We'll do twenty dollars a hand," Sam announced. "Hit and hold?"

Will nodded.

Both men went for their cards. Will glanced at his hand and threw down. "Forty-one."

"Humph!" Sam popped a crisp double sawbuck to Will's side of the table.

Within fifteen minutes Will had doubled down six hands and had amassed over two hundred dollars. He marveled at the ease with which Sam lost his money. The more he lost, the happier Sam seemed to be, childlike in an eerie glee. Yet he played as if he were deadly serious and earnestly trying his best.

Was he a stupid man or an ill man? Both? Certainly he was head up for experience. As the evening progressed, Will wondered more and more about his frenetic host. Between sporadic shouts of joy at winning an occasional hand and curses at frequent losses, Will could not decipher the man.

Sam should fear him. He was a convicted killer. Yet the man exhibited no visible anxiousness. Perhaps it was because of Will's size. But soft living had bent Sam severely out of shape and he could easily be taken by the smaller, younger man. Didn't Sam know about criminals? Didn't his mother inform him on the inadvisability of trusting strangers? Perhaps, in his unhip manner, Sam innately understood the difference between a crime of passion and a crime of possession.

Sam sputtered jocularly, engaging Will in patter about sports and music until Will realized he was the lucky possessor of the entire stack. Will began to sweat and could smell his own stink in the steamy confines of his coveralls.

Sam leaned back in his chair philosophically and removed a second, identical stack of money from the shoe box. Will stared coldly at the man. His eyes glistened in disbelief. What kind of fool did Sam take him for? Had he been suckered? Allowed to win just so Sam could have the satisfaction of winning it back? What else did he have secreted in the shoe box?

Will mentally counted his money. If he wanted to rob the

man, there would've been a fight. Or would there have been? The ease with which it was happening made Will suspect his rationality as much as Sam's. Yet it was happening. And there was the evidence. Irrefutably tangible and unquestionably spendable. Will envisioned someone being invited to Sam's home and relieving him of his cash and his life. How could the man be so stupid as to leave himself open to the possibility?

"Uh—look, Sam it's been nice but I don't enjoy taking your money."

"You think I'm crazy. I just want a chance to get even. Come on, Will. We got hours before Martha gets home. Your deal."

Perhaps this was a seduction of sorts. But why sham? All hints at sexual liaison were absent. How could Will have not detected that? He could not conceive of Sam's coming up with anything beyond Will's sophistication. Will eyed Sam closely. All Sam's gestures and movements were dully, almost dutifully hetero. No, Will surmised, Sam was not that kind of kinky.

Will struggled to remain calm as the money leapt at him. He felt a sudden panic. Was he having one of his searingly vivid prison dreams? They were more real than real. How many times had he awakened to find himself still locked in that metal cage, batting around in his own skull?

His palms began to sweat.

Two hundred shy of acquiring the rest of the second stack, Will put his hands palm-down and refused to pick up his cards.

"Look—just a few more hands and it's quits," Sam leaned across the table. It was not quite a whine. He leaned back, took the top off the box and lifted out two more identically fresh stacks of twenties and waved them in front of Will's disbelieving eyes. Will felt his stomach knot. He nodded.

"Alrighty, here we go!" Sam cheerily began the ritual anew. This time Sam peeped his hand and went down. "Forty-one."

Will downed his hand, his eyes glazing over. "Forty-one. Caught you."

"Shitttttt!"

The evening wore on. Will roasted in a skunk that gradually cooled on his skin into concentrated silence. Sam became more and more animated, chattily recounting school days, his sex life with Martha, his aging parents, and hassles with ungrateful tenants, losing his money as rapidly as he moved his mouth. Again the stacks diminished and Will was a mass of disbelief and cold fear, hardly having heard a word of Sam's feverish monolog.

"I'm quits, Sam. Your luck has failed to turn around." Will wondered what god had blessed him.

Sam let out a petulant "Awwwww. Have I said something to hurt your feelings, Will?"

"No."

"Well, then . . ."

"I can't. I don't want to."

"Man, I thought we was friends."

"Sam, I don't have any friends."

There was a thick dark awkwardness.

"You're a nice guy, Sam. And while I hate to take your money, I will take it and keep it. Because, as you know, I need it. If I didn't, I'd give it back to you. And walk away. Just like that."

"I'm sorry, Will—I didn't realize!" Sam averted his eyes, contrite.

"That's okay, Sam."

Will collected his winnings from the table, assembling them into a hefty wad and burying the bills in the deep hip pocket of his coveralls. He retrieved his hat, unrolled his sleeves and recuffed them.

"Look—I gots over six thousand dollars in that box, maybe more. What am I gonna do with it but have fun? That's what I wants. That's what I buys with it."

"I've got to move on, Sam. Believe me. It's been a pleasure. And I like to play. But you've got your playthings, Sam. A home, two cars, and a good woman. You're in heaven, my man. Learn to use those wings and quit complaining about your halo. Now I must go out into that madness and get mine."

Both men were giddy from the beer and the closeness.

Sam Clark showed Will Clark the door.

"You know where I live—any time you're in the neighborhood."

Will stared into Sam's eyes. Sam met the gaze boldly. "Watch yourself, man. *Watch yourself!*"

Sam stood dazed in Will's words as the stranger made his

getaway. Sam closed the door and quickly began cleaning up the mess. Martha was due any minute. And he had no desire to try and explain something to her that he could not understand himself.

THE DUFUS RUFUS

DILLY stared at the measurement panel on the back of the packet and cursed. She had been in such a big rush she'd neglected to check the size prior to purchase. The smoky pantyhose were one size too small. Even at the proper fit, squeezing into the flimsies without tearing them was always a bother. It had her talking angrily to herself.

"They only make these things for flat-assed women, not somebody got meat on they bones."

And Dilly did, indeed, have meat on her bones. Her healthy thirty-eight inch hips curved out beneath her twenty-four inch waist and were topped by a thirty-six inch bust. Her figure had been known to stop traffic at high noon on more than one occasion—a worthy compliment.

Tonight she intended to stop traffic at Thelma Jo's house party. She appraised her flashy red leather mini-dress which hung outside the closet door. It had cost her two hundred dollars and three months of peanut butter and jelly sandwiches. Dilly considered it well worth the sacrifice. Accented with gold brocade three-inch heels, her long tan legs would knock eyes out for blocks.

Showered, lotioned, powdered and potioned, she began the painstaking process of putting on the pantyhose. Gently, starting with her right foot, she nursed the delicate filmy fabric to mid-calf. She started the left foot, reached mid-calf, then worked some more on the right, easing it along, going back and forth, left to right, careful to avoid snagging them with her one-inch fire engine red fingernails.

"Honey, you gonna blind the night!"

She laughed at herself. Not that she intended to give up

any nooky at all. Not on a bet. She was out strictly for fun and tease. One never knew who'd show up. This was a Hollywood party; who knew what interest she might spark — meaning interest as in bank account.

She reminded herself to be sure and call Thelma Jo by her new name, Shanti. Ex-roomies, Thelma Jo and Dilly finally got stars in their eyes after ten years of treading water in assorted secretarial pools. They decided to make one last stab at stardom before youth deserted them. Thelma Jo urged Dilly to change her name to something more "saleable," but Dilly couldn't quite see it in her heart. If she did change her name, who'd know it was her once she finally became someone? So far it was no big worry.

Dilly stopped for a breather, regarding her sartorial effort. She was up beyond her knees. The last thing she wanted to do was break into a sweat and funk up her freshly dry-blown wildwoman afro. She was prepping herself for the most perilous part of the adventure — thigh bone to crotch, rear-end to navel. She stood, braced herself, and bent forward.

"Come on, Baby, be good to Mama. Mama wants to look hot tonight for the fast track. That's a Baby — easy now, easy."

She had them steady on the outside now, rising, slipping them gently over her hips, sucking in her tummy as tightly as she could.

"Ah-ha!" She felt them snap into place around her waist. Victory.

"Oh, poot!" The little fibrous panty pad was suspended mid-air three inches below her crotch. She walked around in a circle. The gap felt uncomfortably insecure. "Stretch pants, here we come."

She took out the elastic panty from its sachet niche in her dresser drawer and stepped into it. It hugged her, girdle-like, and pulled the pantyhose firmly into place. There would be a little extra heat in her lower depths, but added comfort made such precautions necessary. She zipped into her red leather mini-dress, put on the gold heels, and grabbed up her little beaded gold clutch purse. The results were eye-popping. "Mercy mercy me," she chirped to the mirror.

Parking proved to be a problem at Thelma Jo's. She lived in a transitional neighborhood where posh residential homes were giving way to income property, condominiums and apartment buildings. Parking was inadequate for the new population. When several events took place at once, getting space within a block was impossible. Determined to find something that wouldn't overly tax her three-inch heels, Dilly cruised up and down the dark streets for fifteen minutes.

"Damn, there must be something somewhere!"

Doggedly she turned down the alley behind Thelma Jo's block and peered for a possible spot into which she could cram her gas-guzzler. The dark narrow demi-street was threatened by overgrowth of bushes and weeds. Beyond the cement and stucco caverns of ill-lit garages, she spied a burned out, boarded up building. It was just the spot.

She parallel parked as close as she could to allow others passage without scraping the paint off her highly prized coupe. Satisfied, she dismounted, locked the door behind her and began wobbling carefully up the alley, on the lookout for fox tails, pot holes, or anything that might conceivably flaw her visual perfection.

Dilly felt so good she began to hum a little Motown sound when two leather-gloved hands came out of nowhere, clamped her mouth solidly shut, and jerked her to an awkward standstill.

"Scream bitch and I'll break your neck!"

Dilly's heart thumped so hard she could barely make out his raspy croak. She froze. He lowered one hand, grabbed the clutch purse, then released her to search through it. She turned toward her assailant. The massive muscle-bounder had a stocking over his head mashing his features into a grotesque African mask.

"I ain't got no money."

He looked her up and down. "Shit, dressed like a high-class whore and drivin' that?" He threw the purse down in disgust.

"I'm going to a party!" Dilly was inexplicably defensive.

"All you Hollywood niggers are just alike — all front and no substance."

"You got your nerve."

"I'm wastin' my time. You ain't nothin' but a dufus rufus."

"A what?"

"You heard me — I've got to get something for my trouble. Might as well be pussy."

He grabbed her and began wrestling Dilly to the ground.

"Wait — wait, my hair! Damn, this dress set me back two hundred!" She began to push at him, fighting him off. He grabbed her knee and sent her crashing to the dirt. She let out a squawk as one heel snapped. She began to whine, "My best heels!"

He ignored her pleas and worked his hands briskly up her legs, feeling around to grasp her panties. He reached her crotch and snatched at the panty. The elastic strained but refused to give. Grunting, he took two more vicious jerks.

"Shit, bitch, what you got on?"

"Please — please don't!"

He went hastily back to work, reaching in above her waist, attempting to peel them down around her legs.

"God, don't tear 'em — just don't tear 'em!"

"Then help me get these muthafuckas off."

They both struggled against the stubborn elastic. It was caught at an odd angle, down past her navel, refusing to give free of her healthy rump.

"Bitch, you got some good pussy. I can smell it."

Dilly felt gravel biting her arms, shoulders and exposed mid-back. He caught a fist full of her flesh as well as the elastic when he tried again with a tug-of-war. "Owwwww — that *hurts!*" She yowled.

A light went on a few yards away, beyond a stone fence. They could hear the inquisitive sounds of a door slamming open, footsteps, and loud puzzled whispers.

"You done woke the whole neighborhood."

Disgusted, he jumped to his feet and gave her a swift kick to her rear with his combat boots, managing to shred what was left of her pantyhose. He turned and fled into the dark.

Dilly coughed and snotted as she picked herself up and dusted off her dress. Tearfully she felt around in the dirt for the heel of her shoe and her little clutch purse and found them. Wondering if she'd be able to find a tailor to repair her damaged dress and a shoe shop to repair and refinish her heels, she limped back to the car, unlocked it and gingerly eased into the driver's seat. There was little choice but to return home. Dilly would not allow herself to show at the party in such a muss. She'd phone Thelma Jo tomorrow and tell her what had happened.

As the achy aftermath of her wrestling match with the rapist

226

began to wear through her waning shock, Dilly made a cautious exit from the alley and entered the stream of bumper-to-bumper night-goers. She struggled for focus, her eyes bedazzled by the unusual brightness of lights beckoning from marquees and billboards. Who knew what opportunities had been missed because of that no-account. The dirty sonofabitch may have cost her her one big chance.

As she angrily gripped the wheel, Dilly noticed two nails had been broken in the battle. She let out a little gasp. It was the final insult. She hit the brake and fell against the steering wheel, head in arms. Pain, disappointment and outrage washed over her in waves of sobs. Horns beeped impatiently behind her as Saturday night traffic backed up for miles.

KELELE *

AFRICA wrapped her thighs around Damu's head and trumped, arms thrown toward the ceiling. She undulated and writhed atop his tough muscular shoulders in ecstatic joy.

Yes, Baby—do it. Do it.

He eased her down, around him, his palms turned upward, prayer-like, supporting the spade of her butt. She left a smear of natural perfume across his left cheek, along his chest, his belly, and he lowered her, still, feet balanced and braced in the dance, his nature athrob in anticipation. Face-to-face, she tore lion-like at his lips in mock mauling—her tongue hot licks to either side of his nose. Lower, her legs locked at his waist and his hands moved to encompass hers, her breasts jutting at his lips, begging tongue.

Yes, Baby—do it. Do it.

Surrounding them was the undercurrent of Drum, its soft bbbrrattta bratta brrrrattt. There was a pause, the tense momentary tease, then the man-hands resumed their ballet— bratta brrrrattt atttattt.

Damu moaned and opened his mouth to devour her when he was sharply speared by the sudden loud wail of irrefutable rhythm and blues—a rude music which harshly jarred him awake.

Damu Chui leapt out of bed, confused, looking and feeling around for his vanished Africa, taking note that *that* had been a dream, severely realistic due to: his current state of exhaustion, having been deprived of his first real sleep in days; his acute state of horniness and depression after having broken

---

*Swahili for noise.

with his lovely Africa two weeks earlier because she was too consumptive of his time and creative stuff; his tenderness of ego
after ten hours of loading and unloading crates at the appliance
warehouse where he slaved as a "shipping clerk" downtown;
followed by an intense three hours and thirty minutes of rehearsal
at the Watts Music Center for an up-coming festival in which
he was featured percussionist.

Having shed the unfortunately bland angloism of one David
Smith (rechristening himself Damu Chui or Blood Leopard) he
had put a classless upbringing in a state orphanage, four years
in Viet Nam and a failed fruitless marriage into a metaphorical
coffin, sealed it and buried it in the morass of artistic obsession.

How many years had he buried? How many could he contain? It had been too much, a numbing happenstance, for on
leaving rehearsal at midnight, he discovered that the right rear
tire on his van had unkindly relieved itself of air. Dog tired as
he was, he had wrestled with the spare and the jack alone.
Everyone had fled quickly, afraid to be in that ill-reputed part
of town after dark. Unassisted, Damu changed the tire,
awkwardly wary of protecting the hands that were his livelihood,
his art, his self-defense.

Damu Chui valued his hands above all other parts of his
being. He was not the sort to brag that he could kill a man in
hand-to-hand combat. He had been trained to do so, but even
Nam had not presented an opportunity to translate theory into
fact. Stateside, he allowed his amazingly dense, if small, body
to speak for him. And it spoke well of long hours of discipline
and practice.

Damu believed in the perfection of the body as weapon,
the perfection of hand as tool, the perfection of the spirit-mind
as salvation. And while the first two perfections had been at-
tained, Damu's love of the martial arts was no mere afro-cultural
fad. It was, indeed, love second only to his love of the Drum—his
true tongue in which he was supremely eloquent.

He had not embraced *open hand* as diversion, but as art.
As he embraced his drums/drumming. He had fused it and other
aspects of Asian militarist erudition to himself as he had conga,
bongo and gourd. Indeed, he verged on ascension to mastery.
At last, hard work and sacrifice were realizing profit and modest
success—in money, women, and a growing respect from
musician peers. His was a budding local reputation, a name

230

beginning to appear in places of artistic significance. He was becoming important in his subculture.

But. . . .

A niggah can't get a night's rest.

Not even a dream. It was two-twenty in the morning. Something burst inside him. Damu Chui was maddened. "Shit! Goddamn it!" he screamed, anger manifest as sweat on his palms and forehead.

On more than one occasion, Damu had gathered himself up, dragged himself out into the night, knocked politely on his neighbor's door and had spoken in the severely even tone of a karate master on the brink of demonstrating his lethal expertise.

"Brother-man, would you *please* turn down your stereo!"

His next-door neighbor, Joe Jonesy, congenial enough at first, initially obliged. "Sure man, sorry 'bout that! Most certainly . . . most certainly," closing the door with a cooperative nod. And that would be the end of it until the next time and the next time and days at a time and so on.

It became a ritual harassment. One man worked dawn-to-dusk and needed sleep. One man worked dusk-to-dawn and slept while the other worked. Both men maintained surfaces of cool, nodded gentlemanly when bumping into one another outside their adjoining apartments. Rather than turn their angers on the pseudo-architect who'd hastily redesigned their multi-unit dwelling to squeeze in more residents and squeeze out greater profits; rather than indulge in the Zen of hating landlords, they turned on each other—no longer speaking; or, if speaking, in as few and as cryptic syllables as possible.

"Hey, man."

"Yeah, man."

" 'S up."

"What it is."

"Hrumph."

"Yeah, heard that."

"You too."

"Uh-huh."

"Cool, dude."

"Bro."

"Hrumph."

As minimal as that was, becoming more so over the weeks, each man looked forward to the other's moving out. No matter who vacated first, the other would declare his leaving a victory. As it was, both men were comfortable in their respective situations and both stayed firmly put.

That they had virtually, and coincidentally, the same skin color oddly intensified their antagonism. Usually Afro-Americans of similar skin tone gravitated toward one another in kinship. Perhaps it was because of their features in which were revealed widely diverse heritages. Damu exhibited a strong Nigerian trait in the shape of his head, overall build and the set of his umber eyes. Jonesy's bulk and gray-brown eyes suggested an Irish ancestor.

I bet your mama was a mongoose.

I bet your mama was a cobra.

Daily they crossed one another's paths in a smog of hostile silence, accompanied by the opening and closing of doors as they came and went. It was not long before Damu learned of another reason which reinforced his mounting hate for Mr. Joe Jonesy.

"So this is where you crib, man."

"Yeah."

"How long you been in *this* building?"

"A couple of years."

"You like it?"

"It has its drawback." He thought of his neighbor, one wall over. "But — yeah."

"Well, man — guess who lives next door to you?"

"You mean that dude, Jonesy or whatever-the-fuck his name is?"

"Yeah, Jonesy — that's it! You know what he do for a livin'?"

"No, what?"

"Deal cocaine, man! That dude is a for-real snowman."

"You jive." That explained the man's late hours and loud intrusive music-to-be-high-by. "You jivin' me. How do you know?"

"My partner, Reese, is in tight with the dude, Damu. I've even come through the cat's crib with Reese on a cop-and-blow. I mean, you *know* me. It ain't my thang — a little bush now and again, but . . . Reese, he does a little one-and-one time-to-time."

"I see."

Damu Chui began staring at Joe Jonesy, a new contempt intensifying his glare, giving it keener focus. Joe Jonesy pimped destructive substances to his own community. His own people. He had bought into the lie of racism and had become an implement of it. He had become a part of the sickness of drug dependency that fed on the minds and pocketbooks of his people/their strength, and deprived them of socio-political determination. Joe Jonesy was a loathsome thing who fouled their consciousness. A disease. A blight. A parasite.

In his pursuit of physical perfection, Damu disdained drugs unless used in religious mystical ritual or rite — when perfect unity between world and spirit were mandatory. And it did not go unnoticed by Joe Jonesy that this Damu character now openly sneered at him on chance meetings. There was an aura about his militant little neighbor that made use of the diminutive ludicrous. The man simply was not to be messed with. The man was, in Jonesy's eyes, a maniac. And his continual disturbing presence forced Jonesy to think more and more about his own particular place in the universe and wonder what he had done, other than deal drugs, to cause himself to be cursed with such an uptight clown of a neighbor.

"Velma, get the door."

"Sure, Joe."

She went, exchanged a few soft words, nodded and returned.

"Who was it?"

"That guy next door." She was at the stereo lowering the volume.

"The creep?"

"He didn't seem so bad."

"Whose side are you on?"

"Don't bite my head off, Joe. I just did as asked."

"That crab has been on my ass for months. A niggah spends five grand on some high fidelity and can nevah get maximum wattage out of it."

"That's quite a lot of money to spend on a toy."

"I likes expensive toys, Baby. Like you."

"Oh? Hmmm."

"So my fun is taxed by that pootbutt. It's startin' to get on my nerves."

"Why don't you move, Joe? You've got the money.

Certainly to live more lavishly than this."

"Cuz my set-up's right. And why should I allow that chump to run me out of my territory. I was here *first.*"

"Sure, Joe. You're right. Can we change the subject?"

"Emmm, Velma. What shall we discuss?"

"I'm into doing-the-dirty in a big way. Let's discuss that."

Joe Jonesy saw himself as a Robin Hood of sorts. He robbed from the wickedly middle and upper classes and gave to himself and all within his circle. He provided his parents with sufficient, if reluctantly accepted, cash to pay off thirty-odd years of mortgage, numerous loans, liens and other financial nasties. He had also purchased, as a Christmas gift, a modest used luxury car for their Sunday-goings-to-meeting.

A man about his business, Jonesy kept neat and clean, drove a new car, and was never seen with any women other than the foxiest of foxes or the most stately of queens. He also did a few little things like lay some extra cash on his nephews when their goings got rough. And now and then, he underwrote the cost of a family gathering.

"My Dear, *please.*"

"Joe, why don't you come? Aunt Marybell asks about you all the time."

"Give her my love."

"And your Uncle Sammy."

"My Dear, you know they don't approve of my lifestyle."

"You'll find the right girl, Joe, I know you will."

"Got to run, My Dear."

"Try to make it — if you can."

"I'll try."

Of course he never made it. Five minutes in the presence of those black Christian sheep were more than he had ever been able to tolerate. It amused him to wonder if any of those old countryfied negroes had ever lived with half his passion.

Well, I guess I'll never know.

When family members questioned his apparent solvency, his substantive partnership in a used car lot more than adequately covered his true source of income. It simultaneously explained the freedom he had to come and go as he pleased unhampered by bosses, foremen or the usual others on an employee's roster of "superiors." And that, alone, cloaked him in an aura of inspired respect which resonated along the streets of the poor neighborhood in which he'd been reared, cloaking his parents in safety. The local gangsters did not molest them.

Outside of family, race consciousness was not something Joe Jonesy took time to make an issue of. He accepted the world as he found it, taking risks as he saw fit, to get the things out of life he wanted. Indeed, it did not trouble Jonesy that his co-caine connexion was a member of the Latin *raza,* nor did it trou-ble him that the only language they had in common was the dialectics of cold hard coin and a penchant for dark rum. All that mattered was sustaining the lifestyle he enjoyed. And he enjoyed every facet of it, except Damu Chui's persistent intrusion.

So, as it went down that early Thursday before sunrise, Joe Jonesy, in his usual state of I-don't-give-a-fuck, pulled out his favorite LP for a solo flight. He had made a wonderful score of high grade "nose candy" and felt like having a little private celebration. A glass of Scotch, music and his favorite "lady," cocaine. He opened his personal stash, took his little coke spoon, dipped it into the crystal and lifted it delicately to one naris and then the other, snorting mightily, his pinky stiffly up in the air. Then he went to the stereo and put up the volume a few decibels shy of blast. There was sufficient bass to create a pounding that set the entire wall shared with Damu ashimmy.

The thunder vibes not only rattled Damu's kitchen uten-sils, but the Civil War pistols, Turkish scimitar and other prized objects he had mounted in display on his side of the wall. There was also a leopard's skin, the horn of a wildebeest, a pipe of carved ivory, a palm frond, and the black-felt under phosphorescent-blue air-brushed nude of a busty afro-ed vixen — all atremor to the boop-boop-a-doop.

This, Damu decided, *has to end.*

Clad only in pajama bottoms, he leapt for the scimitar, snat-ched it from the wall, and headed through the door. He did not intend mishap or injury to his precious hands, karate or no karate, on Jonesy's obviously overly hard head.

Kicked back against his sofa, Joe was deeply sweetly aloft on music, eyes closed, transported via *white girl* to a small roman-tic waterfront dive, perched on a stool, microphone in hand, slaying hearts with funky song styling.

The door whammed inward, jolting him out of reverie. The

235

astonished Joe suspected he was still hallucinating as Damu rode into the room on a head-splitting yell, brandishing the scimitar. Damu immediately began hacking away at his amazed victim's five-hundred-dollar three piece suit, instantly evoking blood. It was too real, even though he felt nothing. That was his blood staining the couch. Cursing in surprised outrage, Joe Jonesy fell backward over the couch, to the floor, unaware of his wounds, anesthetized. Was the cocaine in his system working in concert with adrenaline? Or was it that pain is too much of a luxury when one is under assault?

Damu slashed at the stereo, smashing the turntable with the scimitar's handle, creating an electronic buzz which blistered the air. With another slash he severed the wiring and silenced it.

Joe Jonesy roared, "I paid five thousand dollars for that, niggahhhh!" grabbed a lamp and threw it at Damu who deflected it mid-air, propelling it through the gaping doorway where it crashed to the walkway outside.

The violence was heard and brought curses and catcalls from other apartments as the tenants were disturbed.

"Hey, man, what's the matter with you?" Joe Jonesy yelled, fending off another slash with one of the couch pillows. Damu was gone beyond communication. The coffin of emotions he had so neatly interred had made its way to his mind's surface. The lid had sprung open and all manner of foul haunts had seized hold. He did, in fact, no longer appear human, but demon. Damu fiercely did his dance, hacked this way and that, anointed in the splattering vital stuff of his enemy, doom in his eyes.

"Shit, man—what did I do to you?" A horrified Joe Jonesy squealed as Damu leapt at him full force, slashing home mid-torso deeply into his waist, laying open adipose flesh, bloodying Joe's trousers and depriving him of his navel. Damu trumpeted his cry of vengefulness, both men squawking in grotesque duet.

Yes, Baby—do it. Do it.

Joe Jonesy frantically staggered back to escape. Damu took a healthy slice of his leg with the scimitar, severing a ligament. Limping angrily toward his bedroom, Joe raged as much for the demise of his stereo and the brutalization of his suit as his own body. If he lived he would heal, but his stereo and silk suit were forever lost. He half fell through the door, scuttling

236

for the bedstand table. He opened its drawer, snatched out the automatic hand gun he kept there, scrambling to slip the clip of bullets into its butt, bloodying it in his grasp.

Damu leapt after Joe, onto his back, hand and fist, scimitar raised as he repeatedly pummeled Joe's head with the handle. Damu reared back angling to take Joe's head off. Galloping in circles, Joe bucked, tossing Damu to the floor, two feet away, but distance enough for the opening Joe desperately sought. Trusting instinct and blinded by blood oozing down his forehead, into his eyes, Joe fired the automatic.

Damu caught one bullet in his abdomen, and then again, another shot, and then again and then again. His fist froze to the scimitar as he fought to keep his spirit from fleeing an all consumptive pain.

When the gunfire ceased, Joe's apartment filled with cackling onlookers staring in disbelief at the fresh mayhem. Damu was a convulsing sprawl across the bedroom threshold, profusely spouting blood from several raw apertures, his mouth contorted. Above him stood the zombie Joe Jonesy attempting to once more unload an automatic long emptied of missiles, shaking it at his fallen assailant, speechless and sightless, blood everywhere telling of the scimitar's ravage.

"What in hell? Would you look at this."

"I called the police."

"What happened?"

"He left his stash out here on the coffee table. Hey, this is some good shit."

"Hey, man, put that down. Don't touch anything. Wait till the cops get here."

"What *happened*?"

"Your guess is as good. . . ."

"They were both such regular guys."

"Someone sure had a bug up his ass."

"We'd better do somethin' for this one here or he'll bleed to death."

"The other one's dead?"

"If he ain't he might as well be."

Handcuffed in spite of his massive wounds, a wild-eyed Joe Jonesy was pushed into the back of a squad car and sped away to the prison ward at County General Hospital, sirens shrieking.

The coroner's wagon sped off in another direction, transporting the stiffly defiant corpse of Damu Chui, his face twisted in grisly determination as though somewhere somehow seeking repossession of his form to continue combat in the name of a sound night's sleep.

JONESED

Yes, Lord.
It's like this: I've got to have it. I've got to have something. Got to have that good sweet high. I mean, what is life if life is without pleasure? It's not that I need it. No, maybe that's exactly the case. I need it. No, that's not quite right either. I *require* it. The way a title requires society. The way the whore requires her trick. It's something I could live without. But what would life be without it. And that, my dear, is merely a fact of my existence you don't seem to want to take into consideration. Allow me to hip you.

I've always been an upstanding decent soul. I was given a very traditional Christian upbringing. I was taught all the refinements beyond my station. Refinements? The mannerisms, habits and sensibilities of the upper classes/the rich. And my parents were black and poor. Very black and very poor. Of course, they had no harmful intentions. No suspicion they were feeding me a poison of sorts — a social poison developing within me the desire to have things. To accomplish to achieve to aspire. They were giving me morals that frankly did not suit what was to be my full station in life. And, as such, dooming me to this hell I've become resigned to if not accepting of. Can you dig it?

And, it is because of that/this that I find it necessary to indulge in certain underground activities — all to enhance my happenstance. All to salve my soul — so to speak. To provide me with some release from tension, and some respite from the banalities that shape my "working" life. So you see, I've become what I've become, by way of habit, by a modicum of choice. I mean, get with it.

I have selected my indulgences carefully. My physical

239

being/body—such as it is, is not the best it could be, and I've many quirks that require I watch my diet—to a certain extent—but for the most part, I am in fairly adequate shape. I have no desire to destroy myself. I am no advocate of suicide and I do what I do, remember, to make my life palatable; not negate it. That would be utter stupidity. And so, this, therefore, is the basis of my argument. That anyone who has their head about them, can, and should be allowed to do so by Law, indulge in various presently illegal substances without detriment to our society. Can I get an amen?

There are those of us who find no release in "flapping our jaws" on the psychiatrist's couch. There are those of us who are quite readily and easily able to identify our problems. Our problems are so relatively simple, the fact that we have them at all seems to add to our troubled states of mind. I consider myself a prime example of this. My mind is troubled—deeply troubled. And an occasional "cigarette" tends to allow me to better cope with said trouble. Gets me past it. So that I can feel better able to withstand my unfortunate reality.

No, I'm not one of *those*. I'm not inclined to blame it on historical circumstances. That's rather obvious, isn't it? I mean, what can one say. It's been done. Now one must content one's self with dealing with the present. Don't laugh. It's a philosophy that gets me through every day. And that's what's most important, isn't it? That getting through the day. That seeing another sunrise. That certainty that one has, again, met the so-called "enemy" and maintained one's equilibrium.

May I confide in you? Please don't take offense. Please don't think me mad. Perhaps you may see my point. I'm quite lucid, you know, and this is certainly one of my more lucid moments. But I'd like to make a confession at this point.

I hate white people.

Not particular individuals. But clumps of them. That is why I always avoid places where they might appear in great numbers. When I'm in a situation like that—at an amusement park, casino, mall or in some particular institution where they abound, it sickens me to see all that white flesh swimming about or towards me. It's like drowning in a vat of putty. I feel disoriented. I suddenly can't breathe. I start to sweat. Then immediately I grow cold as if I've died on the spot. And God

240

forbid one look at me. I writhe and scorch under their glances. Ain't that too cold?

I mean, when a white person looks at you they look through you. Or they're either full of hostility or misconceptions or fear. And you can see it quite simply all in an instant. Or the "friendly" ones. Those are really horrible. You just know, that upon seeing you, they've thought of their favorite jazz musician or some black friend they met eons ago — a friend, by the way, who has set the limited standard for all they know and see of black folk. Why is it that white people think because they happen to have known or know *one* black person they are suddenly experts on black folk? I've known hundreds of whites, many of them intimately. And I would never say I was an expert on white people. But then, that's beside the point, *n'est-ce pas?* But I digress, Baby.

My point in telling you this is by way of explaining why I indulge in illegal drugs. Why I take the risk of jail. The risk of destroying the little illusion of a decent life I've constructed for myself (compared to what?). Isn't that how this discussion got started?

It's simple. The drugs allow me to tolerate white people. And all the things that they are about. This world of theirs in which you and I are imprisoned. This world to which we belong but own no part of. It takes a good high to melt away the hate. So often a good high puts me in the love mode. As in aphrodisiac. Can you get to that?

What kind of world do I want? Not a world without them. But a world in which I fit. I don't hate them enough to want to obliterate them. No. My dislike, as I prefer to call it, doesn't run quite that deep. In fact, it is more accurate to call it a *distaste*. But I envision a world in which I can simply be myself without having to pretend all the time. It's such a drag. I'm either pretending or explaining. And there's very little else in between. For example, I was hospitalized once for some minor complaint. And there was this nurse, a seemingly wonderful person. Very friendly and all of that and one day she was in my room administering a dose of pain killer when a flash bulletin came on television. Apparently the National Nigger Party or some such was picketing somewhere. It seemed to strike quite a chord in her, while I was quite indifferent to it. I was much more interested in what she was giving me to better my condition.

241

When all of a sudden she turned toward me, rather on me, and asked quite acidly, "What is it you colored people want?" I was thoroughly taken aback/shocked shitless, my dear. I told her that all I wanted was my medication, which she promptly plopped on the table for me to give to myself and left the room in a huff. Now that's quite typical of a white person's behavior. I'm lucky she wasn't a man, I'd've probably had to have a procedure to extract his foot from my ass — as the joke goes. Ain't that a bitch?

Anyhoo. To get on with it. Drugs cut through all this racist bullshit and melt it away. I can face my reality much more readily. And appear sane. Yes, that's what I mean — sane. Surely no reasonable black person can exist in this/their world and remain sane. Not unless they're extremely lucky. Not unless they've been blessed. And I wish it were so in my case. It ain't. So I do the best, the very best I can do under these circumstances. And we'll get to that some other time. Right now, I'm anxious to kick back and fire up a smoke. It's been a long hard day. And I need something to bring me down, to mellow me out. I need something to put mind heart and stomach at ease simultaneously. Some good stuff. So don't look so woeful when I fire up. Don't admonish me about cancer. If I weren't able to get an occasional high, I'd be dead anyway. Dead of frustration, dead of starvation, dead of something or other. I'm giving you the real T.

I'm not saying do as I do and am going to continue doing. I'm merely saying, allow me to do this little bit I do as I please. I'm living in a world that says no to me everytime I turn around. About the only time it says yes is when I'm wasted. And it damn near doesn't make any difference what I'm wasted on. Alcohol is just as good. And if not that, then something else. It's *always gonna be somethang*. I don't give a fuck how many goddamn laws they pass. People like me are always gonna need to be high. We're gonna need that release that keeps us going. That keeps us believing if we can just make it through another day, well, there might be a chance for us to get something out of life other than pain. Now, tell me about it.

242

Printed June 1988 in Santa Barbara & Ann Arbor
for the Black Sparrow Press by Graham Mackintosh
& Edwards Brothers Inc. Design by Barbara Martin.
This edition is published in paper wrappers; there
are 250 hardcover trade copies; 150 hardcover copies
have been numbered & signed by the author; & 26
copies handbound in boards by Earle Gray are
lettered & signed by the author.

Photograph by Michael J. Elderman

SHE was born and raised in a Los Angeles slum known as Watts famed for its August 1965 Rebellion. Following this ethnic insurrection she joined a teenpost and a number of organizations set up to channel the "riotous" energies of young Black Americans into constructive modes. A struggling welfare mother, she was determined to become a writer in spite of horrific odds. A brash, abrasively frank young woman, her few sponsorships were frequently aborted by her naivete, her stubbornness or socio-economic contingencies. Yet, a writer she must be or "die in the effort." Initially venturing into experimental theatre and dance, she backed into scriptwriting when a teleplay scored her a nomination for the NAACP Image Awards and she became the eighth minority member of the Writers' Guild of America, West. Later there would be an Emmy, but her romance with legendary Hollywood went the legendary way of disappointment. Subsequent stabs at success bled literary fellowships from the National Endowment for the Arts and Guggenheim Foundation in poetry. She is presently employed as a medical secretary/transcriber and co-hosts "The Poetry Connexion," an interview program with Austin Straus for Southern California's Pacifica radio station.

Wanda Coleman is the author of *Mad Dog Black Lady* (Black Sparrow, 1979), *Imagoes* (Black Sparrow, 1983) and *Heavy Daughter Blues: Poems & Stories 1968-1986* (Black Sparrow, 1987). *A War of Eyes & Other Stories* is her fourth book, though first collection of fiction.